A LIE FOR A LIE

Also by Jennifer Donaldson

I Know You Remember

A LIE FOR A LIE

JENNIFER DONALDSON

Previously published as *Lies You Never Told Me*

putnam

G. P. PUTNAM'S SONS

G. P. PUTNAM'S SONS
An imprint of Penguin Random House LLC
1745 Broadway, New York, NY 10019
penguinrandomhouse.com

alloyentertainment

Interior design by Eric Ford
Text set in Aldus LT Std

The Library of Congress has cataloged the hardcover edition as follows:
Names: Donaldson, Jennifer (Young adult author), author.
Title: Lies you never told me : a novel / Jennifer Donaldson.
Description: New York, NY : Razorbill, 2018. |
Summary: Told in alternating voices, two teenagers, one in Austin, Texas, and the other in Portland, Oregon, enter dangerous romantic relationships.
Identifiers: LCCN 2018003487 (print) | LCCN 2018012103 (ebook) | ISBN 9780698408494 (E-book) | ISBN 9781595148520 (hardback)
Subjects: | CYAC: Love—Fiction. | Dating (Social customs)—Fiction. | Teacher-student relationships—Fiction.
Classification: LCC PZ7.1.D644 (ebook) | LCC PZ7.1.D644 Li 2018 (print) | DDC [Fic]—dc23
LC record available at https://lccn.loc.gov/2018003487

First published in the United States of America as *Lies You Never Told Me* by Razorbill, an imprint of Penguin Random House LLC, 2018
First paperback edition published as *Lies You Never Told Me* by Razorbill, an imprint of Penguin Random House LLC, 2019
This edition published by G. P. Putnam's Sons, 2026

Manufactured in the United States of America.
BVG

ISBN 9798217114849
1st Printing

The authorized representative in the EU for product safety and compliance is Penguin Random House Ireland, Morrison Chambers, 32 Nassau Street, Dublin D02 YH68, Ireland, https://eu-contact.penguin.ie.

A LIE FOR A LIE

ONE

Gabe

Storm clouds clot the edge of the night sky, stained purple from the city lights; but somehow, right over the yucca-fringed yard, the stars are still visible. I spot Orion there at the center of the sky. It's the only constellation I can consistently pick out: the belt, the sword, the stars dripping away like blood. On the horizon, lightning flutters.

It's late September, the Austin air dense and heavy. I sit in my swim trunks, dangling my feet into the pool. The flagstone patio, the carefully tended native plants, and the high-end bourbon in the monogrammed glass tumbler next to me all belong to my girlfriend. To Sasha. Sasha, whose parents are out of town. Sasha, who's swaying down the path from the house with a wooden tray of snacks, in a black-and-white bikini and a pair of flip-flops.

"Need another drink?" She holds up the crystalline decanter, waving it enticingly.

"Still nursing this one," I say, taking her in. Her long, muscular legs. Her flat stomach and gently rounded hips.

"Lightweight," she says. Her blue eyes sparkle as she pops the stopper out of the heavy bottle and takes a huge swig. "Aren't you getting in?"

"I like to get used to the water first," I say, splashing my legs up and down a few times.

"Oh yeah?" She sets the bottle down on a patio table with a heavy clunk.

"Yeah."

Without warning, she launches herself straight at me. At the last moment she vaults over my head, coming down in a cannonball right in front of me. A wave of cool water washes over me, a shock in the heavy night air. I shake out my hair, laughing, as Sasha surfaces.

"You're gonna get it now." I slide into the water and push off the side. She shrieks and swims away. I launch myself across the pool, my stroke clumsy but strong, my heart racing.

She lets me catch her. I slide my arms around her narrow shoulders, and every cell in my body wakes up with a jolt at the feel of her body against mine. Her skin looks so pale next to my light brown complexion. The strings of her bikini top press hard against my chest. She slides one of her long, smooth legs between mine, and my mind goes silent. Smiling, wordless, she reaches behind her neck and pulls at the knot of her halter, slowly tugging it free. Her bikini top flutters away and lands on the surface of the water, a black-and-white lily pad drifting aimless around us.

"Sasha," I whisper. It's not my first glimpse of her small, perfect breasts. We've messed around plenty of times, in the backseat of my car, in an empty bedroom at a house party, anywhere we can find privacy. But we've never done this so openly, without worrying about time or exposure. Shielded by the foliage, we are open to the sky above.

And then the phone rings.

Sasha's eyes go wide, her mouth flinching into a tight-lipped scowl. "They can leave a message," I say, but she ignores me. She gently detaches herself from my body and wades back to the side of the pool, not even bothering to cover her chest with her arms as she climbs out.

She scoops the phone up from the tray on the patio table, where it glows green between a bowl of tortilla chips and a plate of prepackaged cookies. The citronella torch gutters as she moves near it, the orange light leaving deep shadows across her face.

"Mom," she says.

I swim toward the stairs, my stomach tight. Suddenly the idea of Mrs. Daley hovers over the backyard: her strained smile, her perfect red nails, the way she taps her foot. Sasha's parents are lukewarm about me, at best. I'm not sure if it's the mediocre grades, or the fact that I'm a Chicano skateboarder dating their very white daughter—never mind that I grew up in the same bougie neighborhood as them, never mind that my mom's family has been in the U.S. for generations. They're old money. They could find any of a hundred reasons not to like me.

The dreamlike mood of a moment earlier starts to dissipate. I suddenly realize the clouds have rolled in overhead. Orion is gone, the sky glowering and low.

Sasha still hasn't covered up. I can see gooseflesh along her arms as I climb out of the pool. I pick up the towel hanging on the back of a deck chair, try wrapping it around her, but she pushes me away.

"How's Aunt Patty?" she asks. A ring of black surrounds her eyes where her mascara has smeared. She pauses, her eyes flickering quickly toward me and then away. "What? No, Gabe isn't here. Yeah, I *promise*. Jesus."

Something in her face changes. Her mouth goes slack for one quick second, and then tightens to stone. She takes a few steps away, muttering into the receiver, so low I can't make out what she's saying. My fingers knot anxiously at my sides; I absently pick up the tumbler of bourbon and sip from it. But the biting, burning thrill of the alcohol is gone. Now it hits my stomach like acid.

"Whatever." Sasha's voice rises again, clipped and angry. She ends the call, and for a moment she stands still, phone in one hand.

Then she turns to the patio table and grabs the decanter, throwing it with all her might to the ground. Glass and whiskey explode at her feet, glittering in the moonlight. Before I can say anything, she launches herself across the patio toward the house, stopping just under the eaves and raising both middle fingers into the air.

"Sasha!" I sidestep the broken glass and run toward her.

"They're watching us," she spits. She nods up toward the roof. Sure enough, I can see a tiny red light. A camera. "She checked the security cameras on her laptop."

Watching? A sick, slimy feeling runs over my bare skin. I tug the towel more firmly around my shoulders, feeling exposed. "Holy shit."

She grimaces. "Perverts!" she shouts at the camera. I wonder if there's an audio feed, or if she's just hoping her parents can read her lips.

I imagine her parents sitting in a darkened room, the light of the laptop bleaching their faces. Or maybe they're at her aunt's kitchen table, drinking red wine and laughing at the two of us. The whiskey churns in my gut.

I walk back to the patio furniture and pick up my shirt. It's halfway over my head when I feel Sasha tugging at it.

"You don't have to go," she says. "They're three hours away. What are they going to do, drive all the way back just to kick you out?"

I pull the shirt down over my head and raise an eyebrow at her. "Do *you* want to spend the rest of your junior year grounded?"

She snorts. "They can go ahead and try. It's not like they can make me stay home."

Typical Sasha. She's never been into picking her battles. She prefers conflict so she can show off what a badass she is.

"Yeah, I'm not really feeling this anymore. Let's just call it a night," I say. "Look, tomorrow we'll head out to the Greenbelt—get out of the house, go hiking. Steer clear of cameras."

She steps closer. "Come on, stay. We'll go up to my room. I don't think there're any cameras in there." She slides her arms around my neck. "And if there are, fuck it. We'll give 'em a show."

I gently disentangle myself from her grip. "Yeah, that's not really my thing." I pick up my skateboard from where I had leaned it next to a potted agave. Last summer my best friend Irene painted a winged eyeball across the wood. At the time I thought it looked awesome. Now it makes me think of Mrs. Daley: one more unwanted eye, spying.

"I didn't know you were such a prude," she mutters waspishly. I walk toward the gate at the side of the house.

"It's just not worth getting in trouble over," I say, reaching out to push it open. She darts in front of me, her spine whip-straight.

"Oh, I'm not worth getting in trouble over?" She's working herself up—I can see it in the sharp angles of her limbs, the jut of her chin. If she can't stick it to her parents, she's going to stick it to me.

I put my hands on her shoulders, but she jerks away. "Sasha . . ."

"No, it's okay. I guess I'm not worth the effort."

I glance up to see another camera, under the eaves of the house. Her parents are probably still watching, enjoying the little soap opera that they set off.

"You're *worth* sacrificing one stupid night for," I say. "I'm leaving now so I can still see you later. I mean, you might not care about getting in trouble, but I care if your parents won't let you see me."

She opens her mouth to say something, then shuts it abruptly. For a moment she stands there, her breath heavy, her face pale with anger. Then she grabs me by the collar and pulls me down, pressing her lips to mine.

It's rough and urgent, her tongue pushing forcefully into my mouth. I almost lose my footing but catch myself on the door frame. A part of me recoils deep inside, unnerved. She's doing this to punish her parents; this is her flipping them off, one more time, for the cameras. The idea that they could be watching still makes my skin crawl. But something about her fierceness pulls me in, too, like it always does.

She finally pulls away. Without another word, she walks back across the patio, toward the house.

Out on the street, leaves catch in eddies of wind, skimming the roadway and then lifting off to fly away. It's eerily quiet, and then I realize the crickets have gone silent. It's going to rain.

I throw my skateboard down onto the pavement and kick off. It's a relief to get away. Sasha's engaged in a lifelong war with her mom, a former debutante from an old Dallas family, prim and tight-lipped. I don't like feeling like I'm just a prop in the melodrama.

A sliver of lightning cuts across the clouds just overhead, and a moment later the thunder snarls. I hop up the curb and off it again. I'll have to hurry if I want to get home before the downpour. I lean into the downward slope of the hill.

It comes out of nowhere: a flash of light, and then impact. I am flying. The wind streams around me, seeming for an impossible moment to buoy me up. It's in that infinite moment, caught aloft, that I understand: a car. I've been hit by a car. The headlights surround me like a nimbus, like the light that surrounds the saints in a religious painting.

Then the second impact comes as my body hits the pavement.

The first heavy raindrops splatter around me. An icy chill unfurls through my body, spreading along my arms and legs and coiling the muscles into shivering knots. I don't feel any pain—just the force ricocheting through my bones—but there's something weird about how my arm is twisted. The clouds overhead swirl and glitter, pops of color exploding in their depths now. Or is that just my vision? I try to lift my head, to get a clear glimpse of my arm.

A black shape flutters into view over me, and I struggle to figure out what it is. A bat? A kite? No. An umbrella. The patter of rain on my face ceases as someone holds an umbrella over me. The someone is hard to make out; they keep splitting, dividing, merging back together, all in the strange and shimmery air. I squint up, trying to make out a face.

A cool hand rests on my cheek.

"Shhhhh." The voice is a woman's. A girl's, maybe. "Don't move."

I stare up at her, trying to blink my head clear. The shifting world seems to be tinged with flares of sickening color now, shades of bile and blood at the corners of my vision. I hear a cell phone's key pad and then the girl's voice again. "I need to report an accident."

Lightning streaks across the sky, and in its split-second illumination I see her. She's young, a teenager. Maybe my age. Her face is thin and pale, sharp-angled. Her hair is long and dark. Then the lightning passes and all I can see is the glow of her phone against her cheek, the silhouette of the umbrella against the sky.

And then that starts to fade, too. Her voice gets farther and farther away. She's saying something about my arm, but I can't bring myself to worry too much about it. The sickly colors at the corners of my vision close in, throbbing for a few beats of my heart before I slide away into darkness.

TWO

Elyse

"'Tis almost morning. I would have thee gone," says Brynn Catambay, touching her cheek lightly. "And yet no farther than a wanton's bird, that lets it hop a little from his hand like a poor prisoner in his twisted . . . twisted . . . *shit.*"

"Gyves," I say, reading off the script. "Twisted gyves."

"I don't know why I can't get that." She knocks her forehead lightly with her fist. "What's that even mean?"

"It's like a leash," I say. She looks at me, eyebrows raised. I shrug. "I looked it up the other day. When I was going over lines."

"Only you would prep for an audition by doing research," she says fondly. "Nerd."

It's Friday, early October, and the theater swarms with activity. Last week the drama department announced that East Multnomah High's fall production will be *Romeo and Juliet,* and dozens of us have gathered for the auditions. Most of the drama club is here—Frankie Nguyen, Nessa Washington, and Laura Egan hang out in the wings, running lines, and Kendall Avery sits in the front row on one of the faded theater seats, eyes closed in meditation, which she always claims helps her "get in touch" with the character. There are people I don't know, too. A goth girl with a septum ring sits on the edge of the stage leafing through the audition packet. And there's a guy I recognize from the basketball team, sipping from a bottle of water and laughing in the middle of a gaggle of girls.

Brynn looks around the room and sighs. Everything she does shows just how comfortable she is with the attention of the world on her. Today she's wearing tights printed all over with cats under a puff-sleeved dress. She looks like she's either ready to attend a mad tea party or catch a train at Harajuku Station. If she weren't also unbelievably pretty it wouldn't work. Lucky for her she's got pillowy lips and thick black waves and the innate ability to contour without the use of a mirror.

"Who are these people, anyway? They didn't audition last year when we did *Antigone* or *A Raisin in the Sun*. Do something popular and every poser in Portland comes out of the woodwork."

"Hey, watch it," I joke. "I'm vying for one of those poser spots myself."

"No way!" She frowns at me. "You don't give yourself enough credit, Elyse."

Brynn's always pushing me, always telling me I should go for better parts. She was the one who got me into theater in the first place, back in freshman year, back when I was so shy I couldn't meet anyone's eye. I don't know how she looked at me and saw actress material, but she's stood by that assessment ever since.

"Hey, everybody, welcome." The room quiets down almost immediately. A young, dark-haired man has stepped out onto the stage. His face is smooth and chiseled, his frame lean. He's wearing a button-down shirt and a pair of black-framed glasses, glinting in the spotlight.

My heart speeds up a little. I twist a lock of hair around my finger; the blond looks almost dark against my Portland-pale skin.

"I'm Mr. Hunter. I'm the new drama teacher." He smiles, revealing a dimple in his left cheek. "I know a few of you already, but I'm looking forward to meeting the rest of you. Thanks so much for coming out. Now, some of you are theater veterans by now . . ." A few people laugh, including Brynn. "But even if this is your first-ever audition, don't worry. I want to give everyone a fair chance. So when you come on stage, tell me your name and what part you're trying out for. You'll start off with the monologue you've memorized, and then I'll have you read a little from the script so I can get a good sense of how you approach different characters." He claps his hands a few times. "Okay? Let's get going. Break a leg."

We sit down in the creaky old seats. Next to me, Brynn jogs her leg gently up and down. It's her only sign of nerves. She's used to this by now. She got the lead in *Antigone* last year and starred as Cecily in *The Importance of Being Earnest* the year before, the only time I know of that a freshman's gotten such a big part. She's almost certain to get Juliet.

We watch the parade of would-be actors, some nervous and stuttering, some hamming up every line. A slouching girl with gum in her mouth starts giggling hysterically right in the middle of the "wherefore art thou" speech, and the goth I noticed before barely speaks above a whisper. But Frankie and Laura both nail their readings, and the basketball player does a surprisingly good Tybalt, pacing angrily back and forth across the stage. And when Brynn slides into the spotlight, I can feel the whole room catch its breath. She commands the entire stage, the warm glow picking up the gold in her skin. She somehow makes her Juliet both flirty and innocent, both lovesick and playful. When she comes back to her seat, I hug her with one arm, and she gives a sheepish grin.

"Elyse McCormick?" Mr. Hunter says it like a question. For just a moment, I freeze, my limbs suddenly senseless.

I hate going right after Brynn.

I manage to get on stage without falling flat on my face, which feels like an accomplishment in and of itself. When I'm there, vertigo tugs at my body, turning my stomach over and over. Darkness billows all around me. It flutters in the wings, it wells up from the audience and threatens to overtake me. The spotlight lands on me and I feel, for just a moment, like I've erupted in flame.

"Go ahead." It's Mr. Hunter. I can't see him, but I know he's a few rows back. His voice, coming so clear and so sure from the obscurity, feels like a tuning fork against my spine.

I find myself imagining that he's the only one there—the only eyes, the only voice, the only person in the audience. My focus sharpens to a razor's edge.

"Hi, I'm Elyse, and I'm reading for the part of the nurse," I say. I take a deep breath, raise my chin, and begin. "Even or odd, of all days in the year, come Lammas Eve at night shall she be fourteen . . ."

I can feel the change come over me as I recite the words. It always happens—or it happens when I'm focused, when I've found something in the role to love. My shoulders round forward, my mouth quirks upward into a wistful grin, and I slide into character with ease. People always play Juliet's nurse like she's silly, but to me there's something so sad about her. The first thing she talks about is her own dead child, and then she's hushed and dismissed for speaking so fondly of little Juliet. There's a whole tale of loss and longing beneath the surface, and it's treated like a joke. I feel a little anger creep into my words, and I let it come—I let it flavor the warm, loving language, ever so slightly.

I'm not like Brynn. She's been doing theater since she was seven, a tiny diva in the making. I only started going to drama club because I was looking for something to do, for a way to avoid going straight home after school. I hadn't intended to fall so head over heels in love with it. Brynn was right—there was something in me that wanted to perform, to speak loud and clear at the center of the stage. To be seen. To be heard.

My monologue comes to a close. The air on the stage is almost stifling in the heat of the lights. The nurse fades away, and I'm just me again, awkward and exposed. My hands come together at my heart, anxious and fidgety.

His voice returns. Deep, but light, agile. He must be an actor himself. Our previous drama teacher, Ms. Harris, was an old kook, a free spirit in caftans and shawls who had us pretend to be a leaf on a tree as a theater warm-up. But Mr. Hunter exudes a kind of articulate calm; it's easy to imagine him on stage, speaking poetry to the darkness beyond.

"Thank you, Elyse. Can you go ahead and pick up that script there . . . yes, right by your left foot . . . and read from page forty-two?"

I pick up the packet, leaf through. Then I frown.

"This is Juliet's line," I say.

"I want to hear how you read a few different characters, please. Juliet's just found out that Romeo's been banished for killing Tybalt. Go ahead when you're ready."

I scan the monologue briefly, wishing I could wipe the sweat off my forehead but not wanting to smear my makeup. Juliet, caught between loyalties. Juliet, who's just now realizing the full weight of her decisions. I start to read out loud. "But wherefore, villain, didst thou kill my cousin? That villain cousin would have killed my husband."

I take her on like a mask, and I turn into someone worthy of a spotlight.

When my words finally fade, there's a long silence from the auditorium.

By now my eyes have adjusted a little, and I can just barely make him out, a faceless shape beyond the footlights. He shifts his weight; I hear papers rustling. But his voice betrays nothing.

"Thank you, Elyse. Who's next?"

After everyone's had a chance to audition, Mr. Hunter takes the stage one more time. Now that I can see him clearly again, the spell is broken—all the intensity of his voice replaced with mild-mannered cheerfulness.

"There's so much talent in this room! I'm going to be faced with a very difficult decision in the coming days. I plan to have the casting list up outside the ticket office by end of day Monday. Thanks so much."

The room breaks into scattered applause, and then the lights come up and we're all rubbing our eyes and gathering our things. I pick up my backpack and turn to see Brynn, a slight frown creasing her forehead. She looks at me in mild surprise, as if she's just now noticed something.

"He asked me to read. What was I supposed to do?" I can't quite keep a note of apology out of my voice, even though I know I shouldn't feel bad. That's how auditions work; everyone gets a chance. Even me.

"I didn't say anything." She holds up her hands defensively. "I'm just annoyed because you were *good*. I didn't realize I was about to get upstaged."

I'm spared having to answer by Mr. Hunter, coming down the aisle toward us. He's smiling, eyes sparkling behind his glasses.

"Elyse, can I talk to you privately for a moment?" he asks.

Brynn's eyes narrow slightly. I feel my cheeks grow warm again, my pulse a staccato beat against my temple. "Um . . . okay. Brynn, I'll text you later, okay?"

"Sure," she says. She picks up her purse and slides it slowly over her shoulder, frowning a little. "Bye, Mr. Hunter."

"Good work today, Brynn. Thanks for coming out." He watches Brynn make her way down the aisle.

And then we're alone. The theater suddenly feels cavernous, the two of us huddled close together against the echoing dark. His glasses catch the light just so, and for a moment I can't see his eyes. My fingers twist anxiously around one another. Did I do something wrong? Am I in trouble already?

But when he turns to look at me again he's smiling. My throat feels dry and tight, but I swallow hard and force a smile back.

"I'm not supposed to do this," he says softly. "But I can't resist. I wanted to tell you that you've got the part."

His words don't make sense at first. I stare at him.

"What part?"

"Juliet." He grins. "Don't tell anyone else yet—I'm posting the final decisions next week. But I wanted to see your face when you found out."

My mouth falls open. I shake my head mutely.

"But . . . but I auditioned for the nurse."

"You'd be wasted on the nurse," he says.

I don't know whether to laugh or to cry. A bright, warm

feeling fills my chest. I don't want to be this easy to flatter, but hearing that he thinks I'm talented makes me realize just how hungry I am for exactly that kind of praise.

"I don't know, Mr. Hunter. I've never . . . I've never carried a lead before. You probably want to pick Brynn. She's good. And she's already done some Shakespeare; at theater camp last year she played . . ."

He's shaking his head already. "Brynn *is* good. She's quite good. But she's not what I want in a Juliet. You, Elyse . . . you're really quite remarkable." Our eyes meet. This close I can see that his eyes are hazel, the kind that looks blue, green, and gold in equal measure. For a second I'm unable to move.

"I . . . what if I can't do it?" I whisper. "What if I'm not good enough?"

"I'm not worried about that," he says. He puts a hand on my shoulder and squeezes.

It's starting to sink in, starting to feel real. The lead. He's giving me the lead. A smile spreads slowly across my face.

"You're actually serious?" I ask. "I'm going to be Juliet?"

"Yes," he says.

I can't help it. I throw my arms around his neck, squealing softly. He's taller than me, so I have to stand on my tiptoes.

"Thank you!" I say. "Mr. Hunter, thank you."

"Don't thank me. You earned it. Congratulations, Elyse. I'm really excited to start working with you." He gently disentangles himself from me.

I look up at the stage, the scratches and markings on the wood intimately familiar by now. I can almost picture myself, limned by light, in Juliet's dress. Standing on the balcony. Dancing at the masquerade. Dying in the crypt, heartbroken and beautiful.

"I won't let you down," I say.

He's suddenly serious. He looks me in the eye again, appraising, intent. Then he smiles.

"I know you won't," he says.

THREE

Gabe

"Earth to Gabe." Sasha snaps her fingers in front of my face. "Hey, Jiménez, look alive."

I blink slowly, coming back to the conversation. It's a Sunday afternoon, and a bunch of us are sitting at a picnic table in a gravelly food-truck court in south Austin, sharing brisket and white bread from Reinhardt's. Sasha's holding court, surrounded by her friends. I'm doing my best to look like I'm paying attention, but I've heard this story before. Something about a girl who forgot to take the tags off her leggings for dance tryouts.

"Of course," I say, leaning over to give her a placating kiss. She cups the back of my head a little too hard. "Ow," I say, breaking away. "Careful."

But Sasha just smiles. "Oh, I'm sorry. Did that hurt?"

I give her a look. It's been two weeks since the accident. I got off lucky, with a mild concussion and a dislocated shoulder. They never caught the driver who hit me. They also never found the girl who dialed 911. She'd disappeared by the time the ambulance arrived. So there's no witness, no evidence, no way to find out what really happened that night.

I'm mostly recovered, but my head is still a little foggy, and focusing is hard. And yes, it hurts when someone presses their fingers into my skull.

Sasha turns back to her friends. "So we're all out on the floor going through the group audition, and I look down and I see it." She pauses for dramatic effect. "The *tag* is still there, stuck to her ass. Like a sticker on an apple."

I take a bite of brisket, my eyes glazing slightly. The girls at the table are all eager little Sasha clones: Julia Sherwood dyed her hair Sasha-blond over the summer; Marjorie Chin's got the exact same handbag as Sasha, in a different print. Savannah Johnston and Natalie McAfee watch her closely, hungrily, and when Savannah laughs she throws back her head, just the way Sasha does. They've all heard this story. Most of them were *there* for it; they're all on the Mustang Sallys, our high school drill team. But you don't interrupt Sasha without becoming one of the people she likes to talk about.

My phone rings. It's my dad.

"I'll be right back," I say, unfolding my legs out from under the table.

Sasha watches me with narrowed eyes. "While you're up, get me an iced skinny mocha, no whip."

I nod distractedly. I hope my relief doesn't show as I walk away from them. I don't know if I can listen to another round of recycled gossip.

"Hey, Dad," I say into the receiver, once I'm out of earshot. "What's up?"

But it's not Dad. It's my little sister's voice that comes blaring out of the phone. "Gabe!" Vivi shouts. "Merry Christmas!"

Okay, so it's October—we're nowhere close to Christmas. But who cares? Vivi's almost six, and because she has Down syndrome, her development is a little delayed. But that doesn't mean she's stupid. Who can resist a kid who thinks it's Christmas every time she gets to talk to someone she loves?

"Merry Christmas!" I boom, in my best Santa Claus voice. "What's up, kid?"

The giggle that comes through the phone line is pure gold.

"I wearing tutu!" she squeals.

"Tutu? You mean, like, you're too-too cute?" Not my best work, but she's a pretty easy audience.

She shrieks with laughter, and there's the sound of the phone hitting something. A moment later, my dad picks up.

"She wouldn't wait until tonight to put it on. I'm doing my best to steer her away from messy snacks, but I don't know how long this will last." Dad's tone is joking, but I can also hear the exhaustion in it. Turning Vivi away from something she wants to do is a serious undertaking.

"Told you you should get two dance outfits for her," I say. "One for eating peanut butter, one for performance."

"Thanks for the I-told-you-so. You'll be home by three, right? We need to be at the theater by three thirty. Don't be late."

I hang up the phone. A moment later I get a photo. Vivi grins toothily in her pale pink leotard, a stiff ridge of tulle around her waist. Next to her is her service dog, Rowdy; she's been trying to teach him how to pirouette.

Pink. Nice. That won't show every single stain, I text to my dad.

He texts me back a crying face. I roll my eyes. PhDs aren't supposed to use emojis. Neither are dads, for that matter.

I glance back at Sasha. She thinks I'm spending the whole day with her; I'd forgotten about the dance recital. I realize abruptly that my shoulders are tense, my jaw gritted, and I force myself to relax. She loves Vivi—so maybe it'll be fine. But the truth is, I never know exactly how she'll react to things.

The food court is packed with people snacking on tilapia tacos, bánh mì sliders, chipotle cheese fries, Day-Glo snow cones. The coffee cart is at the other end of the lot, in the shade of a cluster of post oaks. I order the drink from the tattooed barista and stand to the side while she disappears into the truck to make it.

I lean back against the trailer, idly thinking about how I can best break the news to avoid a shitfit. *Hey, Dad reminded me of a thing I've gotta do. I don't want to, but I'll be in big trouble if I don't.* Or maybe: *Come on, Sasha, do it for Vivi.*

She's so totally obsessed with you, it'd mean the world. No one ever went wrong banking on Sasha's vanity.

Then I see something that brings me up short.

There, at a table just a few feet away, is the girl who saved my life.

The sight of her rockets through my brain like a firecracker. A moment ago, I couldn't have described her with any certainty; my memories of that night are murky and shapeless. But now it's like some dark corner of my mind lights up with recognition.

She's alone, crouched over a heavy textbook. Her cheekbones are sharp, her skin wan next to a dark sheaf of hair. Her scuffed purple Keds are the only colorful part about her—otherwise she wears cheap jeans, a black tank top. For a moment I second-guess myself. It can't actually be her. The night of the accident, it was too dark to make much out, and my brain had just been through a blender. For all I know, my savior was a seven-foot-tall dude in a bunny suit and I'm just remembering wrong.

I watch for a moment, take in the way her toe taps slightly along with whatever she's listening to on her headphones. Then she looks up from her book and meets my eyes, and all doubts are gone. Her eyes widen, and her whole body seems to recoil in a short, sharp gasp.

She looks away again quickly, but I'm already sure of it. It's her.

Slowly, half-afraid I'll startle her like some woodland

creature, I step toward her table. "Uh . . . hi," I say. Suddenly I'm not sure how to start. What's the proper icebreaker for meeting a person who saved your life?

She pulls one earbud out, but leaves the other in. I sit down across from her, giving a smile I hope is charming. "I think . . . I think you might be the girl who helped me after my accident a few weeks back. It was over on Briarcliff—a hit-and-run?"

"Sorry. Wrong person." She shoves the earbud back in, looks determinedly down at her book. But she's lying. I can tell. Her mouth is a straight line, but her eyes are wide and almost frightened. I reach across the table and touch her hand to get her attention.

She jerks her hand away like she's been burned. Her pencil falls to the ground.

"Sorry . . ."

"No, it's okay, just . . ."

"Here, I . . ."

We talk over each other for an awkward moment, both leaning down at the same time. I get to it first, and she snatches it out of my hand.

"Look, I just wanted to thank you," I say.

"I don't know what you're talking about," she says, clearly annoyed. "And I've got a lot of homework, so . . ."

A shadow falls across the table. I look up to see Sasha, outline dark against the sun. A few feet behind her, the Sallys are standing in a tight group, glaring at me.

"Uh . . ." I say, stupidly. My heart drops.

"Hey! I was just coming to tell you we're going to the Springs. But I see you might have other plans."

Her voice is as bright as a blade, sharp with false cheer, her lips a blood-red slash on her pale face.

"Hey. Sorry, I was just . . ."

"Don't I know you?" Sasha's talking to the girl, not to me. "You're in third-period computer lab, aren't you?"

I'm almost afraid to look at the girl. I don't want to incite more of Sasha's wrath than I have to. But out of the periphery of my vision I see her nod.

"Yeah, you're the girl that keeps throwing the curve." If I didn't know Sasha, I'd think she sounded impressed, but her eyes gleam dangerously. "What's your name again?"

The girl pauses for a long moment before she answers. "Catherine," she says.

"Yeah, that's right." Sasha turns back to me, smiling. "This one keeps getting perfect scores on the quizzes. We all want to kill her." She says it almost playfully, like it's all friendly teasing, but I know better.

If they didn't before, they will now, I think. But her words give me an idea. "Yeah, I'm in English with her. I was just asking about the homework."

It's risky. She could fact-check pretty easily, catch me in the lie. But her eyes soften a little.

"Like you'll even do the reading," she says. She brushes her hair back over her shoulder. "Where's my drink?"

"Oh . . . yeah." I jump to my feet. The barista long since called my order, and the drink is sitting there on the counter, the ice half-melted. "Here."

Sasha eyes it distastefully, then heaves a sigh. She plunges the straw in like an ice pick and swirls the cup gently. "So, are we going to the Springs or what?"

I swallow hard. "The thing is, Vivi's got a recital. I totally forgot about it, but . . . I have to go to it." I hold up my phone quickly, hoping the tutu picture will derail her a little. "How cute is this?"

Her eyes soften a little. I feel some of the tightness go out of my back as she takes the phone from me. "Oh my God, that's out of control. Look, she put a little tiara on the dog!" She shows the picture around to her friends, and they all coo and croon in appreciation.

"You should come with me," I say hopefully, edging away from the girl at the table. "It'll only be an hour or so, and then we can go to Kerbey Lane after."

Her gaze snaps up. "I'm not eating pancakes on our date night," she says, her voice frosty again.

I fight the urge to roll my eyes. "Okay, then, Asti Trattoria or whatever." Never mind that a meal at Asti will clear out the last of my birthday money. "Whatever you want."

She sighs patiently, like I'm a little kid. "Of course we'll go to Vivi's recital. God, I'm not a monster." She hands the phone back to me and turns to her friends. "You guys have fun at the Springs. We've got to get going."

I finally exhale. Crisis averted. Barely.

"Thanks, Catherine. See you in class." I give the girl a wave and turn to follow Sasha.

Halfway to the parking lot I risk a glance behind me. She's hunched over her notebook again, her hair spilling down over her shoulders to hide her face. But I catch a glimpse of her eyes, wide and wary, as she watches us go.

FOUR

Elyse

I've barely gotten through the doors on Monday morning when Brynn grabs me, sliding her arm through mine.

"The casting list's up," she whispers.

I lick my chapped lips. "Have you looked yet?"

She shakes her head. "Not yet. I was waiting for you."

It's officially my first test as a lead actor: pretending I don't already know that I've been cast.

I could hardly sit still this weekend. One minute I felt like I could fly. The next, I felt like I might puke. I kept picturing what Brynn's face would look like when she found out she wasn't Juliet. When she found out *I* was Juliet. I've been dreading this moment for two days straight.

Now I steel myself, letting my best friend lead me to the ticket office. There's already a crowd. I see Nessa craning her neck to see over someone's shoulder. The basketball player grins widely and nudges a boy standing next to him. One girl is crying.

"You ready for this?" Brynn asks, squeezing my arm.

No. "As ready as I'm going to be," I say, my mouth dry as sand.

Brynn's eyes are bright, hopeful as she stands on her tiptoes to see over the crowd. My heart wrenches in my chest, so sharp for a moment I forget to be happy for myself. I know how much this means to her.

But before I have a chance to say anything, Frankie catches sight of me.

"I knew you'd get it," he says loudly, pulling me into an excited hug. "Your reading was unbelievable!"

I can't see Brynn for a moment, her face disappearing behind Frankie's shoulder while he pulls me close. Other people are looking our way now.

"Congratulations!" Nessa says, grinning. Laura Egan grabs my hands and jumps up and down. I can't help it; a smile blooms across my face at the sight of theirs. I've never been the center of attention before.

"Thanks," I say. "Thanks, everyone."

And then I see Brynn, standing stock-still in front of the casting list. She's facing away from me so all I can see is the back of her head. Over her shoulder I can see my name, hand-written in neat marker.

Juliet. . . . . Elyse McCormick

I scan the rest of the list. Frankie's Romeo; Nessa is Lady Montague; and Laura, Lady Capulet. The basketball player, Trajan Holland, is Tybalt. Brynn's name is halfway down the list.

She's the nurse.

I feel queasy. It's not fair. Brynn works so hard—she rehearses more than anyone I know. She's gone to every drama camp, every theater workshop, every master class she could. I don't understand why Mr. Hunter picked me over her.

I step closer to her, and the people around us get a little quiet. In the time-honored tradition of high school theater club, they are all eager for a whiff of drama. She doesn't turn to look at me; I've never seen her face so still, her expression so blank.

"Brynn . . ." I start. Then I realize I don't know what to say.

She turns to look at me, her eyes glistening with tears. But then all at once she forces a smile. She pulls me into her arms so I can smell the sweet vanilla of her perfume.

"I'm so happy for you," she says softly. And even though her hug is a little wooden, I know she means it.

Tears well up in my own eyes. "You should've gotten it."

"Not this time," she says. "You really did kill that reading." She wipes at her face and laughs softly. "It wasn't mine to get. But next time . . . I'm coming for you."

The rest of the day is surreal. I feel like a minor celebrity—people keep coming up to me and congratulating me. Even people I don't know, or people who aren't involved with theater. For once I don't feel invisible. Somehow the news of my casting has pulled back a curtain and turned on the lights and now I'm on stage, watched as I walk down the hall or answer a question in class. Meg Derrick, the student body president, buys me a cup of coffee from a vending machine before English. And Trajan shoulder checks me lightly as we pass between classes, grinning widely. His gaggle of athlete friends give me the kind of appraising looks that make me blush and straighten up at the same time.

At one point I see Mr. Hunter. It's just after fifth period, and he's in the hallway outside his classroom, monitoring the passing period the way all the teachers are supposed to do. I'm not sure if I should say hi, or wave, or just scurry past as usual, but before I can make up my mind he catches sight of me. A half smile touches his lips, and he winks.

Bubbles fill my chest. I feel like laughing, skipping. But I just smile and hurry past him, remembering the way he talked to me on Friday.

You, Elyse. You're really quite remarkable.

After school I manage to extricate myself from the crowds and head out into the crisp Portland fall. The rains haven't started yet. I pass run-down bungalows with rusted chain-link fences, cars on blocks in half the yards. But even in my neighborhood, with its broken glass on the sidewalk and its weed-choked lawns, the sun is burnished gold against the deep blue sky and the trees are tall and bright and green.

My building is a sagging pink-and-gray box called the Shayla Apartments. I've always assumed Shayla was the daughter or wife or sister of some previous owner. Now the place is owned by a rental company, and the original Shayla is long gone. The parking lot is an expanse of chipped and broken concrete. The unit doors are all tightly shut, strange chemical smells coming out of some.

At mine I stop for a moment, my smile fading. Home sweet home. I stand outside listening for signs of life, hoping against hope to find an empty apartment when I go in. But I'm not surprised when I hear the TV blaring as soon as I crack the door.

My mom's wearing stained sweatpants and an oversized Mickey Mouse T-shirt. She's curled up on the sofa, her eyes vaguely tracking the images on the TV. She's only thirty-four but she looks older. Her hair is fried to an ugly calico orange from too much cheap dye; her bones jut painfully against her dry pink skin. A cigarette smolders in an ashtray teetering on the edge of the coffee table. A quick pulse of anger takes over my good mood.

"Didn't you have a shift today?" I shut the door behind me and immediately start tidying up. Celebrity gossip magazines are splayed out all over the floor, and plates of half-eaten food cluster around the sofa. A pilling, smelly afghan lies heaped on the floor where Mom kicked it off in some fretful dream.

"My back hurts real bad today," she says. She gives this exaggerated grimace, her eyes not quite making it to my face.

I was six when my mom had her car accident. I still remember the brace she had to wear to keep her spine aligned. The crash left her with pulled ligaments, broken bones, and two herniated discs. And because it was her fault—she ran a red light—there was no hope of settlement money to help with the treatment. That was when she started on the Oxy, for the pain.

It's been nine years, but she still spends half her days in a fog. I don't know how much actual pain she's in anymore; it's hard to know if she's still suffering, or if she just likes feeling high.

"Mom, you've got to keep this job." I try to keep my voice calm. Sometimes if I get mad, if I yell, Mom will set off on a whole new binge, trying to numb her hurt feelings. "There's nowhere else that'll take you."

"I know, I know. Tomorrow. I promise."

Tomorrow. The single most overused word in Mom's vocabulary. *Tomorrow I'll go to the doctor. Tomorrow I'll go to work. Tomorrow I'll do those dishes, take out the trash, eat something, change my clothes. Tomorrow I'll stop using.* I grab the cigarette in the ashtray and stab it out almost violently.

"The rate you're going, you're going to set the place on fire before we get evicted."

I stomp into my bedroom and shut the door firmly behind me. I can still hear the TV through the wall. Someone on a game show asks for a vowel. I stick the phone into my stereo dock and turn on Adele to try to drown out the noise.

My room is sparse, but comfortable. There's a small wooden desk I found on the side of the road and spray-painted teal; the cheerful yellow curtains and pillowy duvet were bought out of my movie-theater wages. White fairy lights crisscross a tall bookshelf, stacked high with all my books.

I sink down onto the bed and start unlacing my shoes. I have just enough time to shower before I have to catch the bus. There's a past-due electrical bill on my desk, and the other utilities will be along again soon. Ever since our last eviction, I've taken charge of the household bills.

Sometimes it feels like I'm juggling knives. No, not knives; sharp as they are, knives are light. I'm juggling anvils. Keeping the power on, finishing my homework on time, getting to all my shifts at work, making sure Mom eats enough. Every one is a weight that, any minute, could fall straight on my head.

Tomorrow I'll go through Mom's room, try to find her stash. Flush it. Not that it'll matter; she's got a half dozen doctors ready and willing to prescribe her more. Mom's a mess, but she's a cunning mess, good at manipulating what she needs out of people. But maybe I can slow her down a little.

I take a deep breath, rummage in my bag for my script. Sometimes you have to keep moving so you don't give up entirely. I take a minute to leaf through, scanning the lines. Mr. Hunter's words come drifting back. *You're really quite remarkable.*

But what does that matter? I realize with a dull pang that

the magic of the day has vanished. Shakespeare isn't going to pay the bills. Shakespeare isn't going to help my mom get to work on time, or help her stay clean. I throw the script onto my desk and pick up my towel. Time to get ready for work.

Because Shakespeare isn't going to get me out of this hellhole.

FIVE

Gabe

"You gonna be all healed up in time for Big Bend this Christmas?" asks Caleb Scott, picking the crust off one of his three peanut-butter-and-jelly sandwiches. "I got a new tent. Super lightweight, good for the trail."

It's lunchtime on Tuesday, and we're sitting at a cement table in the outdoor lunch area. The sun is mild in the sky, the heat finally broken. A few yards away a game of ultimate Frisbee rages up and down the lawn. Guitar music drifts aimlessly through the air from where a girl sits under a tree playing.

"Ugh," says Irene Novak, before I can reply. She's next to Caleb, doodling in her history textbook. She's transformed Thomas Jefferson into a psycho clown, penciling a creepy painted leer on his face. "You guys are nuts. A week with no shower, no electricity, no cell coverage? Kill me."

"Yeah, well, that's why you ain't invited," Caleb drawls. He's the only person I know in Austin with an actual Texas accent. "We don't need a repeat of the Enchanted Rock trip."

"Yeah, no kidding," Irene says, peering wryly over the frame of her cat-eye glasses. Her hair is purple this week, short and shaggy around her ears. "Twenty-four hours with nothing but crickets and wind. Never again."

"More like twenty-four hours with crickets, wind, and your bitching." Caleb pauses to shove half his sandwich in his mouth. He's six foot four and built like a tree trunk; the dude never stops eating. "I'm trying to get a little peace and quiet on this trip."

I know better than to take their bickering seriously. Caleb and Irene have been best friends since kindergarten. I don't know how, exactly—they're nothing alike. He's the definition of mellow, a guy whose idea of a good time is stargazing on the edge of town with his dog and a six-pack. Irene, on the other hand, keeps a running, snarky commentary on everything that happens, her hands always busy, always sketching or scrawling. The manic energy comes in handy when she's tagging street signs or stenciling pictures on walls.

"I'm down," I say to Caleb. "My shoulder's still pretty stiff, but I think it'll be fine by then. I just have to talk my mom and dad into it. And, uh, Sasha."

Irene snorts, but doesn't look up from her book. "Better find a backup backpacker, Caleb. Gabe's gonna be home for the holidays."

"Hey, I'm my own man."

She shakes her head sympathetically. "She's not going to let you out of her sight for a whole week. Especially not for Christmas. I mean, what are the holidays without an all-out screaming fight?"

"It's tradition," says Caleb.

Now I remember how they've been friends so long. They have me to gang up on.

"What was it last year? The chocolates you got her were the wrong kind?" Irene says, rolling her eyes.

"Nope, that was Valentine's Day. Christmas was the fact that he went to Midnight Mass with his family instead of taking her out for that carriage ride."

They're both enjoying this too much. "Whatever. It's not like I need her permission to go."

That *really* makes them laugh. I scowl around the table.

Ladies and gentlemen, my supportive best friends.

I've opened my mouth to argue when Caleb nudges me. "Speak of the devil."

I follow his gaze to see Sasha, eyes hidden behind her sunglasses. Heads turn as she steps across the patio. Seeing her walk toward me used to send a hot thrill through my body, crowding out every thought in my head. I wonder when I stopped feeling that way.

"Oh, great! You can ask her now!" Irene's eyes give a wicked sparkle. "Since it's no big deal, right?"

"Ask me what?" Sasha sits on the bench next to me, otherwise ignoring my friends. Her lips are etched out in perfect red lines, a nonchalant pout.

"Uh . . . well . . ." I take off my strapback hat, mess with the brim, push it back on over my curls. Irene's the one who answers.

"Caleb and Gabe here are planning a trip over Christmas break." Irene's voice is cloyingly sweet; she loves a chance to troll Sasha. I shoot her a look, but she ignores me. "They're going backpacking. You don't mind, do you?"

Sasha doesn't even look at Irene. "Obviously I don't. I already told him it was okay."

My stomach twists. It's not true—I haven't said a word to Sasha—but she can't admit Irene knows something before she does.

"Anyway, Christmas doesn't matter. Because we've got our own trip planned for New Year's," she says.

I turn to look at her. "Huh?"

"Yeah, remember?" She takes my hand in both of hers. "You said we could go to Houston. Hit up some clubs, watch the fireworks. Get a hotel room." She says the last part softly, suggestively, but instead of stirring my interest it sets my teeth on edge.

"Uh, no, I don't remember," I say. *Because I never said that,* I finish silently.

"You're such an asshole sometimes." She stands up abruptly. "Whatever. Have a good time in the backwoods. I hope you get murdered by hillbillies." She stalks away, her profile icy with disdain.

"What a lovely girl," Irene says, watching her go. "Are you sure *she's* not the one who ran you down, Gabe?"

"Ha, ha." I throw my sandwich wrapper down on the table. "Thanks a lot, Irene. Now I'm in deep shit."

"Oh, you were going be in trouble no matter when she found out." Irene flips a page in her book and starts to embellish a hair-metal mullet onto a portrait of Dolly Madison. "Relax. She'll be pissed about something else by dinner."

"Great, that's a huge consolation." The first bell rings. I scoop up my books. "I'll see you guys after school."

I head down the hall toward my fourth-period photography class. I've got a whole roll of film to develop today, all of Sasha. Sasha posing with her hands lifting her hair, pin-up style. Sasha posing in her Mustang Sally costume. Sasha posing by pretending not to pose.

Then, ahead of me, I see something that draws me up short: purple Keds, scuffed along the white rubber sole.

My whole body seems to lift up, floating a little at the sight of her. She's walking away from me, but I recognize her dark hair bunching around her backpack, the way her shoulders slope. I pick up my pace, try to catch up, but she disappears into the library before I can say her name.

Hardly anyone uses the library here, aside from a few mousy-looking girls who reshelve materials during their lunch breaks. I've only been in there once, freshman year, when Mr. Doyle brought us down to try to instill in us the magic of reading. We spent the whole time sneaking up on each other in the stacks.

It's silent inside. I guess that's the idea, but after the noise of the hallway it feels almost like a tomb. Like a beige-carpeted, industrial-metal-shelved tomb. A plump-cheeked man wearing a bow tie sits at the front desk. He raises an eyebrow at me as if to say, *Really? You, in a library?* I give him a little wave, hitch up my backpack, and breeze past as if I know just where I'm going.

Catherine's the only one there. She's sitting under a window in a vinyl armchair, her legs curled beneath her. The sunlight skims the top of her head, making a glossy halo in her dark hair. She's reading, her earbuds in again. I watch her for a second, trying to read something in her clothes, her body language, her expression. Trying to figure out something about her. I'm usually pretty good at that kind of thing—but with her, I can't. Her jeans are faded, her dark-blue T-shirt nondescript. She has a plain green backpack, no pins, no patches, no Sharpied song lyrics.

She looks like she's trying to be invisible.

Her eyes dart up from her book and widen when she sees me. I take off my hat again, squeeze the brim. "Hey," I say. "Sorry."

She takes out her earbuds. "What?"

"I said . . . I mean . . ." I take a breath. "I just wanted to say thanks. I didn't mean to freak you out the other day. At the food-truck park. I really just wanted to say thanks."

She puts her feet back on the ground, sits up straight. On guard. But she doesn't close her book or get up to go. She bites the corner of her chapped lower lip.

"I wasn't supposed to be out that night," she whispers finally. "I'm sorry I didn't stick around for the ambulance, but my dad's really strict. If he found out . . ."

"Yeah, no . . . don't worry," I say quickly. "I'm just glad you called them. I was really out of it. I could have been there all night. You saved my life."

She shrugs uncomfortably. The silence stretches out between us for a moment.

"Yeah. I mean, they never caught the guy who ran me down," I say, trying to keep the conversation going. "You didn't happen to see who it was, did you?"

She shakes her head. "I was around the corner when I heard the tires squeal. I didn't even see the car."

"Man. Oh well, I guess I'm just happy to be alive." I sit down on the chair adjacent to her. "What're you reading?"

She holds up the book. I recognize it right away; there are about ten copies of it around my house.

"*One Hundred Years of Solitude*? Cool," I say. "You should read it in Spanish. So much gets lost in the translation."

She raises an eyebrow. I feel my cheeks get warm, and give a sheepish grin. "Or so I've been told," I say. "I've never read it. My father teaches Latin American lit at UT. He named me after García Márquez."

"Gabriel?" she asks. Something about the way she says my name gives me a shiver of pleasure, like a breath on my skin. She catches the music in the syllables.

"Gabe," I say. "Yeah. I can't even read it in English, much less español. It just kills my dad. I'm more of a comic book guy, myself."

"I like comics, too," she says with a small smile. "*The Sandman* is one of my favorite series."

"Oh yeah?" I lean forward. "Have you read *The Wicked and the Divine*? It's kind of like *Sandman*. But with, like, magic rock stars." She shakes her head. "I'll bring you the first issue. You'll love it."

Her eyes light up for a split second, but then they fade again. "No—no, I can't. Thanks. I'll . . . I'll see if they have it at the city library, or something."

The warning bell rings. Two more minutes to get to class. I stand up and linger for a second, waiting to see if I can walk with her toward her next class. She doesn't move.

Almost as if reading my mind, she gives a faint smile. "I have a free period. I spend it in the library getting caught up on homework."

"Getting caught up? I've only ever seen you *do* homework. Do you ever do anything else?" I shift my weight. "You know, besides rescuing strangers by night."

Her face falls back to her hands on her lap. A lock of hair slips past her ear and hangs down in front of her, like a curtain.

"I really have to get back to work," she says softly.

Conversation over. It stings, but I give a careless shrug. "Cool. Well . . . thanks again, Cat. I'll see you around."

I force myself not to look behind me as I walk back to the entrance. But I can't get the image of her out of my mind: the fragile way her shoulders curl around her book, the slate blue of her eyes. That lock of hair, slipping free. I don't know what her deal is, but if she's trying to be invisible, she's failing—at least with me.

SIX

Elyse

"Juliet? *Juliet*. This is your entrance." Mr. Hunter looks up from his clipboard. "Elyse?"

"Oh!" I dart forward, hurrying to join Laura and Brynn at center stage. "Sorry. Here."

Out in the audience, I hear a low giggle. My cheeks burn.

We're only halfway through the first week of rehearsal, but no one else seems to be struggling quite as much as I am. We're still on book, after all. Still reading through all the scenes. It's the easiest it'll ever be. But even with the script in hand I keep losing my place. This is the fifth time I've missed my cue.

". . . where's this girl? What, Juliet!" Brynn says again in an exaggerated tone. Her eyes bore into me like she's trying to telepathically transmit the lines straight into my head.

This must be making her crazy, watching me butcher the role she wanted.

It takes me a moment to find my place on the page. "How now, who . . . um, who calls?" The words come out awkward and stilted. My tongue keeps tripping over itself.

We plow on. Laura, playing Lady Capulet, reads her words with stately grace. And Brynn is actually already off book, her lines memorized. I'm more and more aware of the glare of the lights, the eyes in the darkness beyond the edge of the stage. I don't know what's wrong with me. I've done cold reads plenty of times and done all right, but now that I've got the biggest role of my life I'm a mess.

"Speak briefly. Can you like of Paris' love?" says Laura.

"I'll like to look, if l-l-liking looking . . . no, I mean looking liking . . . I mean . . ." I trail off. "Sorry," I finish lamely.

"How did she get this role again?" It's a stage whisper, meant to be overheard. I don't recognize the voice. It doesn't matter; my gaze drops down to my shoes.

"She got the role because she's good, Kendall." Brynn spins to squint out at the audience. "And it's just a read-through, so why don't you chill?"

The room goes deadly quiet. I can feel all those eyes raking over my body, peering from the darkness. Just last week, I was eager to be seen; I was ready to step into the spotlight. Now it occurs to me that there's a flip side to that attention. Now I realize that there are people waiting—hoping—for me to fail.

"Why don't we call it a day?" Mr. Hunter stands up,

glancing around at everyone. "We've done a lot of good work today, guys. This is all part of the process." His eyes fall on the little cluster of girls where Kendall Avery is sitting. "And I expect everyone here to be supportive along the way."

"Don't let them get to you," Brynn whispers as everyone gathers their stuff to go. "Kendall's hated me since I stole a lead right out of her grasping little hands in sixth grade." She smirks. "She told me a Filipina couldn't be Orphan Annie. She was so mad when the casting list went up."

I stare down at the script. It shakes in my hand.

"This was a mistake," I say softly. I look up at her. "You should've gotten this role. Everyone knows it."

"Well, everyone except Kendall," she jokes. "Kendall thinks Kendall should've gotten it." She gets a look at my expression and softens again. "Oh, come on, Elyse, you know that's not true. Everyone fucks up their first read-through. Especially with Shakespeare. It's hard."

"You didn't," I point out.

She throws her hands out wide. "Yeah, because I've got, like, thirty lines. You just choked because you got stuck in your head. After you've done it about a hundred thousand times, you're going to be amazing." She puts her hands on my shoulders. "Come over Saturday. We'll do the usual."

I finally smile a little. "The usual" means ordering pizza, sharing a beer stolen from her dad's stash, and running lines all night. Except usually I'm the one helping her learn her parts.

Suddenly those eyes in the audience, leering, waiting for me to mess up, don't matter as much.

"You'd do that for me?" I ask.

She frowns. "Uh, obviously," she says. "I kind of owe you for the last, like, year and a half of doing it for me."

I can't help it; I throw my arms around her neck.

"You don't give me any credit at all, do you?" Her voice is muffled against my shoulder. But she hugs me back.

She's right. I'm acting insecure. Brynn's looked out for me from the moment we met, when she stumbled on me crying in the girls' room our first week of freshman year. It was a bad day. My mom's most recent boyfriend had left the night before, giving Mom a black eye as a parting gift. I didn't know anyone at East Multnomah; we'd moved that summer, and all my junior high friends were on the other side of town. My clothes were all stained and old, my jeans too short, my sweater pilling, and at lunch a junior boy had snapped my bra so hard the strap broke. I'd gone to the bathroom to fix it, but instead, I'd just collapsed over the sink, tears pouring down my cheeks. In came this girl in a pink sequined skirt and a T-shirt with a giant sloth face printed in the middle, like a fairy godmother in a Wes Anderson movie, and instead of ignoring me like three other girls had done, she gave me a hug before she even asked my name.

And that was it. I don't know why, I don't know how, but suddenly I was sharing half of her peanut butter sandwich at lunch, and following her to drama club after school, and spending my weekends at her house singing along to musical soundtracks and eating dinner with her family. She was the one who made me audition for my first role; she was the one who coached me on speaking to the back of the room.

So why am I treating her like she's waiting for me to fail?

"Thanks," I whisper.

That's when I hear Mr. Hunter's voice behind me.

"Elyse, can I speak to you for a moment?" he asks.

My stomach dips again. I turn around to face him, expecting disappointment in his eyes. He looks serious. No dimple today. I swallow hard, my throat tight.

Brynn glances at him, then back at me. "Text me later?"

"Yeah, okay." I watch her go, my skin bristling with panic. I can hear Mr. Hunter's voice in my head, crystal clear, telling me his casting was obviously a huge mistake, that I'm not the actress he thought I'd be. I'm so busy letting him harangue me in my head I almost don't hear him when he speaks in real life.

"Are you okay?" He sits down on the edge of the stage.

"Um, yeah." I roll up my script in both hands and tap it idly against my leg. "Sorry about today, Mr. Hunter. I'll do better tomorrow."

"Of course you will. And there's no need to apologize." He leans back against his palms and looks up into the lights. "What you're doing is brave. It's hard to stand up in front of all of your peers and risk making a mistake. It makes you vulnerable. Which, for the record, is partly why I gave you the role."

I cock my head to the side. "What do you mean?"

"I mean you have a vulnerability that some of these other

girls have taken pains to hide. You really get at Juliet's . . . hope. Juliet's not stupid. She knows the risk she's running, and she still takes it. She takes it out of hope and out of love, and it leaves her . . . really exposed."

"It also ends in death," I say.

"Well, sure," he says seriously. "Everything worth doing has the possibility of ending in pain."

I bite the corner of my lip. I want to argue, to say something light, amusing. But I think of my mom fading by the day. I think of how my dad left her in the months after the accident; I think of the one postcard I got from him, written from a prison cell in Idaho. *Put some money in my commissary,* it said. It had arrived two days before my birthday. I think of the treasures I've lost over the years being evicted from apartment after apartment—the tiny diamond studs my grandma gave me, the crumbling cardboard box of secondhand Barbies I'd played with as a little kid. I think of the contours of my life, sparse and small and drab.

"Everything does end in pain, sooner or later," I say softly.

He looks up at me, his eyes flaring slightly. "Not everything." He takes my hand, gives it a quick squeeze before he lets go. "You've got something special, Elyse. You may not know it yet, but I can see it. I believe in you. And with some work, I think the sky's the limit for you."

My breath seizes up in my throat. I don't know what to say.

"Anyway, don't bolt on me because of one bad rehearsal." He rubs his chin thoughtfully. "I have an idea. Why don't you come in Sunday afternoon? Three P.M.? We can work on some of the scenes one-on-one."

"Oh, you don't have to do that," I say quickly, turning pink. I don't want him to think he's got to put in extra work just because I'm not good enough.

"I don't mind," he says. "I'm going to be here anyway—I have a lot of papers to grade. It'll be a nice break. And I think you'll get it really fast without so many people around."

I wrap the end of my ponytail tightly around the tip of my finger. As embarrassed as I am to need extra help, the idea of getting special attention from him makes my toes squirm with pleasure.

"Okay," I say. My voice is soft, but steady again, thank God. "Thanks, Mr. Hunter."

"Great." He finally smiles. It's dazzling. "I'll see you tomorrow."

Tomorrow afternoon. I'll have to go through it all again: the snickering, the staring. The snide whispers. Another burst of anxiety hits me.

If I fail, I'll be worse than invisible. I'll be pathetic.

Almost like he's reading my mind, he gives me a serious look. "You weren't cast by mistake, Elyse."

"Now I just need to prove it to everyone else." I square my shoulders. "Thanks, Mr. Hunter. For everything. I'll see you tomorrow."

I step out of the theater with a fresh sense of determination. Between Brynn and Mr. Hunter, I'm not just going to learn this role. I'm going to own it.

SEVEN

Gabe

"Jesus, Sasha, slow down a little." I brace myself against the dash, gritting my teeth as we hurtle through the darkness. She just laughs and turns the sound system up, Pretty Lights blaring from the speakers, the beat pulsing through my bones.

We're on our way to Savannah Johnston's party in Westlake. Sasha's been particularly prickly all day. This morning, instead of going with her to the mall, I went to my little sister's soccer game. Then I spent the afternoon doing my homework instead of running straight to her. By the time Sasha picked me up in her electric-blue Mini Cooper, she was in a foul mood.

"Scared?" she asks, a thrill in her voice.

I just look out the window at the dark shapes of trees flying past.

She doesn't like being ignored. "Fine. Be that way."

And that's when she snaps the headlights off. The road disappears out from under us. There's nothing around us, no streetlights, no houses, no stores—only rolling hills, hunched forms in the darkness.

"Jesus!" I grip my seat belt in both hands. The car vibrates as it swerves across the rumble strips at the side of the road and then corrects its course. I can hear the engine whine as she presses further and further on the gas pedal. "Sasha! This isn't fucking funny."

She laughs again. The needle creeps up the speed dial. The music is a howling, blaring chaos, thrumming against my skull. For a minute I'm back in the middle of the road, the night of the accident. I'm airborne. I'm flying, out of control, and there's time to think about how hard the ground is beneath me, how heavy and fast the car, how flimsy my body . . .

And then, all at once, the road is back. She's snapped the headlights back on. The car starts to decelerate, still too fast, but not quite so wild.

Sasha says, smirking, "This from my edgy skate-punk boyfriend."

"Did something piss you off tonight?" I ask. "Or are you just in a mood?"

The playful sparkle disappears from her eyes. Her fingers tighten around the driving wheel, the sneer on her face lingering.

"I'm just ready to have some fun," she says. Her voice is low and almost silky. It sends a chill down my spine.

My heart is hammering, but I don't want to make things worse. I stare out the window again, even though there's nothing to watch but my own darkened reflection. We sit in silence for the rest of the drive.

Savannah's house is perched on top of a hill with a sweeping view of downtown Austin.

Inside, the high-ceilinged marble entryway is packed. I see a few people I know, already jumping around to the thud of the music. Noah Delany and Paul Meyer wave at me from the sidelines, holding red Solo cups. Abhay Patel is busy at the DJ booth, adjusting his levels as he mixes Sia's "Chandelier" with some ambient electronic dance number. No sign of Caleb or Irene yet, though I know they were planning to come.

No sign of Catherine, either. But then, she wouldn't be at a party like this. I try not to let my disappointment show.

I turn to look at Sasha, only to see that Julia and Marjorie have already converged. They huddle together, whispering something and laughing. I take deep breaths, try to regain my composure, but a dull nausea tugs my stomach downward.

"Hey, Gabe." Savannah's appeared at my elbow. She's wearing a tight silver dress that looks a lot like Sasha's pale pink one.

"Savannah, you look great," I say, giving her a hug.

"Thanks." She flushes, pleased. "Can you believe how many people are here?"

"Hey, Savannah. Nice dress. Did you raid my closet?"

Sasha's suddenly there in front of us, lips pressed in a smirk. To anyone who didn't know her, her words would sound sincere. But her eyes glint at Savannah, and I instinctively let my arm drop from around Savannah's shoulder.

Savannah tries a tinkling little laugh. I wince at how forced it sounds. "Thanks! Great minds."

Sasha tosses her hair. "Sure. Something like that."

Savannah wilts a little next to me. But then she squares her shoulders, as if steeling herself. "Come on, let's dance." She laces her arm through Sasha's.

"Get me a beer, okay, babe?" Sasha's grip on Savannah is tight. Behind them, a few of the other Mustang Sallys watch through narrowed eyes. All it will take is a word from Sasha to make them turn on Savannah.

It suddenly feels crazy to me, like Savannah's sticking her hand in an alligator's mouth. And then, with disgust, I realize I'm no different. We all act like we're honored to let her treat us like shit.

I make my way through the crowds to the backyard, which is lit with Christmas lights strung through the posts in the wrought iron fence. A bunch of people gather around the keg on the patio. Half the wrestling team is in the kidney-shaped pool with their girlfriends, chicken fighting. Natalie McAfee already has her top off. She falls off Mike Bookout's shoulders with a squeal and a splash. A little further back there's a bonfire pit. I see Caleb and Irene in the group gathered around.

Caleb's roasting a marshmallow over the flames, turning it slowly back and forth for an even golden brown. Irene's got a charred-looking s'more in one hand, a joint in the other.

"Double-fisted partying. Nice," I say. I grab the joint from her and take a drag. The smoke washes over my nerves, smoothing out the tangles.

"You look like hell," Irene says. "What's up?"

"Sasha's in a mood." I take a deep breath. The heat of the flames laps against my skin. "She drove out here like a fucking maniac. Now she's in there torturing the other Sallys or something. I've got to take her a beer in a second."

"Is it my imagination, or is she more psycho than usual?" Irene frowns.

I shrug. "She's pissed that Savannah's having the first big party of the year, I think. It's usually at her house, but her parents have her on a short leash since the whole security camera thing."

"Did you hear she managed to get Tori Spencer kicked off the Sallys? She basically accused Tori of bullying her." Irene pops the last of her s'more into her mouth. "Which doesn't sound like Tori. It sounds like Sasha." Her words are muffled through the marshmallow.

I grimace. "Yeah. She's been laughing about it." Tori was trying to change one of their routines, which meant that Sasha's solo got cut. She went crying to their coach with some crazy story about Tori sabotaging her costume before a game.

Irene shakes her head. "Jesus, what's it gonna take for you to break up with her?"

I don't answer right away. The truth is, I don't know *how* to answer. Because Irene's right. Sasha's appeal has worn thin. I don't know if it's that Sasha's gotten more unstable, or if I'm finally just seeing it for what it is—not some wild, free-spirited energy but something dark and bottomless and boiling. Something with the power to destroy.

That's when Devon Lord, who's standing on the other side of Irene, speaks up, startling all three of us.

"Man, sorry to slide into your conversation like a creep, but it's crazy that you gave Sasha that ring."

Irene, Caleb, and I turn to stare at him.

"What ring?" I ask.

Devon pulls his marshmallow out of the pit. It's a perfect golden brown, even on all sides. He blows on it for a moment, then slides it onto a graham cracker. "That promise ring, or whatever? I don't know, it looked like a big honking diamond."

"How the hell is Gabe gonna afford a diamond?" Irene asks. "He owes me, like, ten thousand dollars for the past three years of Taco Cabana trips. He's never got money."

Devon shrugs.

"Seriously, when did you hear about this?" I realize my voice has gotten loud. People are looking. I grit my teeth and try to calm down. "This is so ridiculous. Like, she had a ring and she was showing it off or something?"

"Yup. In figure drawing yesterday. She kept sort of flitting her hand around." He mimes admiring the back of his hand. "Kept talking about how romantic the whole thing was. Had some big story about how you promised to be with her forever, and you had chocolate-covered strawberries and, like, some song you wrote just for her . . ."

I grimace. "No, man, I didn't do any of that shit. She's . . . she's just messing with you."

But I can't get the image out of my mind. Sasha with a dreamy smile on her face, telling some story that makes it sound like I'm planning to *marry* her someday. Maybe doing it as some kind of joke at first . . . but reveling in the attention. Letting the story spin out of control. Letting everyone believe it. It's not exactly out of character for her.

Almost as if she's reading my mind, Irene turns to look at me. "That's the kind of shit she always pulls when something's out of her control, Gabe."

But before she can finish her sentence, I catch sight of Sasha, emerging from the darkness and into the orange light of the bonfire. Her shoulders are rigid with anger.

"What happened to getting my beer?" she snaps.

Normally, when Sasha comes at me like that, I get flustered. Normally I stammer an apology, sheepishly say goodbye to my friends, hurry to the line at the keg. But this time I can't even speak. I just stare at her.

Her expression falters a little. "What?"

"So where's that promise ring I gave you?" I say.

She tosses her hair and gives an airy laugh. "Oh, that. Give me a break, I was obviously kidding. I found a ring in Mom's safe and thought it'd be funny."

"Sure. Except Devon Lord believed you. So you're not kidding. You're *lying*."

"Devon Lord is dumb as a sack of bricks," she says. "No offense, Devon."

"Uh, taken," he says, frowning.

"And besides . . ." She puts her hand on her hips and stares at me, and even though I know I'm in the right and she is not, I feel like I'm about three inches tall. "Is it so fucking awful for people to think you might do something nice for me once in a while? God, to hear you talk, I've been telling everyone I'm pregnant or you gave me crabs or something."

Is she right? Am I overreacting? I don't even know anymore. I'm never on stable ground with Sasha. I never know how to feel.

And suddenly, that's enough of a reason to be done.

She must see it in my expression. An uncertain look flickers across her face and is gone. Her hands drift away from her hips and she shrinks a little.

"Gabe?" she asks. It's maybe the first time I've heard her sound vulnerable . . . but I don't care anymore.

I look over at Caleb. "You cool to drive, man? I need to get out of here."

"Yeah, man." He glances at Irene, and suddenly they're flanking me. "Let's get outta here."

Sasha shakes her head, lifting her chin angrily. "Don't you even think about leaving me here."

"Okay, Sasha, step aside." Irene tries to shoulder past her. Sasha swells up, her spine going rigid. I push Irene gently behind me.

"Stop," I tell Sasha. My voice comes out almost like a plea; I don't have energy for anything more. "Just . . . stop, okay?"

I turn away from her. I don't look behind me as we walk toward the door. I half expect her to run after me. My shoulders are tensed for it. But she never does, and we get to Caleb's beater without anyone saying a word.

I'm in a car, hurtling in the darkness. The scene shifts and I'm outside of the car and it's barreling toward me. I'm watching Sasha dance, her shorts encrusted in sequins, a white spangled cowboy hat on her head—but partway through the performance she stops and starts to strip. At first I lean forward to watch, a thrill running through me as her long limbs emerge bare and smooth. But then she's angry, her face screwing up into a mask of fury, and she's pulling out her own hair, her eyes swollen, her hands gripping long blond locks and yanking them free. Blood runs down her scalp. She steps toward the edge of the stage, and her eyes meet mine. For a moment we both stare at one another, as if seeing each other for the first time. Then she launches herself like a cat, straight toward me.

I wake sweaty and disoriented. It's pitch-black. Snatches of anxious half dream, half memory grab at me. I'm in my own room, in my own bed. My clock reads 3:42 A.M.; it's only been two hours since Caleb dropped me off.

It's half a second before my eyes adjust and I realize I'm not alone.

Sasha's sitting backward on my desk chair, her legs splayed out on either side of the frame. Her hair is tangled and loose, and her eye makeup is smeared down her cheeks. She looks like a half-mad ghost, blood-hungry, but the smile she gives is calm and almost beatific.

"What are you *doing* here?" I sit up straight, adrenaline shooting through my veins. The darkness feels like it's crowding in on all sides. I pull my blanket up to my chest, even though I'm still fully clothed. "Jesus, how'd you even get in?"

She shrugs. "I have a key."

"You have a . . ." I shake my head. "What key?"

"I had it made a couple of months ago."

"What, did you steal mine and get it duplicated?"

She gives a soft snort, rolling her eyes. "Jesus, Gabe, you act like I'm untrustworthy. Plenty of people leave spare keys with their girlfriends."

I know something is wrong with this line of reasoning, but I'm still so groggy, so confused, I can't quite figure out what. I reach for the bedside lamp, but her voice cuts through the darkness. "Don't!"

Then she stands up from the chair, and I see that she's completely naked.

"I came to make nice," she purrs.

My breath catches in my throat. She is truly beautiful, her body powerful and delicate at the same time. But she's also truly terrifying. The angles of her face disappear into shadow. Her mouth is a tight determined line. And there's something flat and far away in her eyes.

"Sasha, this is nuts," I whisper. "My parents are asleep down the hall."

She moves toward me. Her skin glows in the moonlight. "All I want is to make you happy. You mean everything to me. I *need* you." She leans down, cups my chin in her hand.

I jerk away from her touch. "Don't."

"Oh, Gabe, come on." She rests a knee on the bed next to me. Her flowery perfume winds its way into my nose, into my throat. The sense of claustrophobia intensifies. I push her to the side, gasping for air.

Now she looks genuinely confused. For the first time a hint of self-consciousness seems to cross her features. She presses her knees together and hunches her shoulders. "What's wrong?" she asks. "Why don't you want me?"

I stare at her. I can see that the last question, at least, is dead earnest, and that's what breaks my heart: the fact that she can fight with me all night long, then break into my house convinced I'll still want her. That this will make all our problems go away.

I grope around on the ground until I find her T-shirt, then hand it to her. Silently, she pulls it over her head, tugging it down to cover the tops of her thighs.

"We're done," I say, simply.

She blinks, gripping the bottom hem of her shirt. "What are you talking about?"

"Sasha, we're done. I don't want to do this anymore. The jealousy, the arguments, the head games. It's exhausting." I angle toward her, trying to look her in the face, but she's staring out in space now. "I don't think you even love me anymore. I think you just like playing with me."

She shakes her head, still not looking at me. "No."

"Yes." I put my hands on her shoulders, trying to force her to look at me, but she wrenches out of my grip.

"Forget about it," she hisses. "We're *not* breaking up."

Anger rises up again, all my pity and anxiety and sadness swallowed whole by the rush of it. "You don't get to decide that. It's not up to you."

She smirks at me. It's humorless, hard. "Isn't it, though?"

I shake my head. "I'm done fighting." Then I lean across the bed and snap on the lamp.

Light floods the room. She recoils, squinting. Somehow in the light she doesn't seem so frightening, so unpredictable.

"Find your clothes. I'll walk you out to the front door."

For a minute, it looks like she's going to refuse, and I'm not quite sure what I'll do if that happens. Physically drag her out, kicking and screaming? I don't want to have to explain that one to my parents. I cross my arms over my chest and wait, refusing to look away. Finally, she stands up and walks over to the desk chair. Her underwear and shorts are folded neatly on the desk. I turn away as she pulls them on.

Once she's dressed, I get up off the bed and open the door softly, gesturing for her to go first. Silently, her face as still as a doll's, she walks past me and into the hall.

I follow. At my sister's half-open door, her service dog, Rowdy, pushes his head out of the crack, his tags jingling softly. *Useless dog,* I think. *Aren't you supposed to bark at intruders?* But Sasha pats Rowdy's head as she passes, and he wags up at her. Because Sasha's *not* an intruder; she's one of our pack. And now I have to start the tricky business of extricating myself from her.

In the living room, I open the front door. She stands for another moment and stares at me. Her face is strange and affectless in the dim light.

She puts her arms around my neck and presses her lips to mine. I pull back but her arms are tight, surprisingly strong. She nips at my bottom lip before letting go of me, smiling up at me with a dark glitter in her eye.

"This isn't over," she whispers.

Then she slips through the door and is gone.

EIGHT

Elyse

Sunday afternoon I let myself in the unlocked door in the arts wing and make my way to the theater.

My footfalls echo off the linoleum. There's the sharp smell of the janitor's chemical cleaners; underneath is the memory of body odor and graphite dust and greasy food. It's always weird being in the halls when school's out. There are no windows to let in the late autumn sun; the only illumination is from the emergency lights, dim and almost ambient. The place feels like I'd imagine a tomb does, the silence a rebuke to all the noise and chaos that used to be here.

Mr. Hunter is in the green room beneath the stage, sitting on a steamer trunk and paging through some notes. I linger in the doorway for a few seconds. He's wearing a plain V-neck T-shirt today, no jacket, and it makes him look younger than usual.

"Hey, you made it," he says, his dimple flashing.

"Yeah. Thanks for meeting me," I say.

"Don't mention it. The play is going up in six weeks. I sprung this part on you. I just want to make sure you're ready." I can see the back of his head in the vanity mirrors, his dark hair, his trim shoulders. I can see myself there too, standing awkwardly in front of him. My skin is pasty white in the glaring light. I suddenly hate the outfit I spent the morning picking out—skinny jeans and my favorite blue scarf. So basic.

"Should we head up to the stage?" I shift my weight, not sure if I should sit down or lead the way upstairs. He thinks about it for a moment.

"Let's stay in here so we don't have to mess with the stage lights. We're just reading—we don't need to worry about blocking yet."

I glance around. The green room is the size of a small classroom, brightly lit and decorated with posters of productions past. A shelf of wig heads stands against one wall, the Styrofoam eyes peering cagily out from under wigs and hats; the accrued detritus of decades of theater kids rests on every surface. Coffee cups and makeup kits, good-luck stuffed animals, vases of long-dried roses. An enormous mason jar filled with multicolored bits of ribbon for reasons unknown. It's a cluttered, comfortable place—but it feels suddenly, strangely intimate.

Mr. Hunter pats the spot next to him on the trunk. I sit down. There's no space between us. He smells crisp and outdoorsy, like cedar chips and winter air. I feel the heat of his body radiating toward me.

"I've been trying really hard to memorize the lines," I say. "I think I'm getting there."

He sets down the clipboard.

"I'm not worried about the lines. You're doing great. But you know, we do this play so often we take the characters for granted. Juliet's often played like a generic ingénue. But there's more to her than that. Otherwise it wouldn't be a tragedy."

I frown a little. "I thought it was a tragedy just because it was, you know . . . tragic."

"Yes, but tragic things happen all the time," he says. "Sad things, bad things, happen to people every day. Most of them aren't worth writing a play about. So what is it that's special about Juliet? What is it that makes it worth memorizing three thousand lines of poetry, just to tell this story?"

I look down, my mind spinning madly. I've never been asked a question like this before.

"Well . . . she's beautiful," I say.

He shakes his head. "You can do better than that. Come on—it doesn't have to be in the text of the play. I'm asking you to imagine her internal life. What moves her. What she dreams about." He looks at me seriously. "What does she have in common with you, Elyse?"

"Nothing," I blurt. He raises an eyebrow, and I duck my head. "I mean . . . never mind."

"No. Tell me," he says. He doesn't look mad. In fact, he looks curious. I take a deep breath.

"I just mean she's . . . you know, rich. And pretty. And she has a family that works really hard—too hard, maybe—to protect her. Never mind half the boys in Verona are apparently into her."

He looks thoughtfully out in space. "So Juliet's sheltered. She doesn't know how the world works. And you, Elyse . . . you take care of yourself?"

"I have to," I say. I hesitate. I don't want to say too much. In junior high I let slip that my mom hadn't been home for a week and a half once, and before I knew it I was in foster care for half a year. Mom's a mess, but I can say with certainty that living with her is better than living in a group home. "I mean . . . it's not so bad. I'm not, like, abused or neglected or anything. But my mom works a lot, and my dad . . . he's in prison."

I watch for some sign of shock, or even disgust. I don't talk about my dad very often because when I do, inevitably the other person I'm talking to starts treating me like I'm a daytime talk show guest or something. But Mr. Hunter just nods.

"I didn't see him for a long time before that, so it's not even like I miss him," I say.

"That's got to be hard," Mr. Hunter says. "You know, my dad . . . my dad was not great, either. He was kind of a survivalist type. He thought we should live off the grid, be ready for some kind of armed insurrection or government meltdown or something. I don't know. He was pretty unhinged. So I kind of raised myself too."

"Wow," I say. I try to imagine it. "Did you live out in the woods?"

"On and off," he says. "At least until he died."

His expression is calm and measured, but I see something in his eyes. A quick flash. I'm not sure if it's anger, or sadness.

"I'm sorry," I say.

"Don't be. It's part of what made me who I am." He leans forward, bracing his forearms against his knees. "I learned a lot from my dad, even if I hated him sometimes. You know, now I know how to start a fire without matches. I know I can survive without central heating or running water. I also know I don't *want* to," he says with a chuckle. "But I know I'm a survivor. I think someday you'll look back and see the same thing about yourself."

I look down at my hands in my lap. Will I ever be far enough from this life to be able to look back and see anything with clarity? It's hard to picture. I realize suddenly that when I imagine my future, it looks exactly the same as my present. I won't be in high school, of course; but I'll still be here, on the outskirts of Portland, mopping up spilled Coke in the movie theater every night, going home to see a mother in various states of unconsciousness.

"I think Juliet's lonely, though," I say, wanting to get the spotlight off me and my life. "Like, the nurse can barely even remember how old she is. Her mom doesn't really care if she likes Paris or not. So when Romeo shows up at the party, ready to talk to her directly, she finally feels like someone wants to know who she really is."

"That's a great observation." Mr. Hunter's voice is gentle. "Can I assume you might know something about that feeling?"

I just laugh.

No, it's not the same. Juliet is treated like precious property. I take care of a mom too strung out to even notice me. But still—we're both invisible. We're both hungry to be seen.

He sets down the script. "Okay. Let's try this. Let's do the masquerade scene, between Romeo and Juliet, and I want you to think about that while we go through it. Think about her loneliness—and the idea that someone finally sees her. How's she feeling? What does she want? No, don't answer—just channel that. Ready?"

"Don't you need the script?" I don't know why, but for some reason I'm nervous. My heart is going too fast, and my cheeks are so warm they feel almost scraped raw.

He grins. "I played Romeo in a college production. I still have it all memorized."

Of course he did.

"Ready?" He stands up, and I jump up behind him.

"Yeah. Okay."

He closes his eyes for a few seconds. When he opens them again, his affect has changed. His eyes are soft, his mouth in the slightest pout. He takes my hand, just by the very tips of the fingers. The touch is so light it makes me shiver a little.

"If I profane with my unworthiest hand this holy shrine, the gentle sin is this . . ." he starts. I feel my heart catch, snagged on something in my chest. My breath is short and shallow. "My lips, two blushing pilgrims, ready stand to smooth that rough touch with a tender kiss."

The words spring to my mouth without effort. It surprises me.

"Good pilgrim, you do wrong your hand too much, which mannerly devotion shows in this," I whisper. "For saints have hands that pilgrims' hands do touch, and palm to palm is holy palmers' kiss."

"Have not saints lips, and holy palmers too?" His voice is so tender it's like a feather on the skin. It sends a shiver across my body.

"Ay, pilgrim, lips that they must use in prayer," I say, teasingly.

We're speaking softly. The silence of the school all around us seems to pull us closer together.

"O, then, dear saint, let lips do what hands do. They pray; grant thou, lest faith turn to despair," he whispers.

"Saints do not move, though grant for prayers' sake." My hand drifts up, almost on its own, to lay a single finger on his mouth.

"Then move not, while my prayer's effect I take. Thus from my lips, by thine, my sin is purged."

His lips brush mine.

I feel both syrupy slow and electric. My mind struggles to catch up, but my head is tilting back, my mouth parting breathlessly, and the kiss lingers, his breath warm against my skin, and I think distantly that he tastes sweet and sharp, like ginger, like something you have to have in small amounts . . .

. . . and then the sensation fades. The warmth of his body pulls away like a tide. I'm tugged irresistibly toward it, leaning forward for one split second before I come back to myself. When I open my eyes he's on his feet, striding away from me.

"Shit," he says. "I'm so sorry. I shouldn't have done that." He pulls his hands roughly across his face, his cheeks pink.

My mind's trapped on a loop-de-loop, dizzy and recursive. I kissed a teacher. Or . . . he kissed me. But it was a scene from a play. But he really kissed me. But was he my teacher then, or was he Romeo? From the other side of the room the wig heads look suddenly sly, like they've just spied something illicit.

"I'm so sorry," he says again. "That was over the line." He wrings his hands together, brow furrowed. "You're a remarkable actress. I forget, sometimes, how young you are. I forget this is a high school production."

A flutter of pleasure stirs in my chest. It feels like high praise.

"Then have my lips the sin that they have took," I say softly.

"What?" He shakes his head a little, like he's getting cobwebs out of his face.

"That's my line." I clasp my hands on my knees and give him a small smile. "It's okay, Mr. Hunter. Let's just get back to the reading."

He studies my face, a crease down the middle of his forehead. "Elyse . . ."

"Don't worry about it. I won't tell anyone." I pick up my script again. "It's no big deal. Frankie and I have kissed about fifty times now, running this scene."

It's not the same and we both know it. But the tension is already dissipating. The wig heads are back to being wig heads. The heater kicks on overhead, and just that little bit of ambient noise seems to calm him.

"Well. Let's shift gears, then. Maybe move on to act three." He moves back to where he dropped his clipboard, picks it up and rifles through the script. "I was curious what you think about her relationship with the nurse."

We work for another hour or so, talking about motivations, practicing the cadence of the lines. He's careful to keep his distance this time, moving to the vanity chair. I stay on the steamer trunk. We both make notes in the margins of our scripts. It's all very professional.

But my lips still feel the kiss, its fading pressure, its hunger. And I'm not sure I want to forget it.

NINE

Gabe

"Gabe! Merry Christmas! Pancakes!"

Monday morning I come into the kitchen to see Vivi smeared with maple syrup. Rowdy licks the floor at the base of her special high chair, searching for scraps of fallen pancake. His thick yellow fur looks distinctly sticky.

My mom looks up from the stove, spatula in hand. She gives a distracted smile, a strand of graying hair falling into her eyes, and I'm struck by how tired she looks.

"Morning, Gabe. Sit down, have some breakfast."

"Morning." I lean in and kiss her on the cheek. She's wearing one of her long floral hippie skirts, and there's a smear of pancake batter on her forehead. "I can't, I've got to run. Caleb and Irene are waiting."

She looks a little hurt. I feel a pang of guilt; she must have made the pancakes special for me. She thinks I'm torn up about the breakup and that I'm just trying to be stoic. The truth is, I feel better than I have in weeks.

"Maybe I'll grab a little one for the road," I amend, picking up a silver-dollar-sized pancake and taking a bite. It's perfect, buttery and soft.

"Can you still take Vivi to therapy after school? I hate to ask, but I've got a deadline, and Dad's got a faculty meeting today."

"Yeah, no problem," I say. Mom's worked as a freelance web designer since Vivi was born; it's great, because it's flexible, but it also means she's always either hustling for work, working, or taking care of us. She's spread pretty thin.

"Thanks, kiddo." She's already got the thousand-yard stare, the far-off look that means she's thinking about what she has to do with the rest of her day. "I really appreciate it."

Caleb's Jeep is at the curb, Irene in the front passenger seat. She passes me a bag of breakfast tacos over the console as I climb in the back.

"There's bacon, egg, and cheese, and an avocado and migas," she says. "Extra sustenance for the trials ahead."

"Thanks," I say, rummaging gratefully in the bag. The smell of peppers and eggs fills the car. Caleb's motor coughs and then roars to life, and we jerk away from the curb.

"You hear anything from Sasha yesterday?" Caleb meets my eyes in the rearview. I shake my head.

"No. But apparently the story is that she dumped me at the party. She's all over Facebook going on about how great it feels to be free, about how nothing's dragging her down anymore." I take a bite of my taco and close my eyes in pleasure. "Mmm. Migas."

Irene hoots. "Oh yeah. Feels so great to lose the old ball and chain. So great you break into his house and throw yourself at him like a thirsty bitch."

"I still can't believe she did that, man," Caleb says, shaking his head.

"It's not that unexpected," Irene says. "I'm surprised she didn't put your dog in a stewpot."

"Come on, she's dramatic, but she's not *crazy* crazy," I say. I watch out the window at the Greenbelt whipping past, the treetops tinged with autumn rust. I know I should be at least a little on guard—Sasha can make life really nasty if she's mad. But I'm just relieved to be done with her. Here in the light of day, with Run the Jewels thrumming low on the stereo and my friends ribbing me from the front seat, it's easy to feel like the whole thing was kind of ridiculous. Almost funny, even.

"You ought to tell your parents she broke in so they can get the locks changed," Irene says.

"They've got enough on their plate right now," I say. "I don't want to freak them out."

"Better that than more nighttime visits from your friendly neighborhood succubus," Irene says.

"Nah . . . she's done. It was her last-ditch effort." I finish the first taco and crumple the foil into a little ball just as we pull into the junior parking lot.

The instant I get out of the car I feel exposed. I catch a

glimpse of Marjorie and Emily Chin getting out of their Lexus a few rows over, their heads huddled together in whispered conversation as they stare. A group of band kids, buried under their shiny black instrument cases, goes silent as I walk past. Ben Bloom, who dated Sasha for a few months before me, snickers audibly when he sees me.

So that's the kind of day this is going to be.

Irene and Caleb walk on either side of me, apparently by some kind of unspoken agreement. I force myself to look nonchalant and stuff the last of my taco in my mouth. I wonder what everyone knows—or what they think they know. I don't mind people thinking I've been dumped, but there will be half a dozen embellishments by now.

We're almost to the doors when I see Catherine.

She's alone, as usual. I think she must have some kind of invisibility power that I'm somehow immune to, because no one else seems to notice her. She walks slowly, her thin shoulders slightly stooped under the weight of her backpack. Her long hair coils over her shoulder, a dark question mark against the plain white of her T-shirt.

I peel away from my friends. "Hey, I'll catch up with you guys at lunch, okay?"

"What? Why?" Irene asks, startled. But I don't answer. I'm already cutting across the parking lot toward Catherine. I can feel their eyes on me as I go—their eyes, and everyone else's—but I ignore them all.

"Hi!" I step in beside her. She looks up sharply.

"Uh . . . hi," she says. Her lashes are long and thick, even without makeup; she's got a slight underbite that makes her look pensive. She'd be pretty if there weren't something so brittle in the angles of her face.

"Hey, I've been carrying these around for a week now—I keep meaning to find you and give them to you." I fumble clumsily in my backpack and pull out a small stack of comics in their polypropylene sleeves. "It's that comic I was telling you about."

I hold them out toward her, but she doesn't move to take them.

"Um, thanks. But I can't," she says. "I'm not allowed." She quickens her pace ever so slightly. I match her speed.

"To read comics?" I cock my head. "Are your parents, like, religious or something?"

She doesn't answer.

"Hey, it's no big deal. You can keep them at school, read them at lunch or something. You can even keep them in my locker if you want." I'm still holding the comics out at her. "I don't mind."

She makes no motion to take them. I finally let them fall back to my side.

"Well . . . let me know if you change your mind. I think you'd like them."

She gives me a sidelong look. "You don't even *know* me."

I stop in my tracks. The words crack over me, hostile, jagged. She walks a few steps ahead, then stops too. I see her shoulders lift and fall with a deep breath.

"I'm sorry." She half turns to look at me, her brow

furrowed. "That was . . . rude. But what exactly is it that you want from me?"

I step a little closer and watch as her body tenses. I step back again, holding both my hands up in front of me.

"Look, I don't want to harass you or whatever. I'll keep my distance from now on. I just . . . kind of wanted to get to know you."

She mumbles something. I can't quite make it out.

"What?"

"Nothing." She loops her fingers under the straps of her backpack. "Your girlfriend seems pretty possessive. Does she know you're talking to me?"

"Sasha and I are through. We broke up this weekend," I say.

"You did?" I struggle to read her face. "Oh. I mean . . . I'm sorry."

"Don't be. It wasn't working out." I adjust the straps of my backpack on my shoulders. "Anyway, it's no big deal. It's over. She doesn't care who I talk to."

For a moment she stands there, in the middle of the sidewalk. People give us strange looks as they stream around us toward the school. Then her eyes dart up to my face.

"Do you know Sekrit? The app, I mean?"

"Yeah. I've never used it." I shift my weight. "I usually just text people."

She shakes her head. "It's more private. Secure." She hesitates again. "I'm dollorous00." She spells it out for me.

Then, before I can say anything, she steps close. I get

a whiff of her shampoo. It smells like some kind of fruit—pomegranate or cherries, maybe. I close my eyes, and before I can move she's taken the comics from my hand and disappeared into the crowd.

For a moment I stand there in the glaring morning sun. Then I pull out my phone, ready to download the app and find her there. I'm already writing the first message in my head. It has to be casual—I don't want to freak her out—and maybe funny. But not too funny. Not like I'm saying, *hey, look at me, I'm so funny*. I don't want her to think I'm trying too hard.

But before I can even go to the app store, I see I've got a new Snapchat. It's from a number I don't know. I wonder if it's hers—if she found me already. I open it.

It's a video. At first I can't make anything out—whoever's taking it is behind a chain-link fence, with a large bush obscuring the view. But then the camera refocuses, and I see a playground. A bunch of little kids run laughing across the wood chips, playing tag. They're maybe five—kindergarteners, first graders.

Suddenly I feel cold. I know, somehow, what I will see.

The camera zooms in on one little girl, her curly black hair in pigtails. She looks impossibly tiny against the playground equipment, and she toddles along with a clumsy, stomping gait. The camera is close enough to pick up her laughter.

It's Vivi.

TEN

Elyse

"Leo was so cute when he was younger," Brynn says, taking a handful of popcorn from the large bowl between us.

It's Monday evening, and we're in her living room, taking a break from homework to watch the old *Romeo + Juliet* from the nineties. We're ostensibly watching for "research." It's the party scene—the part where their eyes meet through the fish tank, Claire Danes in her angel wings, Leonardo in his armor.

"He's still pretty cute," I say. "Did you see *Gatsby*? He looks good in a suit."

Brynn sticks her tongue out. "Too old."

"He's not that old," I mumble. My cheeks burn, but she's not looking.

I spent the rest of the day yesterday trying to decide if the kiss had really happened, or if it'd been a dream. Outside of the close air of the green room it seemed so unlikely. But I could still feel it—could still close my eyes and feel the pressure of our mouths touching. He was right—it was crossing the line. It shouldn't have happened. But I've gone over the memory again and again, my heart tripping in my chest every time.

I haven't mentioned it to Brynn. I'm not sure why—I don't think she'd tell anyone. But it feels safer to cradle the secret close, to keep it protected.

"Your one-on-one session must have done you some good," Brynn says suddenly, almost as if reading my mind.

My hand freezes halfway to the popcorn bowl. "What do you mean?" This afternoon I worked as hard as I could to keep things normal, even though the sight of Mr. Hunter filled my chest with bubbles. I barely talked to him, and only when he had something to say about the play. But Brynn knew me better than anyone else. Maybe she'd seen through it.

She doesn't even glance at me. "I mean, you're off book for act one now. And you sound really good."

"Oh. Oh, thanks." I catch my breath again. "Yeah, we just ran lines. It was helpful."

Brynn is wearing a pair of pajama bottoms printed all over with fluffy cartoon sheep. Her hair is pinned up in a sloppy bun, her face is makeup free, and her glasses are crooked on her nose. It's 7:45. It took her less than five minutes to get out of her vintage swing dress and wipe her lipstick off when we got in the door from rehearsal. As far as I know I'm the only person she lets see her like this besides her family.

She glances at me now, raising an eyebrow. "What's up with you? You're all twitchy."

"Just tired," I say. "My brain is full."

"Girl, please, you've got four acts to go." She sits up, folding her legs under her. "Anyway, we need a break. Not a watching-old-movies break. Like, a find-a-Sadie-Hawkins-dress break. Want to hit the vintage shops this weekend?"

I slump back against the overstuffed sofa. "Oh God, that's coming up? We just got done with homecoming. What's the student council's crepe paper budget, anyway?"

She chews the edge of her thumbnail. "I'm thinking about asking Trajan."

"Trajan? Like, the star basketball player currently playing Tybalt?" I laugh. "You're going to have to find six-inch heels, or else you'll be slow-dancing with his bellybutton." Trajan's got to be at least six foot five.

She smirks. "There's something about a guy who could throw you over his shoulder, though. You know? I mean, not like in a caveman way. More in a sexy fireman way. Anyway, what about you?"

"I'm not so into sexy firemen. I'm more of a hot-cop kind of girl," I say.

"No, I mean . . . who do you want to go after?"

The image of Mr. Hunter floats up before my eyes. Which is ridiculous. Because even if we *would* go together, we *couldn't*.

I pull a pillow down over my face. "I'm too tired to go to a dance. I'm too tired for anything except rehearsal. I am a line-memorizing robot."

She rolls her eyes. "Oh, come on. It's not even a lot of work. Find a dress, then come over and let me do your hair and makeup. Boom. Dance-ready."

"Maybe they'll let me wear my Juliet costume and I can wander around the dance running lines from the masquerade scene," I say. "I can multitask."

"You can at least help me find a dress," Brynn says. "Come on, you haven't gone with me in forever."

"Because vintage shopping with you sucks. All I find are moth-eaten housedresses covered in, like, bloodstains and cat hair and black mold. Meanwhile you always manage to find some amazing dress in perfect condition and magically in your size." I shake my head. "It's like you have a superpower. A very limited but very useful superpower."

"Remember that Pierre Cardin I found last summer? Oh man, they didn't even know what they had." She gets a faraway look in her eyes.

I purse my lips. "It's so unfair."

I look away from the TV, the lines echoing in my head. *Then move not, while my prayer's effect I take. Thus from my lips, by thine, my sin is purged.* The scene is layered now, memories overlapping across it. I think of rehearsal, of the chaste peck Frankie gives me, of the feeling of intense focus I get when I'm diving into the role; I think of Mr. Hunter, his lips on mine. I think of the row of wig heads in the green room, watching like an audience, wondering how it will end.

"You girls doing okay?" Mrs. Catambay appears in the doorway. She's a tiny, plump woman with warm sepia skin, and as usual, she's holding a tray laden with food—paciencia cookies and dried bananas and the coconut crackers she knows I love. She comes in and sets it down on the coffee table.

"Mom. We're fine," Brynn says, rolling her eyes. "We don't need to eat every snack in the house."

"Ooh. I love this movie." Mrs. Catambay pauses in front of the TV and gives a little sigh. "Your dad and I used to make out to the soundtrack."

"Ew!" Brynn clamps her hands over her ears.

"You should be grateful we did," Mrs. Catambay goes on, a wicked glint in her eyes. "You wouldn't be here if it weren't for that Des'ree song."

"Oh my God, you have to stop," Brynn groans.

They joust like this all the time. It's partly a bit, partly not. They get on each other's nerves and crack each other up at the same time. I can't even imagine talking this way with my own mom.

"How have you been, Elyse?" Mrs. Catambay turns her attention to me, her eyes twinkling warmly. "I feel like I haven't seen you in a while. School going okay?"

"Yes, ma'am." Mrs. Catambay's always been warm and welcoming toward me. She never says anything about my mom, but she knows things aren't great at home; she takes pains to feed me and fuss over me. But even though the Catambays are playful and casual with each other, I can't quite get the hang of the "normal family" patter. I'm always a little too formal. Luckily Brynn's mom thinks it's hilarious.

"You hear that? *Ma'am*. I am a ma'am, Brynn." She points triumphantly at me. "This is what a respectful child looks like."

"She just doesn't know any better," returns Brynn. Then she throws a pillow at her mom. "Go away. We're trying to learn our lines."

Mrs. Catambay just laughs.

"I'll be in the kitchen Skyping with your *lola*," she says. "Elyse, help yourself to anything else you want, since my ingrate daughter will probably forget to offer you anything." She kisses the top of Brynn's head and whisks out of the room.

"Sorry," Brynn says. Her bun is askew from the mauling, but she doesn't bother to fix it. At home she is completely without a care about her image.

"You know I love your mom," I say. "She always reminds me of Lorelei Gilmore."

"Jesus, don't tell her that, she'll never shut up." She gives me a sidelong look. "How's *your* mom doing?"

"It's been bad lately." Mom's been particularly out of it. She hasn't been to work in a few weeks—I'm assuming she's lost her job. I had to take on extra shifts at the movie theater to make sure we could pay our bills.

I don't have to tell Brynn all this. She knows what "bad" means.

"That sucks." She exhales loudly. And while Mrs. Catambay is out of the room, ostensibly not listening, and while she would insist that Brynn's a terrible hostess who doesn't pay attention to her guests, I know that when I leave here I'll have a bag full of food. Tons of snacks; a bunch of perfectly good fruit they'll claim is "about to go bad;" a Tupperware container full of leftover adobo because "Mom made too much." And I know it'll be impossible to tell who's responsible—Brynn or Mrs. Catambay—because no matter what they say about each other, they're peas in a pod.

I rest my head against Brynn's. The rhythm of her breath against my shoulder soothes me. On the screen, Leo and Claire dodge into an elevator and kiss, narrowly evading Lady Capulet. I think about my own kiss again—the feel of Mr. Hunter's five-o'clock shadow against my face, the woodsy smell of him. I imagine telling Brynn about it. What would she say? It'd almost be worth it just to be less in my own head about the whole thing, just to hear it out loud. It'd make it feel more real.

But what if she thinks it's gross? What if she can tell I liked it anyway?

I press my lips together tightly, as if I might tell her in spite of myself. She glances at me and her brow furrows.

"You know you can crash here any time things get too crappy," she says softly. It takes me a minute to realize she's talking about my mom.

"Thanks," I say. Then I smile. "You really are the best."

She throws a piece of popcorn into her mouth, catching it neatly.

"Yeah," she says. "I know."

ELEVEN

Gabe

"All students will make their way to the B gym for this afternoon's pep rally. Again, all students must make their way to the B gym quickly and quietly . . ."

Principal Degroot's voice is nearly drowned out over the intercom by the noise in the halls. It's the Friday before homecoming, and the last two hours of the school day are devoted to the manic religious experience that is Texas football. Everyone's wearing blue and red, Mustang colors; a few people even have painted faces and bright-colored wigs. The tide moves relentlessly toward the gym.

"Ready?" Caleb says, straightening up from the vending machine with his arms full of Doritos and Hostess cakes. Irene snags a bag off the top and opens it.

"Ready," I agree.

We make our way upstream, against the crowd.

The three of us don't exactly have an abundance of school spirit. The game itself is fun enough—who doesn't like watching two-hundred-pound dudes brutalize each other?—but the other parts of it, the tribalism and theatrics and rah-rah-rah, are lame. Of course, dating Sasha, I had to go to every single event so I could watch her dance. But now I am free to blow off any and all pep-related activities.

I imagine the crush in the gym, the mass of kids piled into the bleachers while cheerleaders tumble below. The football team will come running out through a big paper banner and everyone will chant, "Wat-er-LOO! Wat-er-LOO!" And then the Mustang Sallys will come out in formation, kicking and strutting to the marching band's rendition of some cheesy pop song. I can picture Sasha there in the center in her cowboy hat and sequined vest, her smile painted on, her skin glowing in all that luminous attention.

I've been trying to avoid her since the breakup. It's not easy. Every time I turn a corner she's there, her pale eyes sending a freeze ray right in my direction. She knows my schedule by heart, so I have to assume she's going out of her way to bump into me. I've started ducking into the bathroom every time I see a hint of blond curly hair. I don't want anything to do with her.

Because while I can't prove she sent that Snapchat message, I don't know who else it could be.

I'm not scared. I'm pissed. I don't trust myself to talk to

her. When I imagine it—when I think about the video, the implicit threat to my little sister, my fingers twitch convulsively. I want to grab Sasha by the shoulders, to shake her, to make clear what I will do to her if she comes near Vivi. And that would be trouble.

But I haven't gotten any further messages from the mystery number . . . so I have to believe it was just a pathetic, fumbling attempt to get my attention. The death rattle of a bad relationship.

"Hey, man, there's that girl." Caleb's voice interrupts my reverie.

I shake my head, look up at him. "Huh?"

He's a full five inches taller than me; he can see over the crowd and down the hall more easily than I can. He nods to the left. "That girl. You know, the one you chased across the parking lot Monday."

My head snaps to follow his gaze. There she is, curled protectively around a stack of books: Catherine. She strikes me the way she does every time—some camouflaged forest animal, quiet in the shadows, hard to make out but fascinating once seen.

I've been messaging with her all week now—mostly light, innocuous stuff. Videos of baby sloths, pictures of my food, dumb memes from Reddit. Anything I can think of to start a conversation. She's mostly just responded with smiley faces, or vague, noncommittal words. *Cute! LOL.* But here and there we've had an actual exchange. When I sent a picture of Vivi hugging Rowdy around the neck, she said:

dollorous00: I don't know if I'm more jealous of the dog or your sister. Pure love.

And another time:

daredevil_atx: Anyone ever tell you you look like Natalie Dormer from Game of Thrones?
dollorous00: Ha . . . no? But thank you.
daredevil_atx: She's my favorite. Though Sansa Stark's pretty badass now that she's dressing like a supervillain.
dollorous00: I HATE Sansa! She's the WORST.
daredevil_atx: No spoilers! I'm behind by a season and I plan to binge watch the rest this weekend. You should come over and watch with me.

A suggestion that we should hang out was apparently too much too soon, though, because I haven't heard from her since that one.

Now I stop in my tracks. "Hey, Catherine! Cat!"

It seems to take her a minute to register my voice. She blinks, then gives a little wave without slowing down.

But this time I'm not going to let her slip by me. I push my way across the hall. "Trust me, you can skip the pep rally. Spoiler alert: Waterloo High will Go-Fight-Win. Our opposition will be pushed Way, Way Back. We will score many goal units that way."

In spite of herself, the corner of her mouth twitches up.

"But how am I ever going to learn how to spell *victory* if I don't go?"

"Wait, wait, is that a joke?" I feign incredulity. "School spirit is good on you. It really brings out your inner snark."

She glances up and down the hall, stepping back as a guy in a red-and-blue clown wig walks between us, howling. "This is nuts. No one at my old school cared about football."

"Must not have been in Texas, then," I say. "This is pretty tame. Last year we fought our rivals from just outside Houston. There was livestock loose in the hallways. Seriously—their mascot's a ram, and some dumbshit thought it was going to be a good idea to sacrifice a sheep . . ."

"Oh no . . ." She looks simultaneously horrified and amused.

"Don't worry, it survived. It got loose, ate half the band's sheet music, and took a crap on the Mustang mosaic in the middle of the cafeteria before the 4-H kids managed to wrangle it into submission. I hear it's living in Tori Spencer's backyard now. Keeps the grass trimmed."

She laughs.

For that moment it's like the crowd becomes so many cardboard cutouts around us. The chaos gets swallowed, and in its vacuum all I can hear is her laughter. It's soft, musical, muted—a tune escaping from a mine, from somewhere deep and dark.

And then I come back to myself as Caleb and Irene come up behind me. "Hey. What's the holdup, Jiménez?" Irene asks.

"Hey. Uh, this is Catherine. I was just trying to convince her to come with us instead of going to the rally."

Irene gives her an appraising smirk. I feel unaccountably nervous. It's not like I need my friends to approve of some girl I've got a crush on—but then, since they were right all along about Sasha, maybe I *should* wait for their thumbs-up.

Finally, Irene nods. "Come on, then."

I feel myself relax. Catherine glances from Irene back to me, uncertain. Caleb holds up a package of Ding Dongs and shakes it enticingly.

"We've got snacks," he says.

A shy smile unfolds over her face. She tucks her books under one arm.

"Okay," she says. "Where are we going?"

Technically, the Lower Courtyard isn't really a courtyard. It's a spot under the social sciences wing that's built over a dip in the landscape and supported by pillars, with an entrance to the ground floor that barely ever gets used. It's functionally a shaded patio for smokers, skate punks, art freaks, and burnouts.

Over time the place has gotten decorated in a haphazard, communal kind of way. A handful of mismatched deck chairs sit at random angles to each other. Someone's left a bucket of colored chalk down there, and the concrete is covered in smeared and faded scrawls. *Smash the patriarchy! Mara + Colton 4Eva. Degroot suxxxxxxx!* There's a broken pogo stick leaning against the wall, and someone has wound chili-pepper-shaped string lights around two of the pillars, though the bulbs are all burned out.

Irene shakes her head at the chalk graffiti. "Amateurs." She dumps out the bucket of chalk and picks up a pastel green, running it in quick graceful lines over the concrete. Caleb releases the armful of snacks onto a three-legged card table propped up with cinder blocks and picks up a bag of pretzels. I glance at Catherine; she's smiling a little, looking around the Courtyard. A warm hum fills my chest.

"You're new, right?" Irene asks, glancing up at Catherine as she draws. "Where'd you go last year?"

"Oh . . . last year I lived in Eureka. It's in Northern California." She scuffs her feet. I pull a pink plastic lawn chair out and gesture to it with mock gallantry, and she sits. I plop down next to her on an upended milk crate.

"Cool," says Caleb. "I got a cousin in Eureka. Maddy Scott? You ever meet her? She's a year behind us."

Catherine shakes her head. "No, I don't . . . I mean, we lived right outside Eureka. Kind of, uh, rural."

"Rural Humboldt County. You must have some stories," Caleb says. "I bet you got a contact high just walking down the street."

Catherine's eyes fall to her lap, where her fingers twist anxiously. I give Caleb a look, willing him to stop putting her on the spot.

"Anyway," I say pointedly. "Hey, so, I'm halfway through *One Hundred Years of Solitude."*

Her face lights up a little. "Isn't it amazing?"

"Yeah, except it's more like One Hundred Years of Dudes with the Same Name. I can't figure out who's who."

She grins. "I know, I had that problem too. I had to make a flow chart."

"Whoa, whoa. Back up," says Irene. "Gabe's reading? A, like, book?"

"A, like, five-hundred-page book," I say haughtily. "It's been known to happen."

"Uh huh," Irene says. She looks up at Catherine. "Have you read *Love in the Time of Cholera*? I like that one even better."

"No, but it's on my list," Catherine says. "Maybe I'll pick it up over Christmas break."

"You have to really savor it. It's slow and dense and gorgeous." Irene picks up a yellow piece of chalk and starts to color something in. "Why aren't you in AP English with me? If you're reading García Márquez you're better qualified than, like, ninety percent of the idiots in there."

I could kill both of my best friends right now. But Catherine just gives a little shrug. "My grades weren't good enough last year. My mom died in the middle of the semester and I . . . I didn't really recover very quickly."

Irene stops what she's doing and looks up. "That sucks, dude." She pushes her cat-eye glasses up her nose. "My dad died when I was twelve. Car crash. The idiot was driving home drunk from a Longhorns game. It was totally his fault, so I couldn't even be mad at someone else. I basically refused to leave the house all summer. These two were the only people who'd still talk to me after that." She jerks her head at me and Caleb. "Everyone else was too weirded out."

Catherine nods eagerly. "Yeah, I felt like such a . . . such a freak. Still do, kind of. Most people don't get it."

Okay . . . maybe I spoke too soon. Because the tension suddenly leaves Catherine's jaw, and her eyes are round and earnest.

"Yeah, well, most people are morons." Irene studies her, then starts to draw again. "That why you moved here?"

"Yeah. Dad thought we needed a change of scene." She kicks her legs gently, brushing her hair to one side. "It's okay here, I guess. But I miss the trees back home."

"The redwoods are amazing," Caleb says. "But Texas is okay. You should check out Hamilton Pool—it's just outside town. Big limestone grotto. Snapping turtles, jackrabbits, catfish."

"That sounds beautiful," she says.

And just like that, she's chatting with my friends. I'm not sure if I'm grateful or jealous. How is it that they've gotten this girl out of her shell more in five minutes than I have in a week? But soon I'm laughing with everyone else while Irene and Caleb retell our best stories: the time the three of us stole a golf cart from the country club and drove it up and down the halls at school, dressed in argyle sweater vests and plaid pants; the time Caleb got arrested because he was staring at some fireflies so intently the cops thought he was on drugs.

The time we climbed out on the train trestle over Town Lake to help Irene paint giant octopus tentacles coming up from the water and I almost fell. By the time the bell rings we're laughing our asses off.

Caleb glances at Irene, then back at Catherine. "Hey, what're you doing after school? Weather's still good. Why don't we all head out to Hamilton Pool?"

"Yeah!" I sit up straight. "We totally should. It's awesome. And we can go to Rosie's on the way back. It's this dope TexMex dive. I saw Willie Nelson there once."

Catherine looks a little startled. She picks up her books and hugs them to her chest, almost unconsciously.

"That sounds . . . amazing. I really wish I could. But I have to get home."

Irene shakes her head. "What's so great about home? Your new best friends aren't there. They're going to Hamilton Pool and possibly getting high with an aging country music star. Just think about what you could miss out on."

"Trust me. I'm already regretting it." She chews the corner of her lip, then shakes her head and gets up to go. "Maybe another time. This has been really fun."

"You know where to find us." Irene gives her a little wave.

I scramble to my feet. "Can I walk you a little ways?"

She's quiet for a long moment, and my stomach lurches.

"Okay," she finally says.

I don't even hear Caleb and Irene saying goodbye. There's nothing but Catherine, casting her long shadow next to mine.

We make our way toward the street. Greasy-looking clouds obscure the sun overhead. A thin breeze shifts the branches of the box shrubs lining the walkway.

"Your friends seem nice," she says shyly.

"Really? Because based on this afternoon, they seem more like career criminals," I joke.

She doesn't smile. "No—I can tell. They care about each other. You all care about each other."

There's a note of such sadness in her voice when she says this that I come up short for a moment. It strikes me that I've never met anyone who seemed as lonely as her.

And then I'm moving before I can think twice about it. My arms slide around her. I pull her close. For a moment she's bony against my chest, hard and unyielding. But then, just as I'm about to let go, she softens. I close my eyes. In the dark behind my lids there's just the smell of her shampoo, like sun-ripened fruit, and the warmth of her body against mine.

She steps away, and I stagger a little.

"I've got to get home. I'll see you."

"Yeah." I watch her make her way up the street, her gait a little faster than usual. She turns a corner and disappears out of view.

I stand there, my brain shorted out, my body alive with the memory of hers. My phone vibrates, and I reach for it in a fog.

But when I see what it is, my focus comes rushing back,

razor sharp. It's another Snap from an unknown number. A still frame this time—a picture of me and Catherine at the bus stop. A picture from mere seconds ago. In it, Catherine's moving out of my arms. But whoever sent the message has modified the image.

There's a skull, superimposed over Catherine's face.

TWELVE

Elyse

On Friday afternoon Mr. Hunter announces to the cast that he's managed to score free tickets to a matinee production of *No Exit*, and we should all come if we can. "Sorry it's last-minute," he says. "I didn't know if I could get the whole group in or not."

So I spend Saturday morning trying to figure out what to wear. Last year I bought a short, curve-hugging LBD on markdown at Nordstrom, and I've never yet had the guts to wear it in public. I put it on and take it off three times before I finally steel myself and rip off the tags. I manage to curl my hair without burning myself for once, so it falls in soft waves around my shoulders, and I swipe red lipstick across my mouth. My dark-blue eyes pop from thick, dark lashes.

I barely recognize myself in the mirror. For a half-beat of my heart, I think, *God, I don't just look pretty; I look glamorous.* But the very thought makes me blush. It's too much. Too drastic a change. It's ridiculous. I'm heading to my closet to change into something else when I hear Brynn's quick double honk from the parking lot.

No time. I have to go.

Outside my bedroom the smell of unwashed clothes and cigarette smoke stings my nostrils. My mother lies sprawled across the sofa, wearing the same dirty T-shirt and athletic shorts she's had on for almost a week. She snores softly. The TV's tuned to what looks like a police procedural, music low and ominous.

I move softly, trying to ease over the creaking floorboards without waking her. But at the door I pause, biting my lip. The temperature in the apartment is icy, and we can't afford to turn up the thermostat. Sighing, I take a green-and-yellow afghan off the back of the couch and spread it over her.

Mom stirs, her eyelids fluttering with the effort it takes to open them. "That's a new outfit. Where you going?"

"To a play," I say, tucking the edges of the afghan under her shoulders a little snugger than necessary. "Did you eat anything today?"

But she's already nodded off again.

I hesitate for a moment, trying to gauge how far gone she is this time. Brynn's waiting, though. I quickly grab the cigarette lighter off the table and slip it into my purse—at least I can keep her from accidentally setting the couch on fire—and head out the door.

Brynn does a double take when I hop into the passenger seat.

"Wow" is all she says.

I flip down the visor mirror, check my makeup and my hair. It hasn't gotten messed up in the ninety seconds since I left my bedroom. I keep fighting the certainty that the mascara is smeared, the lipstick on my teeth. "Is it okay?"

"Uh, yeah, you look amazing." She gives a sideways grin. "Your legs look about twenty feet long in that dress."

She's wearing a lime-green pencil dress, her hair in thick, 1940s-style victory rolls around her face. "You've got to teach me how to do that to my hair sometime," I say.

She gives me another long look, then shakes her head. "It doesn't look like I need to teach you anything," she says, putting the car into gear.

The theater's in a hip little row of cafés and shops in a neighborhood lined with Victorian houses. We park and join the others just outside the ticket office. I don't see Mr. Hunter; he must be running late.

Kendall gives me an up-and-down glance. "Jesus, Elyse, it's just a matinee. What'd you do, rob a Saks?"

I feel my cheeks get warm. I open my mouth to snap back, but before I can, I see Mr. Hunter, and all other thoughts disappear from my mind.

He gives a half-distracted, half-wry grin when he sees us from down the street. Somehow he's both sophisticated and sheepish—stylish in slim-cut jeans and a blazer, his hair mussed from running. He looks like how I've always imagined a writer or a professor: like someone who sits in the big picture window at Powell's drinking black coffee, watching people pass on the sidewalk outside and taking notes in a Moleskine.

"Sorry I'm late!" He steps up to the box office and gives the cashier a dazzling smile. "We should be on the list."

He doesn't even look my way. I realize I'm standing on my toes, leaning toward him, a plant craning for light. I force myself to relax.

It's not like he's going to ogle me or tell me I look hot. Not in front of everyone. But I can't help it. I can feel myself shrinking, my shoulders drawing up against my body. I feel suddenly ridiculous. Everyone's looking at me, and even though that was the point, it doesn't feel as fun as I'd hoped. The heels, the lipstick—it's all too much, it's two P.M. on a Saturday. I feel wildly overdressed, even standing next to Brynn in her vintage clothes and pin-up-girl hair.

I hug my purse under my arm and follow everyone into the theater. It's small, a cramped, claustrophobic space perfect for Sartre. Mr. Hunter leads the way, handing the usher our tickets and herding us into a row near the back. Brynn sits next to Trajan. I watch as she leans over and says something that makes him laugh. I sit on the other side of her, tucking my purse under the chair and looking down at my lap. The low susurrus of conversation weaves around me in the dim house lights.

I feel someone settle in next to me. I look up, expecting to see Frankie or Nessa or Laura, one of my other friends, but when I see Mr. Hunter my pulse swells like a tide. He doesn't look my way, and I barely have enough time to register him when the lights go down and everything disappears from view.

The seats are close together. In that brief moment of darkness I feel the heat of his body radiating toward me. I feel his breath, rising and falling. I don't let myself lean toward him. But I don't shy away from the contact. My elbow touches his across the armrest, and even with his sleeve between us, it makes me breathless.

The first two actors step out on stage. "So here we are?" says Garcin.

"Yes, Mr. Garcin," says the valet.

"And this is what it looks like?"

I barely register their voices. I can't track what's happening on the stage. I stare blindly forward as the other characters join them, one by one, filling up the nightmarish little room. Out of the corner of my eye I watch Mr. Hunter's profile, his aquiline nose, his dark, thick eyebrows. The stage lights shift and change color, sending wild shadows across his face.

My mind wheels around wildly, soaring over the theater. I know that I'm supposed to forget that kiss. He said it was a mistake, and he was right. But being so near him now, in the dark . . . I touch my lips, remembering.

I know it can't happen again. But I want proof. Proof that it wasn't all in my head—a dream, a fantasy.

Proof that, for just a moment, he wanted to touch me.

I shift my weight toward him, just a little. It's barely noticeable. I could deny it if I had to. I slide my arm onto the armrest, as if I didn't notice his elbow there on the edge. I breathe in his smell, cedar and citrus and something else, a dark musky note.

His chair creaks softly as he shifts his weight too. And then it's like every connection in my brain lights up at once, a Christmas tree surging to life, twinkling and brilliant, because his hand brushes against mine, our skin touches, and everything in the world vanishes but that tiny point of contact.

On stage the actors are yelling at each other about something, but I don't care. His hand draws gently away again, and I'm left wondering if it was an accident or not. My head spins. He's never once looked my way. His eyes are locked on the stage.

But it felt so much like a caress. Deliberate and soft and gentle.

As if from far away, I hear Garcin's famous one-liner: "Hell is other people!" Soon the audience is clapping and whistling. The actors step forward to bow. The warmth between us dissipates as Mr. Hunter gets to his feet, applauding.

The house lights go up. Mr. Hunter turns to say something to Nessa, who's sitting on the other side of him. I fight down a surge of jealousy. Why won't he just *look* at me?

"That was amazing," Brynn says breathlessly.

"Yeah, great," I say, distracted. She doesn't notice. We stand up and start crowding toward the exits. "Crap, I left my purse."

I turn around, and walk right into Mr. Hunter. His hands land on my hips.

For just a moment, I think I see a flash of longing in his eyes.

Then he smiles, jerking his hands away. "Sorry about that," he says, bluntly cheerful. "You startled me."

"It's . . . okay." I straighten up. I've been praying for his gaze all day. Now it moves over my face, making me visible, beautiful.

"Sorry, I just need to get my purse."

He steps back so I can squeeze by, and when I turn around he's gone, along with the rest of my friends, out to the lobby. I stand there for a moment, letting my heart slow its manic staccato flutter.

I don't know anymore what's real and what's my imagination, what's a kiss and what's a performance. I don't know if I'm just hoping, wishing, for him to think I'm special. For him to look at me and touch me and want me. But I can't deny one thing, not even to myself.

I want it to be real.

THIRTEEN

Gabe

I don't have any classes with Sasha this semester, but I still know her schedule. So Monday after lunch I wait outside her figure-drawing class until I see her coming down the hall.

I'm acting against every bit of good advice I've ever gotten, including my own. But I've thought about it all weekend. Breaking into my room to freak me out was one thing. Stalking my little sister—and Catherine—is another. I can't let it go.

She smiles when she sees me, but she doesn't pick up her pace. When she gets to the door of the classroom it looks for a minute like she's going to saunter right past me. I grab her arm; when her eyes widen I realize I'm squeezing harder than I meant to. I let go.

"Knock it off with the Snaps," I growl.

She cocks her head. "What's your problem?"

"Don't be cute," I say. I fight to keep my voice steady. The sight of her arched brows makes me want to push her away as hard as I can. "Leave my friends and my family alone, Sasha."

She smooths an invisible wrinkle from her skirt. "I seriously don't know what you're talking about."

I grit my teeth. "Whatever. If I hear from you again I'm going to the cops."

She shakes her head, looking almost sad. "Gabe, come on, there's no need for this. I'm totally over it, okay? I've moved on. I'm dating someone new. So whoever's messing with you . . . it's not me."

"You're so over it you break into my house?" I say.

She glances away.

"That was . . . not cool. I was drunk, I was upset. You blindsided me. I'm sorry I freaked you out."

Now I'm the one who's blindsided. I've never heard Sasha apologize for anything.

She peers almost shyly up at me, through a canopy of lashes. "Anyway. I'm over it now. And . . . I'd like it if we could be friends."

She looks so earnest—and I want to believe her. I want this to be over.

But I also don't trust her.

"Fat chance," I say. I adjust my baseball cap, take a few steps backward. "Just stay away from us."

I turn away before she can answer.

•••

"Yummy!" Vivi says, her eyes wide as the waiter sets a steaming plate of cheese enchiladas in front of her.

"Yummy indeed. Now be careful, *mija,* it's hot." Dad leans over to tuck a napkin into the front of Vivi's shirt. "Let it sit for a minute."

We're at my sister's favorite restaurant, El Rancho, to celebrate her sixth birthday. The faux-hacienda is packed, as always, the air thrumming with conversation and music. Every now and then a loud groan erupts from the crowd watching soccer at the bar. I keep catching my dad's eyes flitting over to the TV. Mexico's playing tonight, so if the margaritas keep coming we might be in for some truly foul Spanish swear words. Dad's lived in the States his entire life, but his own father used to play for the Liga MX, the top-tier soccer league in Mexico, before he and my grandma moved to L.A., so it's safe to say he's a total fanatic.

I take my phone out of my pocket, glancing down to see if there are any messages I've missed. It's become a nervous tic. There's nothing, though—nothing on my Snapchat, and, disappointingly, nothing new on my Sekrit. I haven't heard from Catherine since yesterday afternoon. I quickly reread our old conversation.

daredevil_atx: Hey, no randos have been texting you, have they?

dollorous00: Besides you, you mean?

daredevil_atx: :P

dollorous00: No, no one's been texting me. Why?

daredevil_atx: No reason. I just want to make sure I'm your only rando. Rando Calrissian. William Rando Hearst. Rando Baggins.

dolorous00: Don't worry. You've definitely managed to be the BIGGEST rando, in any case.

So at least Sasha hasn't been hounding Catherine directly. I wonder if I should warn her—if I should give her a heads-up that I may have accidentally brought the wrath of the drill team down upon her. But there's no need to freak her out if Sasha isn't actively messing with her. And Sasha claims she's done. The question is whether I can believe her or not.

My little sister's wearing a plastic rhinestone tiara, and a cluster of bright balloons is tied to the back of her chair, fanning out like a throne. She looks like a tiny princess in Crayola colors.

"Happy birthday me!" she says, kicking her feet out.

"Happy birthday you," I agree. "Did your class like the treats, Vivi?" Last night I baked and frosted three dozen chocolate-and-banana cupcakes, each with a *Little Mermaid* paper cutout stuck into the top with a toothpick. I'm a pretty good baker, but it took me forever to finish them. When she came downstairs this morning and saw them, though, the look on her face made the whole thing worth it.

"Yup," she says.

"Except one little girl demanded a *Frozen* cupcake instead," Mom says. "There were tears when I told her we were an Ariel household. Tears, and judgment."

"There's no accounting for taste." I pick up a tortilla, bouncing it from hand to hand to keep from burning my fingers.

And then, almost like an apparition, I see Catherine float past the bar, and nothing else even registers.

Just behind her is a tall, bearded man in a plaid button-down. His stride is heavy, authoritative. He pulls out her chair for her. She sits automatically, like a wind-up doll.

A waitress brings a basket of chips to their table, and Catherine dips one in the salsa. The man watches her, his brow furrowed in what looks like disapproval. Or disappointment? Either way, he leans in to talk to her, but she doesn't look up from the menu.

"'Scuse me," I mutter. "I need to run to the bathroom." I push myself back from the table and drop my napkin onto my empty plate. My parents don't even look up; Dad's taking pictures, and Mom's trying to get a glob of enchilada sauce out of Vivi's hair.

I walk around the wide edge of the room. Catherine's back is to me now, but I can see the man's face. His eyes are hidden behind his glasses, light glinting off the lenses. As I approach, I can just make out what he's saying.

"Can you please just relax and try to have a nice evening?" He trails off as he sees me. I take a deep breath and put on my best parent-charming smile.

"Sorry, I didn't mean to interrupt," I say, rubbing the back of my neck with an aw-shucks grin. "I just saw Catherine and thought I'd say hi."

I glance down at her, and something jerks in my chest. The expression on her face isn't just shy, or nervous.

She's staring at me in wide-eyed horror.

"Well, hello." The man's voice is softer than I expected, almost gentle. "Do you two know each other from school?"

My eyes dart to Catherine. Now, mired in a mistake I don't understand, I don't know what to say. She gives a tight little nod.

"Yes, sir. I'm Gabe Jiménez." I gesture back to my own table, where my sister is playing with the tiny plastic animals that always fill her pockets, galloping a blue elephant across her plate. "We're out for my little sister's birthday."

Catherine's staring back down at the table, but the man watches me steadily.

"That's nice. How's the food here? I've heard the queso is great."

"Oh yeah, best in town," I say. I turn an open, friendly face toward him, but inside my pockets my fingers clench. Why won't she look at me?

It's that moment when the mariachi band approaches my family's table, buckles and tassels bright against their dark jackets. The vihuela strums a few opening chords, and the band erupts into "Las Mañanitas." A small flan appears from the kitchen, a single candle flickering from the center. Vivi claps her hands, off-rhythm with the music.

Catherine's father gives a tight smile.

"Looks like you'd better get back to your family, Gabe. It was nice to meet you. I hope your sister has a happy birthday."

There's no way to argue with that. I give them both an awkward wave, and head back to my table. I feel the man's eyes follow me all the way.

I barely hear the music, barely notice my little sister's delighted squeal. Dad takes pictures of Vivi with the mariachi while Mom sings along. The candlelight lights up Vivi's face. Her arms pump up and down in spontaneous, uncontrolled joy.

"Make a wish!" Dad says, as the music comes to its robust finale. Vivi leans forward and blows her candle out in one sputtering breath. I absentmindedly join in the applause. I sneak another glance at Catherine and her father. They're talking now, both leaning in over the salsa dish. His lips move quickly, angrily. She shakes her head no. He grimaces, slapping his palm lightly on the table.

"Gabe, yummy!" Vivi's holding up a huge quivering spoonful of flan to my lips. Most of it ends up on my chin, but I make a big show of wiping it off with my finger and then popping it in my mouth.

"So yummy!" I say. "Boy, they're sugaring you right up before bedtime, aren't they? Maybe we should just leave her here. I'm sure the mariachi will look after her."

She laughs and bounces in her seat.

I don't risk another glance at Catherine's table until we're on our way out. She and her dad have their entrées, and they sit, unspeaking, picking at their food. I will her to look up at me, but her eyes remain resolutely downcast.

As I pass, her dad's eyes narrow in my direction. I feel it like a jab to the ribs, sharp and hostile.

He doesn't look away until I'm out the door.

FOURTEEN

Elyse

"That was great, Elyse," says Mr. Hunter. "Can we try it again?"

It's Monday—the first time I've seen Mr. Hunter since the matinee. Since those few brief moments of contact. I've been counting down the seconds to get here. Desperate to be in a room with him, to be near him. To see if anything has changed.

Now I'm not sure why I was so anxious to see him. Because nothing has happened.

"Let's start from 'Come, night,'" he says. "And when Brynn comes in, let's really slow down when she tells you Tybalt is dead. Remember, you think she's telling you Romeo's dead. It's a big moment."

"Sure." I roll my neck back and forth, trying to release some of the tension in my shoulders. I step back to my mark and take a deep breath.

"Come, night. Come, Romeo. Come, thou day in night . . ." I meet Mr. Hunter's eyes as I say the lines. I try to read any sign of desire in the curve of his mouth, the arch of his brow.

I feel like I'm losing my mind. Like I've got a fever and I can't really think straight—I can only tumble blindly from one fantasy to the next. One minute I'm sure that he knows how I feel, and that he feels the same. The next he's giving me the same mildly friendly look he gives everyone in the play—dispassionate, detached.

But the way his hand lingered against mine, there in the dark of the theater . . .

"Oh, I have bought the mansion of a love, but not possessed it." I step to the edge of the stage and reach out my hands beseechingly. "And though I am sold, not yet enjoyed."

I think I see something in his eyes—a ripple in the water, like a fish I just missed seeing jump. But then he looks down at his clipboard and scribbles a hasty note. My hands fall back to my sides as Brynn hurries to the center of the stage, all aflutter with the news of Romeo's banishment.

"Good!" His voice cuts through the scene. "Good. Elyse, you looked absolutely heartbroken there. That's exactly what we want. That's perfect."

"Great," I say softly. Perfectly and absolutely heartbroken. I think I can manage.

He gives out a few notes to other actors. I'm barely listening. I watch him put a hand on Laura's shoulder; watch him grin at Frankie, dimples popping. I'm trying to see some difference in the way he talks to them and the way he talks to me, and if I'm honest, I can't.

"Elyse. Hey, where are you?"

I come back to myself with a little jolt. Brynn's standing next to me, knit cupcake scarf wrapped around her neck, jacket buttoned tight. "Sorry, what?"

"Do. You. Want. To. Get. Coffee?" she asks.

"I shouldn't. I have work tonight," I say. "I've got to get home."

"Boo." She scowls. "Your schedule sucks."

"Yeah, well, my whole life kind of sucks, so I don't know what to tell you." I watch as Mr. Hunter bursts into laughter at something Frankie's just said. All the moments I've mistaken for connection feel farther and farther away by the second.

She stares at me. "Are you okay?"

I take a deep breath and sigh. "Yeah. Yeah, I'm just tired. I've been pulling the eight-to-midnight shift to make ends meet while Mom's out of work."

"Hmm." She doesn't look convinced. I tear my eyes away from Mr. Hunter and try to focus.

"Really," I say. "But it's just a few more nights. I'll be able to catch up on my sleep this weekend."

"No you won't," she says. "You'll be able to catch up on Mrs. Cowan's ten-page *Wuthering Heights* essay."

I groan. She's right.

"See?" I say. "My whole life kind of sucks."

•••

I trudge home in the twilight, my backpack a heavy weight on my shoulders. A thin drizzle wets my sweater. Everything smells leafy and green in the rain, even in the traffic. It's the smell I most associate with fall.

I climb the steps to my apartment and unlock the door.

"Where the hell have you been?"

My mom stands in the middle of the living room, eyes wide and staring.

This morning I left her on the sofa, drifting in and out of consciousness. I'd expected to find her mild and stoned now. But here she is, looking not so much alert as half-wild. I take an involuntary step backward as she comes toward me.

"Hi to you too," I say. I take a deep breath and shut the door firmly behind me. The TV mutters madly from one corner. Mom obviously hasn't showered in days; a rich, earthy stench is starting to roll off her. I drop my backpack next to the door and step around her into the apartment.

Mom tries to whirl around, but she's unsteady, her feet tripping into a little jig to keep her balance. "I'm not playing. Where've you been all night?"

"All night?" I shake my head. "What are you talking about?"

"Don't play cute with me!" Her voice is a sudden scream, ripping loose from somewhere deep inside her. My fingers tense into fists at my sides. "It's six in the morning, Elyse. I'm not an idiot. Where have you *been*?"

I stare at her. I can't help it: I burst into scornful laughter. All my fear and worry and confusion vanishes in a rush of anger.

"Jesus, Mom. You're *high*. It's six at night. I was home last night at *eleven*. We even had a conversation, though I'm not surprised you don't remember." I snort, crossing my arms over my chest. "I just got home from play practice."

Mom wavers a little, her eyes going out of focus for just a moment. Then she regains her own outrage. "Don't lie to me, Elyse. I can always tell when you lie."

"I'm not lying!" I stride back to the door and throw it open. "Look outside, Mom. Rush hour traffic on the road. Light source in the west. It's six P.M. and I just got home from school. And you've been so fucked up for the last week you don't know how to tell time."

I slam the door shut, more forcefully this time. "And even if it were six A.M., don't think for a minute that you get to tell me what to do with my life. You've been so checked out for the past decade you've long since lost *that* privilege."

Breath heaving, I stomp to the small kitchen, separated from the living room by a chipped Formica-topped island. I jerk open a cabinet and pull out a metal pot, a box of spaghetti. I'm not hungry now, but I can take it to work and heat it up there—better than another meal of popcorn and Sour Patch Kids. I keep my back to the living room, not wanting to look at my mother.

I bring the water to a boil and add the noodles, my hands trembling with anger.

It's not until I pour the noodles out into the colander that I realize my mom is crying.

"I try so hard," Mom whimpers. "And I still always mess it up. I just . . . I always mess it up."

My shoulders sag, my resolve collapsing like it always does. I look up to see my mother standing like a forlorn child in the middle of the living room, covering her mouth with one hand. Her skin is pink and tear-streaked. I take a deep breath.

"Sit down, Mom. I'll put on some coffee."

Mom doesn't move. I ignore her, pouring water into the coffeemaker, turning it on. Then I fix a bowl of noodles and sauce and set it on the island. "Come on. Eat something. You look like a scarecrow."

"I can't." Mom's voice is breathless, tragic. I slap my palm against the Formica.

"You have to. You haven't eaten in ages. Come on, just a few bites." I push the bowl a few inches toward the bar stools on the other side. The Oxy always kills her appetite, but if I can talk her into eating just a little, drinking some coffee, it might help sober her up. "Please?"

The *please* seems to do it. She doesn't sit, but she walks forward a few steps and takes up the fork in one hand. Tears still wet on her face, she coils a few strands of pasta around the tines. Then she pauses with it halfway to her lips.

"I don't . . . I don't know what to do," she whimpers.

I pour a cup of coffee and push it across the counter. "I think you need some help. Maybe . . . I mean, maybe you could look into going to a meeting, or . . ."

She grimaces. "A twelve-step thing? You don't know what they're like, Elyse. Full of sanctimonious, preachy . . ."

"You have to do something!" I snap. I grit my teeth. "You can't go on like this. I'm going to come home and find you dead on the floor one of these days. Have you ever thought about what that'd be like for *me*?"

Her hand shakes. She sends a tiny spray of spaghetti sauce over her already stained shirt. "I know how much I can take."

I laugh humorlessly. "Oh yeah, you know your limits, huh? You don't even know what time it is. So pardon me if I don't buy it."

For a long moment she's silent, staring at the fork with its few sad strands of spaghetti. Then, finally, she gets it into her mouth and chews. She washes it down with a swallow of hot black coffee.

"Okay," she says, finally, her voice very small.

"Okay what?" I brace myself against the island counter.

"Okay, I'll . . . I'll find a meeting. I'll stop. I'll do better." She puts the fork down with a clatter and rubs her face with both hands. "I'm sorry, Elyse. I really am."

I bite my lip. We've had the same argument before. She always makes the same promises, and I buy it almost every time. I want to believe things can change. I want to believe, so badly.

I pull the plate of pasta back toward me and take a bite. The canned sauce is bland, but it's better than nothing.

"I'll call in sick tonight," I say. "Help you get showered,

make sure your dinner stays down. And then tomorrow, we'll find you a meeting. Okay?"

She looks up at me, her eyes red and watery. For a moment I think about walking around the island to hug her, but I decide not to.

"I swear," she says again, picking up the coffee mug and cradling it in both hands. "I swear, Elyse, this time I'm going to get clean."

I know I can't believe her. I've heard the same thing so many times now.

But it's hard not to hope, when I want to so badly.

FIFTEEN

Gabe

Tuesday afternoon I walk slowly along a residential street, stepping cautiously behind parked cars and doing my best to look as nonchalant as possible.

Six or seven blocks ahead of me Catherine is making her way home from school, her head down, a dark coil of hair down her back.

I haven't heard from her since last night at the restaurant. I've been texting her all day. Sorry if I got you in trouble last night. Your dad's not mad at you, is he? He looks intense. But no response. I couldn't find her at lunch, either. I wasn't even certain she was at school today.

So when I saw her hurry past the window of Ruby's Donuts, where I was brooding over a jelly-filled after school, I slid off the stool and went out to follow.

The neighborhood is old, the light dappling through big shade trees. I stop abruptly when she pauses and tilts her face up toward the sun. For just a few moments I see her in profile. She encircles her hair with one hand and pulls it back. I haven't seen her so exposed before. From here I can see the delicate line of her throat, the wide and thoughtful curve of her lips. Then she lets go and vanishes behind that long, dark curtain again.

I feel kind of creepy as I trail after her. After all—according to Sekrit, she's gotten my messages. If she wants to talk to me, she will. But I have to know she's okay. And . . . maybe more than that, I want to know where she lives. I want to know what she does when I'm not around. I want to know her stories, her secrets.

She stops at a shabby yellow cottage. It's the smallest house on the block, with a ramshackle wooden porch and oak roots pushing up through the asphalt walkway. A mailbox at the curb reads *Barstow.* At the door she pulls out a set of keys and starts to open the door.

I don't know why she looks around. I don't make a sound—I'm careful to hold back. But some impulse keeps her on the doorstep as she glances up.

The keys fall out of her hand when she sees me. She gasps, fumbles at them, her whole body going taut as a violin string. Her eyes dart wildly up and down the street.

I give a weak wave as she takes a step toward me.

"What are you doing here?" she hisses.

"I'm . . ."

She doesn't let me finish. "You have to go. If he sees you . . ."

"Who, your dad?" I ask.

She walks quickly up to me, pushing at my shoulder. "Gabe, please. I can't talk to you here. If he comes home I'll be in big trouble."

My blood pounds in my ear. I've made a mistake in coming here. I've made things worse for her. But still, I fight the urge to touch her. I want to pull her into my arms and make sure she's intact. "I'm sorry. I wanted . . . I wanted to see if you were okay."

She closes her eyes for a moment.

Then she opens them again. "Meet me at Pease Park in thirty minutes," she whispers. "Near the bridge."

Then she turns and runs into the house, slamming the door behind her.

The park is quiet. I sit on a picnic table in a clearing, my feet on the bench, leaning on my knees. I can hear the muffled sounds of traffic in the distance, but closer in it's just birdsong and breeze.

I force myself not to jump up and go to her when she finally appears.

She glances nervously around, rubbing her shoulders even though it's a warm day. She sits down next to me, so close our legs touch.

For a few minutes neither of us says anything. I lean back against my hands and look up at the clouds.

"I'm sorry about the other night," she finally says.

"It's okay."

"No, it's not." She sighs. She twists a lock of hair between two fingers. "I didn't mean to ghost on you. I just . . . I freaked out, and I didn't know what to say."

"I'm sorry too. I shouldn't have followed you. But I had to see you," I say.

She picks at a hole in her jeans.

"Why was your dad so pissed, anyway?" I ask. "I mean, that wasn't my imagination, right? He was definitely not happy."

"No, he wasn't." Her hands fall still in her lap, as if they've suddenly gotten self-conscious. "I'm not really supposed to talk to boys, is the thing."

"What, are you supposed to avoid one half of the population?" I frown. "That's nuts."

She gives a hollow laugh. "I'm lucky. He *wanted* to homeschool me. When we moved here I begged to go to public school. He finally gave in, but it was on a bunch of conditions. No dating, no flirting, no extracurriculars. I have a six P.M. curfew."

"Six?" I spit. "I mean, what if you want to . . ."

"Want to what?" She looks up at me. "I can't go *out*, Gabe. That's what I'm trying to tell you. I . . . I really like you. But this isn't going to work."

The words jerk me back and forth. I soar for a moment before the crash. *I like you . . . but*. "What're you saying?"

"I'm saying I don't get to be a normal girl, okay? If I were . . ." She blushes, looks down. "You deserve to be with someone fun and easygoing and . . . and normal. Someone who can actually talk to you in public. But that's not me. My life is . . . complicated."

"I don't care," I say immediately. "I don't mind complicated."

"You don't understand. If we got caught . . ."

"We'll be careful," I insist. "I won't let anyone hurt you, Catherine."

Her eyes fill with tears. She brushes them away with the back of her hand. "That's sweet. But there's nothing you can do. He'll move us again—I know he will. I told you we came here from California, but the truth is, we lived three other places before *that*. Every time I get attached to something, or someone—every time I might be just an iota out of his control—he finds some excuse to yank me out of school and hit the road again." She looks up at me, a few teardrops clinging in her lashes. "If he finds out I like you, he'll take you away from me, too."

"He won't find out," I say urgently, knowing even as I say it that I can't promise that.

"And Sasha . . ."

"I told you, Sasha and I are through," I say quickly.

Her forehead crinkles, and I have to fight not to reach a fingertip up, to smooth the worry away. "Are you sure about that?"

My body goes rigid. "Why? What's she been saying?"

She shakes her head. "She's been really friendly in astronomy—sitting next to me, trying to start up conversations. She invited me to go to the mall with her the other day. Obviously I made an excuse. But something about it is . . . off. I don't know, maybe it's all in my head. But I get the feeling she's seen us . . . talking. Girls like that scare me. I can't get in the middle of whatever is going on between you two. I can't invite more chaos into my life."

I hesitate, thinking about the Snap I got last week. The picture of Catherine with a death's head. But Sasha'd seemed so earnest when I asked her about it. *Whoever's messing with you . . . it's not me.* I don't know who else would do something like that. But I want to believe it. More than that . . . I want Catherine to believe it.

"She's over me," I say. "She's dating someone else now. You don't have to worry."

She gives a rueful laugh. "See, but this is the point. Between Sasha and my dad, maybe it's just a sign. Now's not our time. If I'd met you . . . God, if I'd met you any other time in my life, I'd be . . ."

I wait for her to finish the sentence. She doesn't.

"No one else gets to decide if we're right for each other," I say fiercely. I picture her dad again, his jaw tense, his eyes cold shards. I picture Sasha, smirking. Both of them so sure they can control us. Both of them so sure they're in charge. "I won't let fear keep me from someone who makes me feel like this."

I'm suddenly hyperaware of the way our legs and hands touch, of the warm smell of pomegranates in her hair, of her pale and narrow face turned toward mine. The dark gray-blue of her irises seems lit from within, like some luminous deep-cave crystal.

Our lips find each other. The kiss is light and lingering, her breath warm on my mouth. We never fully break apart, our foreheads resting against each other. Her eyes close. My pulse drums in my ear.

"This isn't the stupidest thing I've ever done," she says. "But it's close."

SIXTEEN

Elyse

Thursday afternoon there's a soft, almost tentative knock at the front door.

I've been out of school for three days. I'm trying to help my mom through the worst parts of detox; she's been shaky and weak and crouched over a toilet vomiting almost the whole time. Neither one of us has made it to work, which is scary because we don't have much padding in our bank account—but more frustrating to me is missing three days of play rehearsal. I told Brynn to tell everyone I had strep throat, and she reassured me that Mr. Hunter was rearranging the schedule so they could focus on scenes without me in them—but I hate feeling like I'm letting everyone down.

At least I've had a chance to finally clean up the apartment. Mom's in bed, so I've been taking loads of clothes down to the laundry room, vacuuming the floor, throwing out all the detritus that's collected around the living room. It's not magically transforming into Downton Abbey, but it's an improvement.

When I hear the knock I pause with the duster in my hand, listening. The knock comes again, a little louder this time. I set down the duster and go to open the door.

It's Mr. Hunter.

I'm so surprised I just stand there and stare. He's got a black umbrella unfurled, his shoes damp in the rain. His golden-green eyes are warm and curious. I'm suddenly hyperaware of my own getup: sweatpants, a bandana tied over my greasy hair.

"Hey, Elyse. Sorry to just stop by like this." He smiles, and the dimple appears in his cheek. "I've been worried about you. I thought I'd swing by and bring some soup." He holds up a plastic tub, steaming in the cold.

"Mr. Hunter. Uh . . . thank you. That's so . . ." I stammer.

That's when Mom's door swings open, and she staggers out in her sweats. Her hair is plastered to her forehead. She doesn't even look at us—just disappears into the bathroom. I can hear her banging around inside. Then I hear the unspeakable sound of her losing the toast and egg I managed to coax her to eat this morning.

Mr. Hunter stares at the closed bathroom door. I try to convince my body that now's the time to dissolve, to vanish into thin air. To disappear into the shadows. But I'm still corporeal a moment later, still standing with the door open and the cold air rushing in and the soup tub held out, stranded midair between us.

I grab him by the arm and spin him around. "Mom, I'm going to check on the laundry. I'll be back in a minute!" I shout, following him out and shutting the door firmly behind me.

The rain patters lightly on his umbrella overhead. The sweat I'd worked up cleaning the apartment grows clammy out here in the chill air. I close my eyes and feel the tremble start along the surface of my skin and work its way down, until I'm shaking all over, cold to the bone, scared and exhausted.

"So," he says softly. "You're not sick. Your mom is."

"I know that's not an excused absence, Mr. Hunter, and I'm really . . ." I start to apologize, but he holds up a hand.

"Let's go get a cup of coffee, okay?"

I shake my head. "I can't leave my mom."

"Just for a few minutes. Come on, you look like you need it." He rests his palm in the center of my back. It takes little pressure to propel me forward; I let him push me gently toward the stairs.

He opens the door of his plain white sedan for me, and wordlessly I climb in the passenger seat. When he starts the car he turns the heat up full blast.

We don't say anything for a few minutes. My fingers twist together in my lap. I'm afraid to look at him. I'm not sure what's worse: that he caught me in a lie, or that he knows what my life is like. If he ever really thought I was special, now he knows just where I come from.

The car glides through the rain, stoplights smearing into bloody streaks as we pass. I still feel the apartment clinging to me, the smell of sweat, the tang of sickness. The sticky, cloying feeling of shame.

It's not until we're in line at the drive-through that he says anything. "You must be worried about her. Not a lot of kids stay home to take care of their parents."

I stare down at my hands.

"She's detoxing," I say. "From Oxy. We've done it a few times before, but this time it's really bad. She's been sick for days."

I've never told anyone except Brynn. It's dangerous to tell a teacher; he could report my mom to CPS. He could tell the school counselor. Hell, if he were an asshole, he could let it slip at rehearsal and tell everyone.

But the way he looks at me, it's like he really sees me. Like he knows me. And after fighting so long to keep my family problems hidden from the world, it's a relief to finally say them out loud.

I peek at him from the corner of my eye. He doesn't look mad. His brow is crinkled in a look of sympathy. Not pity—sympathy. I know the difference.

Before he can say anything we're at the window. He smiles at the barista. "Black coffee, please. And . . . what can I get you?" he asks me.

I shake my head. "I'm okay. Thanks."

"How about a grande mocha?" he says to the barista. He looks back at me. "You don't have to drink it if you don't want. But it might warm you up."

We wait in silence for our drinks. When the barista comes back, Mr. Hunter hands me my cup before paying. It warms my fingers, filling the car with the smell of sugar and coffee.

He pulls into a parking space and lets the car idle. Then he turns in his seat to face me. "Elyse, I'm glad you told me."

"Please don't tell anyone else," I say, a shot of panic ricocheting through my chest. "Not anyone. My mom's . . . complicated, but I don't want to lose her again. I don't want to get taken away."

"I won't." He takes the lid off his coffee to let it cool, resting it in the cup holder. "Your secret's safe with me."

Tears well up at the corners of my eyes. "It's just . . . it's so hard. It's hard when she's high. It's hard when she's not high. I have to take care of everything."

He nods. "I know. It's not fair, Elyse. You're taking on more than your friends can even imagine. I don't know how you're doing it."

"I don't, either. Some days it doesn't feel like I am." I give a brittle laugh. "Sometimes I just wish I could pack up and leave. Leave my mom, my friends. Go somewhere where I have no ties, so I'd be free to just . . . be whoever I wanted to be. I know that's awful."

"It's not awful, it's normal. I get the feeling you've been taking care of your mom for a long time. It's a heavy burden to bear." He looks intently down at me. "I told you about my dad, how we lived. God, all I ever wanted was to be normal. To have a TV and to get prepackaged cereal at the grocery store and to turn on the thermostat when it was too cold. That wasn't going to happen with him. So when I was sixteen I ran away."

"You . . . did?" My eyes go wide.

He nods. "I hitchhiked into Missoula. Lived in a tent for a whole summer and showered at the YMCA. I found under-the-table work—that was the good thing about growing up with a survivalist. I knew how to do a lot of odd jobs. Carpentry, basic repair work. By the end of the summer I applied for emancipation and got my GED."

"Wow," I say. I try to picture him as a sixteen-year-old, and it's impossible. "That's brave."

"It was better than staying with my parents." His gaze goes faraway for a few seconds, then sharpens again. "Point is, it's possible. You could leave. You're already taking care of yourself; it'd probably be easy for you."

I try to imagine it. Where would I go? What would I do to make money? I don't want to work in a movie theater for the rest of my life. And I don't want to be on my own—not really. I just want to have what normal people have.

"Not that I'm recommending it," he says suddenly, looking closely at my expression. He smiles a little. "I don't exactly want to lose my lead. It's too late to recast."

"Don't worry. Brynn knows my part by heart," I say, but I keep my voice light so he knows I'm teasing.

His eyes meet mine. "Brynn's not the one I want."

The words hang in the air. Every sensation feels heightened beyond bearing. The seat belt is too tight, the upholstery rough against my skin. The coffee cup feels molten, resting on my thigh. My body aches, but for what, I don't know.

"I need to get back," I whisper. "My mom . . ."

"Sure." He starts the car again, but before he backs out, he turns to look at me, one more time. "Here, give me your phone."

I hand it over. He types his number in.

"Call me anytime. If you need anything. Even if you just need to talk." He hands it back to me. "There's no pressure. But if I can help, I will."

"Thanks," I say softly. I cradle the phone in my palm. It's probably my imagination, but it still feels warm from his touch.

When I put it back in my pocket, the weight of it there is reassuring. It feels like ballast. I finally muster a little smile.

"Thanks," I say.

He turns his eyes back to the road.

"Don't mention it," he says.

SEVENTEEN

Gabe

"I'm looking for Gabriel Gee-minez?" says the girl in the doorway, pronouncing it Anglo-style with a soft *G*. Mr. Perlman stops in the middle of his lecture on the electoral process to nod in my direction.

It's Friday afternoon, almost the end of the day, and my mind has been a million miles away from U.S. government and civics. I'm staring out the window, wondering what Catherine's doing in her sixth-period English class. It's been a little over a week since our kiss in the park, and while we've messaged back and forth every day since, I've managed to see her only during lunch.

I raise my hand, and the girl steps forward and gives me a folded piece of pink paper, an office memo. "Thanks," I whisper before opening it.

Your mother called to say you don't need to pick up your sister today, she can do it.

I can't believe my luck. Usually my Fridays are spent Vivi-sitting; Mom has a standing work meeting, so I pick Vivi up and play with her all afternoon. I love my sister to death, but there are better uses I can think of for my Friday afternoon than hanging out with a six-year-old, no matter how cool that six-year-old may be.

Like, for instance: seeing Catherine, if she can get away.

"So can anyone explain to me how a presidential candidate can win the popular vote, but still lose the election?" Mr. Perlman leans back against the chalkboard, looking around the room hopefully, but my mind's already wandering. I have my phone out under my desk. Can you meet after school? Going nuts and I have to see you.

A few minutes later, the response comes back.

Scupture Falls, 3pm.

After a rain, Sculpture Falls turns into a swimming hole, crowded with families and dogs splashing through the shallows. But right now it's bone-dry. The creek bed is exposed, bare in the sun. On a day like today, there's usually no one around.

She's already there when I arrive, wearing a frayed men's button-down shirt and her scuffed-up Keds. Something in her stance has changed. She's not so curled into herself. She thumbs her backpack straps as she sees me come down the trail, biting her lip and smiling at the same time.

"Hey," I say.

"Hey." Her eyes flicker down for a moment, then turn up toward me, up through her thick lashes. My breath snags in my throat.

"Come on." I take her hand, walk her carefully over the uneven ground to the limestone outcropping that's usually covered by the falls. Over the years the water has carved it into all sorts of strange, flowing shapes. We sit on the edge, legs dangling over the side.

"It's so peaceful here," she says. "This was the first place I felt safe when I moved to Austin."

"Yeah?" I smile. "Me too, actually. I mean, it was the first place I felt like myself, after my sister was born."

She cocks her head inquisitively. I hesitate for a moment. "I'm not super proud of this, but . . . I had a hard time when Vivi was little. I don't know if you've had the pleasure of a meeting a special-needs toddler before, but take your average toddler insanity and multiply it by about a million. I kind of . . . wasn't very nice."

The memories still make my cheeks burn. The way I'd back away from her when she reached out toward me, always just out of reach, just to torment her. The way I'd blame things on her—like when I knocked down my mom's Día de los Muertos altar, breaking one of the clay skeletons inside, or when I tracked mud all over the rug of my dad's study.

"Some of it was jealousy. She took so much of my parents' attention, and I was used to being an only child. And some of it was that I was . . . embarrassed. God, that's such a shitty thing to say. I was an idiot." I shake my head. "Anyway . . . in junior high, I met Caleb, and he started bringing me down here. Sometimes to swim, sometimes just to hike the trails. Something about it helped me get centered. And . . . you know, I guess once I started being a little happier, I was finally able to see what a great little kid Vivi was. But I've never really forgiven myself for being such a jerk."

I wonder for a second if I've talked too much. Catherine is quiet, looking down at her lap. But she leans against my shoulder, her hair spilling out across my chest

"I so get that," she whispers. "It's hard to forgive yourself for stuff like that. God, there are things I wish I could just . . . scrub off the past. I don't want to think of myself as the kind of person that could do . . . some of the things I've done. But there are some things . . . once you've done them, you're branded with them forever."

I look down at her, almost amused. "What could *you* have done that's that bad?"

She turns her face toward my chest so I can't see her expression.

"I've made plenty of mistakes," she says.

For a moment I don't say anything. I don't know what she's thinking about, but I have a feeling it's more than cheating on a math test. I don't want to say the wrong thing. But my fingers curl protectively around the back of her head.

"Yeah, but, Cat . . . everyone deserves a second chance," I say.

She lifts her head to look up at me. Her storm-blue eyes pull me in. She smiles then, a tiny curve of the lips. My heart swoops.

And then we're kissing again, soft at first, tentative, then hungry, our mouths opening against each other. She presses against my chest and we lay back against the warm stone. My hands move over her, searching, running through her silky hair, playing down her spine, cupping the small swell of her hip. Every thought in my head is crowded out by the smell of her, the taste of her, the feel of her skin against mine. Her fingers slip inside my T-shirt and graze my stomach, and I catch my breath.

My phone shrills in the quiet. I fumble for it, thinking I'll send the call to voice mail. But when I check the screen and see it's my mom, something keeps me from ignoring the call. I answer.

"Hey, what's going . . ."

"Where are you guys?" My mom's voice is annoyed. I glance automatically around the clearing.

"I'm at the Greenbelt with some friends. What's up?"

The line's silent for a moment. Catherine cocks her head inquisitively, but I just frown.

"You took Vivi to the Greenbelt?" asks Mom after a moment.

"Vivi? No." I adjust the phone so it's closer to my ear. "I got your message. I've been out with some . . ."

"It's almost five!" Her voice is louder now. "Her school's been out for three hours, Gabe!"

"Wait . . ." I sit up a little straighter. "Are you saying she's not with you?"

"Hold on. I'm calling her school." She hangs up without waiting for my reply.

A panicky, metallic taste is rising up in my throat. I hold my breath, staring straight ahead. Something lands lightly on my back, and I half turn to see Catherine, her hand resting on my shirt.

"Is everything okay?" she asks.

"I guess I was supposed to get my little sister." I frown, fumbling in my pocket for the note from the office, but it's not there. I must have thrown it away. "She's probably been waiting for hours for someone to get her. Fuck." I stand up. "We have to head back to the car. I'll have to pick her up on the way home."

But we've gone just a little way down the trail when the phone rings again. It's my mom.

"Get home right now."

Her tone sends a shock down my spine. She's not mad. She's scared.

"What's wrong?"

My mother takes a deep, shuddering breath.

"She's missing, Gabe. Vivi's missing."

EIGHTEEN

Elyse

The night is cold, the sky laced with clouds, when I step out into the movie theater's parking lot. Fake-butter smell is embedded in my hair and clothes, and my soles cling to the asphalt with every step, sticky with sugar. Fridays are both the easiest and hardest shifts to pull—the pace is hectic enough to make it go fast, but I always end up with an aching back and feet in the process. Tonight I spent six hours running from one side of concessions to the other while customers barked orders. I burned my hand on the hot dog warmer, and then the soda machine broke, so I had to spend the rest of my shift telling people that no, they couldn't get a Pepsi. My ears still throb, even out here in the quiet darkness.

"Night," I say to the little cluster of co-workers who just ended their shift. They mill around, lighting cigarettes, bitching about the cold. Most of them are a few years older than me. It scares me sometimes, how at home I feel with them; it scares me that I might be here forever.

"Sure you don't want to go with us to IHOP?" Rita Solano, my fellow concessions lackey, asks. She's one of the few girls my age who works there, a whip-smart dropout with four little siblings she's helping to raise. "You look like you could use a break."

I think about it. They'll all sit at the diner until three in the morning, slugging back bottomless cups of coffee and sharing plates of cheese fries. I go out with them sometimes, and it's usually chill. Fun to gossip, to be out late, to crack jokes at each other's expense. Fun to feel connected to other people trapped in wage-slave hell. But I feel like I'm asleep on my feet. Plus Mom's at home. She's feeling better—less nauseous, at least—but she's still pretty delicate. I can't leave her alone for the night.

"I'm tired," I say. "I've gotta go home. I'll see you Monday night, though."

She gives a little wave and turns back to the others, their laughter rising up in an echoing chorus.

It makes the parking lot feel especially lonely, walking away from the light and the noise, across the dark expanse to the bus stop. Exhaustion weighs me down, but I tuck my purse under my arm and walk quickly. I've been riding the bus home from work all year, sometimes in the middle of the night, and while nothing bad's ever happened, the theater's in a pretty shitty neighborhood. I've been propositioned more than once—and a guy followed me all the way down the street making kissing noises at me. The best thing to do is to get on the bus as quick as I can. There's one at 1:47, and if I miss it the next one won't be along for a half hour.

I hear the motor of a starting engine. Rita's Camaro roars past me, honking, and a few other cars trail behind her. Then there's silence. I look up and down the empty expanse of the parking lot, shivering in my thin coat. The distant lights of the street are bright but glamourless.

There's a single car parked in the middle of the lot. Must be a customer's car. Maybe the driver walked to the dive bar down the street after the movie, leaving the car behind. But as I pass it I see something move inside.

Someone's sitting in the driver's seat.

My pulse picks up. I change course, angling as far away from the car as I can. It's probably just a drunk, trying to sober up before hitting the road. Or maybe someone living out of their car, trying to find a place to sleep for the night. But even though I can't make out the driver's features, I can sense his attention on me—can imagine his eyes burning as they follow me. I fight the urge to bolt.

The engine growls to life. A strangled whimper comes unbidden from my throat, my breath coming quicker now. I grip my cell phone in my fingers, ready to call 911 if I have to. *You're overreacting. It's nothing.* But I pick up the pace, tucking my head down and making a beeline for the road.

When I hear tires crunching slowly behind me I can't hold it in any longer. I break into a run. I drop my backpack and tear toward the bright lights of the road. It feels impossibly far away. My feet slam against the concrete. A sharp pinch shoots through my lungs.

I hear shouting. It takes me a moment to recognize my name.

"Elyse. Elyse!"

The engine dies behind me, but the lights don't turn off. I slow to a trot and turn to look behind me.

It's Mr. Hunter.

I can just make out his features in the glare of the headlights. He gets out of the car and walks over to my backpack, stooping to pick it up. I stop where I am and stare. The adrenaline still shudders down my limbs, but its intensity shifts. I'm no longer feeling fight-or-flight; instead, a warm tingle of anticipation tickles through my veins.

"I'm so sorry." He walks over and hands me my bag. "I didn't mean to scare you. I thought you saw my face. I should've parked near a light."

"What are you doing here?" I realize as soon as it's out of my mouth that it's a dumb way to ask the question. What I really mean is, *Why are you lingering in a dark parking lot?* But he either doesn't pick up on that or ignores it.

"Seeing a movie. I didn't know you worked here."

"I didn't see you in there. You must not have gotten any popcorn."

He grins. "Don't tell anyone, but I smuggled in a box of Junior Mints."

My hands fly up to my mouth in mock astonishment. "Breaching the sacred trust between moviegoer and concessions? Mr. Hunter, I am shocked. Shocked!"

He laughs. "Want a ride home?"

My exhaustion lifts off me, as if by magic. I walk around to the passenger side door and climb in.

The streetlights flutter through the car and vanish as we drive under them. His radio is on very low, an old Smiths song thrumming along with the hum of wheels on pavement. I watch him out of the corner of my eyes, leaning back against the headrest.

"You really take the bus home in the middle of the night?" he asks. "Seems kind of dangerous."

"It's not so bad," I say. "The drivers keep an eye out for me. And it's only about a fifteen-minute ride."

"Hm," he says, frowning.

"Hey, you're the one who keeps telling me how easy it was to get emancipated at sixteen," I say.

"Touché." He glances at me, his glasses catching the light for a moment so I can't see his eyes. "How're things at home?"

"A little better," I say. "Mom felt good enough to make a meeting this afternoon."

"NA?" he asks.

"Yeah. I went with her—just to give her some support."

He frowns, but doesn't say anything. I raise an eyebrow.

"You don't approve?" I ask.

"It's not that." His fingers tap the edges of the steering wheel. "I just worry that you're taking her sobriety on your own shoulders a little bit. You know you're not responsible for her."

I look out the window, biting the edge of my thumbnail.

"I'm sorry. I shouldn't have said anything," he says quickly. "It's not my place."

"No, you're right. I always feel like somehow, this time, I can make her stay clean. If I just figure out the right mixture of meetings and nagging and support, if I can just will her to try a little harder . . . if I can make things perfect. If I can be perfect."

"And how's that been working?" he asks.

I give a little laugh. "About as well as you'd think."

We pull into the parking lot of my apartment complex. My heart sinks; the ride was too short. He parks in an empty spot, but he doesn't turn off the engine.

"Look, Elyse, I can't tell you how to feel. What you're going through is . . . really hard. But if I could encourage you to do anything . . ." He pauses. "It'd be to protect yourself."

"What do you mean?" I turn sideways in the seat to look at him.

"Just don't let yourself believe any of this is your fault. Or your responsibility," he says carefully. "It's really noble to want to help your mom. But her sickness isn't something you can control. And if you let yourself get pulled into her mess, it'll hold you back."

I look down at my backpack on my lap.

"I . . . I can't just let her fend for herself."

"I know." His hand comes to rest gently on my elbow. I draw in my breath a little. "Just . . . make sure you don't sacrifice your own hopes for hers. That's all."

I glance up at him. The car suddenly seems very small, our faces very near one another.

"Thanks, Mr. Hunter."

"Aiden," he says. "You can call me Aiden. At least when we're not at school."

"Aiden." Maybe it's all the Shakespeare I've been reciting, but I love the rhythm, the shape, the poetry. Aiden.

We sit in silence for a moment. I know I need to get out, but I don't want to. Not yet.

I don't know why—maybe it's the residual adrenaline from being startled, or maybe it's the memory of the kiss, brief and breathless in the green room. Maybe it's the curve of his lips in the moonlight, the lock of hair resting carelessly against his forehead. Maybe it's just the exhaustion kicking in and making me foolish.

What it feels like, though, is bravery.

I lean across the console and kiss him, a quick, nervous peck on the side of his mouth. "There." I laugh. "Now we're even."

He looks down at me, his lips parted in surprise. And I think, *Oh God, I've done it now. I've made it awful. Now I'll be in trouble, and lose everything, and he'll never want to see me again . . .*

But then his hand is cradling the back of my head and our lips are together, and I taste chocolate and peppermint, and lose myself in the softness of the kiss, the softness of our lips together. His mouth plays against mine without pressure. His tongue traces the gentlest line and then disappears. A sound escapes from my throat.

Abruptly, he stops. He looks around. The parking lot is quiet, but there are lights on in some of the windows.

"We shouldn't do this here," he whispers. But he doesn't move away. He runs a fingertip along my cheek, and I shiver.

"No one's watching." I lean up toward him, and we kiss again, but this time he keeps it short.

"We can't risk it." He gently shifts away from me. "Sunday. I'll pick you up at nine."

"Where will we go?" I ask. He smiles and shakes his head.

"It'll be a surprise. Now go on—get upstairs before someone starts to wonder about my car."

I want to kiss him again, but it feels like a dismissal. The last thing I want is to seem desperate, needy, grasping—even though it's almost painful to rip myself away. I grab my backpack from between my legs.

"Okay. Sunday." I open the door and get out. But before I close it behind me, I lean down to peer back at him. "Aiden."

NINETEEN

Gabe

The living room blazes with light. I sit next to my mom on the red flower-print sofa, my hands clutching my knees. Two uniformed officers sit in the chairs on the other side of the coffee table, one balancing a mug of tea on her knee.

"No one at the school saw where she went," says one of the officers, a young woman with wheat-colored hair and a hawklike nose. Her nameplate reads HUNTINGTON. "Her teacher says she left with a young woman, brunette, in her teens or early twenties."

"Why'd they let her go with someone they didn't know?" I ask. "Why didn't they call Mom, or me?"

"She's in a mainstream classroom," says the other officer, a guy named Larson. He's pale and balding, with a long, muscular jaw. "They have lots of kids to keep an eye on. And they said she seemed to know the woman picking her up."

It doesn't make sense. I've gone through everyone I can think of, everyone Vivi might know and trust, but they're all either too old or they don't have brown hair. And Vivi's trusting, but she knows not to go with strangers.

"Why weren't you there, Gabe?" Mom wipes at her face, looking at me with round, bewildered eyes. I wish I could disappear under that gaze.

"I told you. I got a message from the office. They said it was from *you*." My head spins. I try to remember exactly what it said. "You said you were picking her up."

"I don't know what you're talking about. I was stuck in a meeting all afternoon. And why wouldn't I call your cell if I had a message for you?"

The question stops me in my tracks. I hadn't even thought of that. I'd been so eager to hear I had an afternoon free—so excited to get a chance to see Catherine—that I hadn't stopped to consider.

Before I can say anything, my mom bursts into another torrent of tears. Her shoulders shudder, her breath coming in sharp gasps.

"Mrs. Jiménez, please. We need you to stay calm. *Vivienne* needs you to stay calm," says Huntington.

"It's Vivi. She goes by Vivi," I say. Mom gives a little gasp of pain at the name.

"Vivi," repeats the woman. "I'm sorry. Vivi. But look—we need you to be calm in case we find her and she needs our help. You can't do anything for her if you're too upset."

I hear the words, but my brain refuses to imagine what that might mean. *If she needs our help.* If she's hurt, somehow. If she's . . .

A knock comes at the door.

No one moves for a moment. Mom stares across the room, trembling. The two cops seem to be communicating silently with each other. I'm the one who finally gets up and goes to see who it is.

A slender brunette girl stands next to Vivi, holding her hand. Rowdy lingers next to Vivi's shins, tail low and anxious.

Vivi has a towering ice cream cone she's licking evenly around each side, like I taught her. Her face is dirty and one pigtail sags low, but she beams up at me.

I look again at the brunette, and I realize with a jolt that it's Sasha. Smiling.

The color doesn't suit her. She looks sallow, like spoiled milk. She wears cut-off shorts, a snug plaid shirt, more casual than she usually dresses. For just a sliver of a second her eyes glitter with malice.

Then she turns a thousand-watt smile past me, toward my mom.

"Hey, guys, we're . . ." She trails off as her eyes fall to the cops. "Oh my God, has something happened? What's going on?"

Rowdy low-crawls across the room and disappears into his crate. Mom jumps up and grabs Vivi, squeezing her so tightly the ice cream wobbles dangerously.

The numb, detached feeling that's had hold of me lets go. The world constricts to a tiny, blood-red point with Sasha at its center. She looks up at me with wide-eyed confusion, not a trace of menace in her expression.

"What's going on?" she asks. "Why are the cops here?"

Officer Larson stands up and steps toward her. "And who are you, miss?"

"I'm Sasha Daley." She looks around from person to person. "I'm Gabe's girlfriend. Or . . . I mean, I was." She gives a soft, melancholy laugh. "Now we're just friends."

Larson scribbles something in his notebook. "Did you take this little girl from her school this afternoon?"

Her expression is so earnest, so ingénue-perfect that, for a split second, I actually wonder if this really is just some big misunderstanding—if she really is as confused as she looks. "Yeah, I did. Why? Did I . . . did I do something wrong?"

Larson glances at his partner, then back at Sasha. "Well, no one seemed to know where she was. Did you talk to her mother about this?"

She shakes her head. "No. I . . . I thought it was all worked out." She looks at me, almost beseechingly. "Gabe said he was busy and asked me to pick her up and watch her for the afternoon."

My mouth drops open, but for a second nothing comes out. All I can do is shake my head. Everyone's looking at me now.

"Gabe?" asks my mother. I can't look at her. I can't see anything in the room but Sasha. Sasha, whose brow is crumpled now like she's about to cry.

"She's lying," I say. I fight to keep my voice controlled. It feels like my muscles are filled with something molten. I've never wanted to hit anything so badly in my life. "We broke up. Almost a month ago. Why would I ask her to get my sister? I don't want her anywhere near my family."

Real tears spring to Sasha's eyes now. "Why would you say something like that?"

"Because you're lying!" It comes out as a shout. Larson shifts his weight a little, but I can't help it. My fists are knotted at my sides. "I never told you to pick her up!"

"We were at your locker, right before sixth period!" She looks at my mom. "Mrs. Jiménez, I'm so sorry. He asked me to watch her all afternoon or I would have brought her back sooner. I didn't know you'd be so scared."

Vivi hasn't stopped licking her ice cream, but she looks up at the sound of Sasha's anguish. A worried expression works its way onto her face. She breaks away from Mom and staggers back to Sasha, putting her arms around her waist.

"Don't cry, Sash," she croons. "It okay."

Larson looks around the room in exasperation. "Okay, so it seems to me we have a miscommunication . . ."

"It's not a miscommunication," I insist. "I never told her she could take my sister. This is *kidnapping*." My jaw is so tight I can feel my teeth screeching against each other. I stand for a moment, trying to breathe deep. Trying to calm down.

"Stay away from my family." I look right at Sasha. Daring her to smirk, to show the slightest bit of pleasure in this. Daring her to give me the slightest sign that this is part of her game.

Tears brim at the edge of her eyes. She wipes them away with the back of her hand.

Officer Huntington moves gently between us. "Ms. Daley, why don't you step out to the front porch with me. I'll need a statement before you go, but then I think you can head home. Everyone here's had a really long and difficult day."

"Okay." Sasha gives Vivi one last squeeze. "Bye, kiddo."

Vivi smiles and lays her head against Sasha's hip for a moment before being let go. She lets our mother scoop her back up and waves with her ice cream cone, a ribbon of chocolate winding down her fist. "Bye, Sash!"

Sasha pauses in the doorway, the cop just behind her. She looks at Vivi, but I know her words are meant for me.

"It was fun," she says. "I'll see you again soon."

TWENTY

Elyse

I stand at the edge of the ocean, the wind whipping through my hair. The frigid water sweeps around my feet and pulls the sand out from under my toes. It's a strange sensation, having the earth wrested out from under me. Feeling the tide's gentle but inexorable power.

I hug my jacket tighter around my shoulders and glance over at Aiden. He stands a few feet away, hands in his pocket.

He's quiet today. When he picked me up a few blocks from my apartment, we didn't kiss—not in the middle of Portland, in broad daylight—but his hand reached across the console to hold mine. He held it most of the way to Cannon Beach. I relished the contact. His fingers were warm, calloused in some places and soft in others. But I also wasn't sure what to say. The kiss changed everything. Or at least, it feels like it did. What did he expect from me? What did he want?

Now, on the beach, he notices me looking, and smiles. I feel suddenly shy; I look down at my legs, at the sea foam swirling around my ankles. The air is chill and foggy, the water the gray-green of patina. But then he's stepping close to me, tucking a lock of my hair behind my ear, and I look up. It feels brazen, ostentatious. The line his fingertips etch across my cheek burns.

"Are you warm enough?" he asks.

It's a simple question, a practical one. But I know what he's really asking. *Are you okay? Are you scared? Are you happy? Are you still on board with this?*

"Yes," I say, resting my hand on his broad chest.

We walk up and down the beach, looking at seashells and driftwood tangled with kelp. Haystack Rock looms across the sand, a barnacled hunchback wheeling with gulls. I trace our names in the sand with a stick and watch the water wear them away. It feels daring, putting our two names so close together, even if it's so easily erased.

Afterward, we get lunch in a bistro, plates of pasta and fresh, hot bread. We walk slowly through the little town, peeking into shop windows. There aren't many people on the street, and a lot of stores are boarded up for the winter.

"I've never been here before," I say. He does a double take.

"Really? It's so close!"

"Yeah, but my mom . . ." I shrug. "We don't take a lot of road trips."

"Right." He shakes his head. "I bet there are places all over the state you haven't seen. Crater Lake? Opal Creek? Boardman State Park? Please tell me you've at least been to the Gorge."

I laugh. "Yeah, I went to Multnomah Falls with my class in junior high."

He just shakes his head. "There's so much more than just Multnomah Falls." He looks down at me for a long moment, then covers my hand with his and takes it to his mouth, kissing the palm. "I'll show you."

"Show me everything," I say.

He smiles, tucks an arm around my waist. I lean in against him.

Then he jerks away so suddenly I almost fall over.

Before I can say anything, he's dodged into the bookstore just behind us. I freeze in surprise, the chill of the air sharp where a moment ago his arm kept me warm. I'm about to follow him when I see what he must have seen.

Kendall Avery is coming out of a restaurant with her family, just across the street.

Her parents look like they just stepped out of an L.L.Bean catalog, all fleece vests and worn, clean boots. Two little kids with the same red hair as Kendall play tag around a statue of a bear, giggling. Kendall herself stares down at her phone, looking bored and sour.

My feet feel glued to the spot. It doesn't look like she's seen me—seen *us*—but I can't be sure. What if she snapped a picture of Aiden with his arm around my waist and is posting it on Instagram right now? What if she's texting everyone in the drama department? What if she's calling the principal, or the cops?

A moment later she looks up, and her eyes widen. I let out a heavy breath. It's obvious she's just noticed me for the first time.

I realize I should move away from the bookstore—that I should put as much distance between myself and Aiden as possible. So I head up the sidewalk to meet her.

"Hey," I say.

She just stares. "What are you doing here?"

"Visiting the beach." I gesture in the direction of the pounding surf.

"By yourself?" She glances around. For a moment I think she's skeptical—that she suspects something is off. Then I realize she's just being a bitch. *By yourself? No friends or family? So sad.*

I feign coolness, shrugging. "Yeah. Sometimes you just want some peace and quiet, you know?"

My lack of interest in taking her bait seems to disarm her. She glances at her siblings, rolling her eyes. "Tell me about it. We're here visiting my aunt for the weekend. I've been stuck in a bedroom with those brats for two days now."

"Good times," I say. She snorts.

"Yeah. Whatever." She glances at her parents; they're busy trying to herd the kids into the car seats in the back of a minivan. "I could probably get away for a little while. If you wanted to go hang out or something."

It's an unexpected invitation. I don't know if it's a peace offering, or if she's just desperate to talk to someone she's not related to for a little while. I hesitate. I can't ditch Aiden, obviously, but I don't want to hurt her feelings.

"Uh . . . that'd be cool, but I have to head back to town pretty soon. I have a shift tonight."

I can tell she doesn't believe me. Her lips press hard together. "Okay, whatever. It was just an idea."

She turns before I can say anything and shoves her little sister out of the way, climbing into the back of the minivan.

I stand still and watch as they pull away from the curb a few minutes later. I'm too relieved to feel guilty about the lie.

Aiden texts me to meet him at the car in an hour. I suppose he wants to make sure the Averys are totally gone. When I climb into the passenger seat, he's already there, wearing a baseball cap and a pair of shades.

"That was . . ."

"Close," I finish. "I know."

He sighs. "We'll have to be more careful."

I don't say anything. It felt so right, holding hands, holding each other without fear. How is this going to work? Where can we be together, if not here?

He reaches across the console and touches my shoulder, almost like he's reading my mind. "Hey," he says. "It'll be okay. We'll figure this out." He pauses, then takes off the sunglasses so I can see his eyes. "You're worth the risk."

My heart gives a lurch. It's so easy to ignore my doubts when he touches me. When I look into those hazel eyes, the same gray-green as the foam that skims the beach.

I hesitate. Then I nod.

"*We're* worth the risk," I say.

TWENTY-ONE

Gabe

It's Monday, just before third period, and I stand in the Lower Courtyard, bouncing on the balls of my feet. Waiting.

A soft breeze whisks stray leaves across the concrete. The only other people in the Courtyard are a couple of girls surreptitiously sharing a joint. One of them gives me a nod, gestures invitingly, but I just shake my head. Once upon a time, maybe, but now I have other things on my mind.

Finally, the door swings open. One of the girls pinches out the joint reflexively, then looks relieved when it's only Catherine.

"Hey," I say.

"Hey."

She steps close to me, biting the corner of a fingernail. She looks like she hasn't slept well; dark circles cradle her eyes, and she's paler than usual. Her hair hangs limp around her narrow face. I haven't seen her since Friday, but we've been messaging back and forth. Talking about what happened with Vivi. With Sasha.

"You okay?" she asks. She leans against a pillar, cocks her head sideways like a bird.

"Yeah. In trouble with my parents, but that's nothing new. And . . . you know, I feel like an idiot." I'd fallen for Sasha's trick without a second thought. I'd been so eager to be with Catherine. I'd been careless. "But Vivi's fine. It was just a dumb prank."

I take a deep breath and sit down on one of the lawn chairs as the third-period bell echoes through the Courtyard. The stoner girls head inside, leaving behind the faint smell of weed and Nag Champa.

All weekend I tried to persuade my parents that Sasha is trouble—that they should press charges or issue a restraining order or at least get an alarm installed—but they wouldn't listen to me. My mom just keeps saying to leave it alone, that Vivi's safe and that's all that matters. My dad can't seem to get it through his head that I never told Sasha to pick Vivi up. "You didn't say *anything* that could have led her to misunderstand?" he asked, again and again. "Maybe you weren't paying attention." I even told them about her breaking into the house the night of the party, but they blew it off, like it was just some dumb, petty drama.

"Gabe, seriously," Mom finally said. "Drop it. We don't want to make more trouble. Let's just be grateful it's over."

So I gave up trying to argue with them.

For her part, Sasha's been on her best behavior since that night. No more Snaps. No more nocturnal visits. Just a radio silence that I find almost as unnerving.

"A dumb prank?" Catherine runs her fingers nervously through her hair. "Gabe, she faked a call to the office, pretending to be your mom, so she could take your little sister. That's not a prank, that's . . . really messed up." She takes a deep breath. "I'm not even sure we should be here together. If she sees us . . ."

"Has she said something to you?" I look up sharply.

She frowns a little. "No. But she's obviously not over you. And she's obviously unstable. Gabe, I . . . I really like you, but I can't afford this kind of drama."

I lick my chapped lips, frustrated.

"She's not dumb enough to keep escalating this. She came pretty close to getting busted by the cops last Friday. Trust me, it's over," I say.

Catherine looks at me skeptically, but she doesn't answer. I put my arms around her and pull her to my chest.

"We shouldn't be doing this out in the open," she whispers, but she doesn't pull away.

"No one's down here. No one's watching." I press my lips to hers. The kiss is soft and lingering and for a moment nothing else in the world matters.

And then something we can't ignore permeates.

"Gabriel Jiménez, Gabriel Jiménez." The receptionist's nasal voice blares over the intercom, just outside the door.

"Please come to the principal's office. Gabriel Jiménez, to the principal's office."

For a moment I stand still, listening. My stomach does a rapid roller-coaster drop. Last time I got a message from the office it was a trick. But the *principal* wouldn't page me if there wasn't something important going on.

Catherine looks up at me, her face stark and scared. "What's going on?"

I gently disentangle myself from her. "I'd better go see." I tuck a lock of her hair behind her ear. "You should go inside." I don't add that I'm scared to leave her alone—I don't want to freak her out even more.

"Are you going to be okay?"

I lean in to kiss her one last time, but I don't answer her question. I don't know how to.

When I arrive at the office, lunch is over, and the halls are clear. I pause at the receptionist's desk, leaning over to announce myself, but before I can say anything the door to Principal DeGroot's office swings open.

It's not the principal who steps out. It's Sasha.

It looks like she's been crying. Her cheeks are pink and blotchy, and she has a balled-up tissue in her hand. When she sees me there, she pauses in the doorway for just a moment. Then she shakes her head, and hurries past me to the hall.

I watch her go, my heart thudding painfully in my chest.

Now Principal DeGroot fills the doorway, a heavy-jowled brick wall of a man. I've never had any run-ins with DeGroot before—the few times I've gotten in trouble have been minor enough to be handled by a detention or two. But Irene's been in his office so often she might as well have a plaque on the door herself, and according to her, DeGroot's a hard-ass, big on order and discipline, but not unwilling to listen.

"Mr. Jiménez?" I nod, trying to stay calm.

"Yes, sir."

DeGroot opens his door a little wider and gestures for me to step in.

The room is dimly lit, the overhead fluorescents off and a handful of table lamps lighting the small room. A large tapestry on one wall depicts Waterloo's rearing-mustang logo. The desk is almost spartan, empty except for a half-full coffee mug, a computer, a digital camera, and a bronze football-shaped paperweight. DeGroot moves behind his desk and lowers his bulk in a chair that looks way too small for him. It groans under his weight.

"Please, have a seat." He nods to one of the simple wooden chairs on the far side of his desk. I sit down.

I can't hold back any longer. "Is everyone okay?" I blurt. I'm on the edge of my chair, clutching at the sides of the seat with both hands. DeGroot, who's still settling in, goes motionless.

"That's an interesting question," he says. "What makes you think someone might not be okay?"

"I don't know," I say. "I thought maybe . . . maybe my family . . ."

The principal seems to be studying me carefully, his brow slightly furrowed. "So you have no idea why you've been called down here?" he asks. I shake my head.

For a long moment, the principal doesn't say anything. I get the feeling he's trying to wait me out—letting the moment drag on so I might say something. I shift my weight, unclench my fists from the sides of the chair and rest them in my lap as calmly as I can.

Finally, DeGroot picks up the camera. It's an older model, large and heavy-looking. He starts pushing buttons. Then he holds it across the table toward me, screen-first.

I take it almost numbly. When my eyes adjust to the screen, my whole body gives a jerk of horror.

It's a picture of a locker, hanging open, the door dangling by one hinge. The first thing I see is red. Red, dripping down the inside of the door. A red, pulpy mess, lumped on the bottom. On the small screen it looks like a pound of flesh. I stare down at it, my eyes trying to make sense of what I'm looking at, trying to parse out the image.

"What . . . what is this?"

DeGroot leans forward, clasping his fingers together. "I don't know, Mr. Jiménez. Why don't you tell me?"

I look up at the principal, shaking my head. The man's face is hard to read, a slab of blank stone, but his voice is low and serious. After another long, silent moment, he reaches under the desk and pulls out a crumpled scrap of paper. It's flecked with dark red, the same dark red as in the picture.

I don't want to touch it. But when I lean closer to inspect it, I can see that the blood is fake. The color is spot-on, but the viscosity of it isn't quite right; it looks like the concoction Irene and I once made out of corn syrup and food coloring, fake blood for a short horror movie we filmed together and put on YouTube. I had played a hapless victim of Bloody Mary, the demon who lived inside the mirror, and I can still remember how gummy the blood was, how it felt drying on my skin over the course of the long afternoon.

The note is short, scrawled in untidy pencil.

STAY AWAY FROM ME AND MY FAMILY YOU BITCH OR ELSE.

"It's fake," I say, looking up at the principal. "The blood."

The principal's expression doesn't change. Talk about a poker face. "If it weren't, you wouldn't be here talking to me. You'd be talking to the cops."

I shake my head. "But I didn't have anything to do with this. I don't . . . I don't know what this is about."

"That's not what Sasha Daley says," says DeGroot.

I stare back at the picture. Sure enough, now I can see it—the picture of Zayn Malik she'd taped inside her locker, now running with fake blood. And that's her Mustang Sallys warm-up jacket—torn to shreds, but still identifiable. It's Sasha's locker. And I realize suddenly that I'm the one who supposedly vandalized it.

"I didn't have anything to do with this," I say, pushing the camera back across the desk. "I'd never do something like this."

DeGroot's eyebrows lift slightly, but other than that he betrays no real surprise. "Ms. Daley says you two broke up recently."

"Yeah, we did. A month ago," I say. "But this is crazy. Why would I mess up her locker? I just want her to leave me alone."

DeGroot nods. "I see. Ms. Daley also said there was a misunderstanding last week. She spent some time with your family, and you reacted pretty badly to that."

My skin gets hot with anger. "She didn't 'spend time with my family,' she kidnapped my little sister. She took Vivi without telling anyone she was going to do it. Yeah, I reacted badly. Who wouldn't?"

The principal takes off his glasses and sets them upside down on the desk in front of him. He pinches the bridge of his nose for a moment, and then sighs.

"Look, Mr. Jiménez, I know that breakups can be difficult. There are a lot of emotions running high." He clasps his hands in front of him again. "But harassment is a very serious problem, and we don't take it lightly at Waterloo. No matter what happened between the two of you, this is not an acceptable way to react."

"But she's the one harassing *me*." I can't help it. The words burst out of me in a blast of justified outrage, but they sound nasty as soon as they're out, defensive and entitled.

"I don't care about the he-said, she-said," says DeGroot, holding up his hands with a placating motion. "It doesn't matter anymore who said what, Mr. Jiménez. The fact is, I can't prove you had anything to do with her locker, so all I can do is issue the following warning. This is a learning environment. This behavior is disruptive. Whatever has happened between you and Sasha in the past, you need to steer clear of one another now, do you understand me? Stay away from her. Don't talk to her, don't look at her. If she tries to talk to you, just walk away. Because if I catch wind of anything else like this, I will be forced to get the police involved, and I don't think either of you want that." He leans back in his chair. It groans under his weight. "Am I being perfectly clear?"

I slap my hands on my legs in frustration. "So tell her to leave *me* alone."

DeGroot looks at me, unflappable. "I have. And please control your temper while you're in my office. I won't be yelled at."

I stare at him for a moment. I'm seized by a desire to argue, to make the principal understand that I'm innocent. But I can tell that DeGroot thinks this is some kind of tit-for-tat, back-and-forth spat between me and Sasha. That the locker is a vengeful prank gone too far. I wonder how Sasha played it. Dabbing her eyes, telling in a choked voice how she'd found the locker broken open and destroyed. Mentioning her volatile ex-boyfriend, how upset I'd been that she'd dared speak to my family after the breakup.

"Am I being perfectly clear?" DeGroot asks again.

Finally, I nod. "Yes, sir. I understand."

"All right. Head on to class now. Mrs. Murray will give you a pass so you won't be marked tardy." DeGroot stands up from his desk. "I hope I don't have a reason to see you again, Gabe."

I don't trust myself to answer. I grab my backpack by one strap and step out of the office. My fury mutes the sounds of the hallway. I barely notice as a sophomore slams into me, eyes on her phone. She looks up to apologize, but the words die on her lips; I have no doubt my rage is plain for anyone to see.

I slow only when I get to my locker, my steps faltering. The lock is missing and the door is slightly open. The noise of the hallway comes back with one sharp blast, the loud shouts of kids returning from lunch, the clang of lockers, and the distant strains of a Sia song from someone's headphones. I hold my breath as I open the door fully. Everything is exactly as I left it—my textbooks piled haphazardly, my jacket on the hook, the peace sign carved on the side wall. Everything except for a crisp white envelope tucked neatly in the back corner.

After a moment's hesitation, I rip the envelope open, the paper thick and pulpy in my trembling hands. The pain comes swift and sharp as a small metallic object tumbles out, embedding itself in my palm before clattering to the floor with a hollow *ping*. It's a razor blade, the edge now stained with my blood.

I whirl around, pressing the cuff of my jacket to my palm to stanch the bleeding. And then I see her, at the very end of the corridor. She leans against the bulletin board as students stream around her, rushing to fourth period.

Sasha's eyes lock on mine, a smile playing on her lips. She blows me a kiss and then disappears into the crowd.

TWENTY-TWO

Elyse

"The thing is, Trajan's smarter than most jocks." Brynn leans on her palm, elbow on the table next to a towering stack of books. "Did you know he's going to Stanford next year? He wants to study chemistry, which, like, yuck. But he's also super into literature and stuff."

It's Wednesday night, and we're at Central Library after rehearsal, trying to study. I love the old sandstone-and-marble building; it gives off a studious, serious air that the boxy modern branch down the street from my apartment lacks. We're on the third floor, surrounded by heavy wooden book stands and globes and glass displays of early editions.

My phone vibrates softly on the table. I glance down at the screen.

I can't stop thinking about you.

And even though there's no name associated with the number, a smile touches my lips.

We haven't been able to see each other outside rehearsal since Cannon Beach last weekend, but Aiden and I have been texting all week. We have to be careful. I can't put any identifying information in my phone; I can't list his name, can't have a photo of the two of us—though I do have a perfectly innocent picture of him on stage, going over the notes of the last few rehearsals. He texts only from a burner. That way, if someone gets suspicious, we won't get in trouble.

Brynn hasn't even noticed. "Like, we've been talking about Shakespeare a lot. You know he's in AP English? But he also reads plays for fun. The other night we read the seduction scene from *Richard III* together, and it was so freaking hot."

"That's the nerdiest date I've ever heard of," I say.

"I know. Isn't it great?" She grins. "Maybe we can talk Mr. Hunter into doing that one next year. I mean, *Romeo and Juliet*'s okay, but it's definitely not the most sophisticated play Shakespeare ever wrote."

"I like *Romeo and Juliet*!" I protest.

"It's about dumb people making dumb decisions." She shrugs. "I'd much rather do *Midsummer.* Or *Much Ado about Nothing.* Oh man, I'd kill to play Beatrice."

I don't know why, but it irritates me. *"A Midsummer Night's Dream* is about someone falling in love with a donkey. I'm not sure that counts as sophisticated."

She laughs lightly. "Well, that's not what it's *about*. It's a little more complicated than that."

The faint note of condescension rankles my nerves. "I've read the play, Brynn. I know what it's about."

"Okay, okay, don't get huffy." She smirks a little. "Juliet is a very important role, too. No one's disparaging your part."

"You literally just said she's a dumb person making dumb decisions," I point out.

A crease forms in the middle of her forehead. "Look, can you stop making this about you for half a second? I'm trying to tell you that Trajan and I are, like, official. So can you maybe be happy for me?"

What I want to say? *Why does hearing about you and Trajan require an elaborate sidebar about how the play I'm starring in is trash? And why do I have to drop everything to care about your latest conquest?*

But what I do say, after a long pause?

"Sorry. I *am* happy for you . . . he's really cute. And he sounds awesome."

She looks mostly placated, but the remnants of a frown linger on her brow.

"What's been up with you lately? You've been distracted nonstop."

"I'm just feeling anxious since we're so close to opening night, I guess." I grab my ponytail and take it out of its elastic, then redo it, my fingers fidgety. "That, plus Mom, plus homework, plus my life in general."

She seems satisfied with the answer. She reaches across the table and pats my forearm. "It's a lot. But you're going to be great. You're perfect for this role."

I purse my lips and restrain myself from pointing out, once again, that she just told me Juliet was an idiot.

But at least my secret is still safe.

When I get home a few hours later, Mom is in the kitchen, smoking into the exhaust fan. When she sees me she puts out the cigarette and straightens up.

"Hi," she says. "How was your day?"

"Fine," I say. Then I look around and see that the island is set with plates and cutlery and serving ware. My eyes widen. "What's . . . all this?"

"I thought we could eat dinner together." She smiles shyly. "If you wanted to, I mean."

I stare at the spread. She hasn't cooked in about five years. I'm sort of impressed she still remembers how. It's a simple meal—baked chicken breasts, steamed broccoli, Pillsbury biscuits—but it smells good. My stomach rumbles.

"Sure," I say, putting down my backpack and swinging myself up into one of the barstools at the island. "It looks great. Thanks."

She sits down across from me, and silently we start to load our plates. She still looks a little sickly; her skin is pasty-pale, her hands a little shaky. But she looks worlds better than she did last week.

"So. Uh, when is opening night for that play?" she asks, spreading butter over a biscuit.

I blink. "What play?"

She gives a nervous laugh. "*Your* play, dummy. You know, the one you're *in*?"

Somehow I never imagined Mom coming to the performance. She hasn't set foot in my school at all since freshman year, much less come to any plays or concerts. It's hard to picture her in the auditorium, surrounded by the other parents. What will she wear? Will she fidget through the whole thing, all her nervous tics out on display?

Will she want to meet Aiden?

I'm taking too long to answer. Mom's face falls. She sets down the biscuit and looks away. "I mean . . . if you want me to come."

"Of course I want you to come," I blurt out. "I just . . . I didn't know you'd want to. It's the Thursday before Thanksgiving."

She gives me a slightly surprised look. "You're the lead, Elyse. Of *course* I want to see it."

It's no use pointing out that until last week, she didn't even know I was in a play. It'd just hurt her feelings. And while there are moments I want to yell at her, moments I want to hold her accountable for all the ways she's hurt me, I also know from experience that there's no faster way to send her spiraling back into despair.

And at least she's trying.

"Okay. I'll get you on the list." I decide to let myself be excited. Finally, my mom's going to see me in the spotlight.

We eat in silence a little longer. The chicken is a tiny bit dry, but the seasoning's good. The broccoli is crisp and bright. It's the best meal I've had in ages.

"Elyse?"

I look up. Mom's biting the corner of her thumbnail, looking nervous. I hold my breath, waiting for some confession to come. Did she get more pills? Did she fall off the wagon? If so, we'll have to find an NA meeting tonight. Which will mean, once again, no homework. Though that would be the least of my worries.

"I just wanted to say . . . to say thank you. For last week. For helping me. I know it's been hard." She rubs her face a little, and I can see how exhausted she is. "I know it's been hard for a long time."

I look down at my plate. "It's okay, Mom."

"No, it's not. I know I can't really make things up to you. And Jesus, I'm really dreading that ninth step." She takes a deep breath and laughs nervously. We both know the Twelve Steps by heart by now; nine is making amends to people you've hurt. "Because you and I will have a lot of shit to talk about. But this time I . . . I'm going to do it. This time I'm going to be better."

Usually, I try not to think too much about the past. The memories of my mother drifting in and out of consciousness, or selling my things when she needed cash, or disappearing for days at a time are painful. But even more painful are the happy memories. I usually stave those off. I have to, if I'm going to stay realistic, if I'm going to keep from false hope. But now for some reason they play across my mind, projected like a film reel. Mom taking me to the zoo when I was two or three, marveling at how many of the animals I could name from memory. Mom holding me in her lap at the movies. Mom making me bologna sandwiches with the gross plasticky edge of the meat peeled off. Mom lying in bed next to me, rubbing my back until I fell asleep.

I put down my fork and take her hand. It's chilled, almost scaly-dry. I make a mental note to buy her some lotion next time I get paid—something that smells good, that feels like silk. Not to reward her—she doesn't deserve a reward just for staying sober. But because that's the sort of gift you give your mom, when you want her to know you love her.

"Remember the rules," I say. "One day at a time, right?"

We both smile. We've both made fun of NA's cheesy sayings over the years. But the fact of the matter is, there's no other way for us to figure this relationship out. One day at a time. Because even though I want to hope and I want to believe in her, we both know how fragile the future can be.

"Okay," she says. She squeezes my hand. "One day at a time."

TWENTY-THREE

Gabe

"Again!" shouts Vivi, shrieking with laughter. "Again!"

"All right, you ready?" Caleb puts his hands under her arms and swoops her up to the hoop. She dunks her little foam basketball with both hands.

"Vivi makes the goal!" Irene yells. She's sitting at the table, watching them play. Rowdy runs in circles around the yard.

It's late Friday afternoon, and we're at my house, the slate on the patio still warm with the fading sun. Vivi's pigtails are lopsided, her cheeks flushed pink. My parents are at a faculty banquet, and I'm babysitting for the night. I don't mind. Caleb and Irene are over to keep us company, we have pizza money on the counter, and the fact that Sasha's been watching my every move has left me less eager than usual to go out.

"Gabe! Gabe, ball!" Vivi squeals, pointing. Rowdy's scooped up the ball and torn off running across the yard, tail wagging. I take off after him, and we play an exaggerated game of keep-away, much to Vivi's delight.

Ding-dong. I can hear the doorbell inside the house. My stomach flip-flops.

"I'll get it," I say quickly. "Be right back."

I try to keep my excitement down as I run to the front door. It could be anyone. It could be a FedEx guy, or a Jehovah's Witness, or the little kids from next door wanting to know if Vivi can come play.

But it's not.

Catherine stands uncertainly on the doormat, rubbing the back of one bare leg with the toe of her sneaker.

"You came," I breathe.

"I came." She smiles a little bit. "Dad had work tonight."

We've been extra cautious at school since I found the razor in my locker. I don't talk to her in the halls anymore—I don't even look at her, if I can help it. It's maddening. But tonight her dad is out on a job—he's a handyman, and there's been some kind of plumbing emergency at a duplex on the edge of town that's going to take him all night.

So she's here.

"You didn't *tell* me this was gonna be a boy-girl party." Irene's voice comes from behind me, mock-scandalized. "I don't know if I should be here."

"Hi, Irene," Catherine says. She glances behind her, toward the street. "We should get inside."

"You're right. Come on." I open the door a little wider and let her in.

It's somehow surreal to see her in my house. I'm used to seeing her in the woods, under the trees. My high-ceilinged living room, lined with my dad's books, my mom's cheerful folk art collection, my sister's toy animals, seems too bright, too loud, for someone like her. She glances around, and her face is hard to read.

That's when Vivi and Caleb come clattering in, Rowdy on their heels. "Gabe! Gabe, I got ball!" says my sister, holding it up over her head. She skids to a halt as she sees Catherine, her eyes getting big.

"Vivi, this is Catherine. My, uh, friend," I say.

Catherine kneels down in front of my sister. "I've heard so much about you, Vivi."

Vivi studies her face for a moment, taking her in. Vivi loved Sasha, who used to bring presents every time she came over—a pink dress, an Elsa doll, glitter ChapStick. I hold my breath, wondering how this will go—if Vivi will hate Catherine, if Catherine will be awkward, if somehow this whole thing was a bad idea. But then my sister breaks into an enormous smile.

"Hi!" she says. She holds up the ball, wet with dog drool. I'm about to jump in and intercept it, but Catherine doesn't skip a beat. She takes it, bounces it a few times in her palm.

"So where's the hoop?" she asks. "And whose team am I on?"

•••

We play outside until it gets dark, and then retreat to the den. At first I'm tense in spite of myself. It's not that I'm ashamed of Vivi, or afraid Catherine will turn out to be a bitch or something—but I have a long-ingrained, knee-jerk anxiety every time I bring someone new home. I want to protect my little sister. I also don't want my friends to think I'm boring or lame.

But it's not long before I relax. Catherine rolls with everything. She plays *Dance Central* with Vivi about five hundred times. Then, when we order pizza and settle down in front of the TV, she doesn't bat an eye when Vivi immediately cues up *The Little Mermaid*. She even joins in when Irene, Caleb, Vivi, and I sing along—her voice is soft but pitch-perfect, sweet.

By ten Vivi's asleep, half on the sofa, half on my lap. I gather her up in my arms to take her to her bed. My heart gives a quick lurch when Catherine gets up to go with me.

"We'll be back," I say. Irene has the remote and is already switching to Adult Swim.

"No hurry," she says, without even glancing at me. "We know where the fridge is."

My sister is limp in my arms, her head against my shoulder. I take her to her purple bedroom and tuck her in. She stirs a little in her sleep, then falls still. Catherine lingers behind me, watching, smiling.

"She's such a sweet kid," she whispers, when I step back out into the hall.

"Thanks. Yeah." I lace my fingers through hers.

She catches sight of my door, painted with green and pink graffiti streaks. "Is this your room?"

My heart trips a beat or two, but I try to keep my cool. "Yeah. You want to see it?"

She nods shyly. I take her hand.

My desk light casts a warm glow across the smooth denim bedspread, the dresser appliquéd with skate stickers, the Justice League action figures posed on my desk. I shut the door gently behind us, then wonder if I should have left it open—if she'll think I'm being a creeper or something. But she's already looking around the room, smiling.

"It's so *neat*," she says.

"Yeah, so?" I feign a scowl. "What, you think just because I'm a dude I don't like hospital corners?"

She runs her hand along the back of my desk chair. "It's just that I don't know a lot of people under thirty with a labeling machine." She picks up my label maker and types something into it. Then she hits "Print." ANAL RETENTIVE, it says.

"Fine. You know my dark secret. I'm the world's only OCD skate punk." I put the label on my forehead and stick my tongue out. "Fight the man. But maybe do it with color-coded Post-it notes."

She laughs.

Then she reaches up and peels the sticker off my forehead. I take the label maker from her and set it on the desk, using it as an excuse to step closer to her. My hands slide around to the small of her back. Her breath is thin, shallow; her arms wrap around my neck.

We kiss. It starts slow but builds quickly, chemical reactions setting each other off in a cascade, energy and heat releasing from every touch. She grips my shirt in her fingers. I feel drunk and desperate and dizzy. I clutch her hips and pull her close.

CRASH.

We've bumped into the desk. My Green Lantern clatters against Wonder Woman, and they both tumble to the ground. I give a start, but then we both laugh, and we're leaning toward each other again, about to kiss, about to touch, when I see something that stops me cold.

She pauses and opens her eyes, looking confused. "What's the matter?"

I don't answer. My hands drop away from her sides. Suddenly my whole body feels like it's made of stone, heavy and numb.

I reach across my desk and pick up the thing that was sitting behind my action figures. A black box. On the front, a small reflective circle, a single dilated eye. The whole thing no bigger than a matchbook.

Catherine blinks. "Is that . . ."

"Yeah," I say.

A camera.

TWENTY-FOUR

Elyse

"Don't squirm."

I stand on a block in front of the green room's full-length mirror while Oksana Ivchenko, the girl heading up the costume department, sticks a pin into the heavy brocade dress. It's gold and white—it looks like it's made from some kind of upholstery fabric, but Oksana's made it look elegant. The French neckline dips low, and the trumpet sleeves drape beautifully around my wrists. I tuck my hair experimentally into an updo, and suddenly, there she is.

Juliet.

We're one week out from opening night, and the costume crew is here in full force. A few feet away, a skinny boy with elaborately gelled hair is taking Laura's measurements. Brynn sits at one of the vanities, rotating the chair slowly left and right as she waits her turn. Kendall and the other girls, the extras and bit players, are digging through a box of accessories, looking for things that might work for them.

There's a general buzz of excitement in the room. This is when it all starts to feel real. Doing final fittings, working on hair and makeup design, going through the last few rehearsals. This is when the pieces come together.

"Ow!" One of Oksana's pins jabs my hip. I give a little jump.

"I told you, stop squirming." Oksana frowns at the spot where she stuck me. "Don't bleed on my fabric."

"Sorry." I stand motionless, but I'm still smiling in the mirror. I can't help it. Up until now I couldn't have pictured this.

Brynn looks up at me with eyes narrowed. "You really do look amazing," she says grudgingly. "God, you know it kills me to say that."

As always, she's both kidding and not. Her own costume is a bland gray dress and a wimple. It covers her whole body. It's weird to see her like that, out of her usual peacock colors. She somehow looks shorter, diminished.

The door swings open, and Aiden steps in. Brynn gives a little shriek.

"Mr. Hunter, we're changing in here," she says.

Quickly he covers his eyes. "Sorry! Sorry! I just wanted to see how the costumes are coming."

My cheeks get warm at the sight of him. He's been in the shop, taking a look at the sets and props this afternoon, and his sleeve are rolled up to his elbows. The smell of wood shavings clings to him.

"Is everyone decent?" he asks.

"As decent as we get around here," quips Laura. He takes his hand from his eyes.

"Sorry," he says again, chastened. "I wasn't thinking."

Brynn's eyes go hard and narrow. She's never been particularly shy, and she's not remotely naked, so I'm not sure what her problem is.

"What do you think?" Oksana asks. I turn my attention back to Mr. Hunter, meeting his eyes in the mirror. My face is lurid pink; it clashes with my dress. I'm sure everyone in the room has to notice.

"It's great." His voice is brisk and delighted—professional and detached. So much so that I start to wonder if I look as good as I think I do. Is he just humoring me? Humoring Oksana? I don't want to look "great." I want to look *beautiful.*

"We'll do a white petticoat," says Oksana. "And I've got a beaded net that'll look good against her hair."

He nods thoughtfully. "It's quite striking. Good job, Oksana."

Oksana makes an affirmative little grunt in the back of her throat. "Okay, Juliet, step down. I'll take it in tonight."

I hop off the block. The skirt skims the floor, covering my toes. I feel like bolting into the changing room so I can hide my face. But before I can, Aiden steps close.

"It's perfect." His voice is still brisk, but it's softer, gentler.

No one eavesdropping would think anything of it, but I feel the caress in the words.

"Thank you," I whisper.

I wish more than anything that we were alone. So that he could turn me around and look at the costume from every angle. So I could run my fingers through his hair. But we can't even risk standing next to each other too long. I step away and into the changing room. By the time I come back out, he's gone.

And weirdly, Kendall and Brynn are sitting side by side.

The sight of them together hits me hard. It doesn't make any sense—it's like seeing a cat riding on a dog. They lean toward each other, Kendall speaking quick and low, Brynn's eyes wide, and for a moment I'm sure that they're talking about me.

"Hey," I say, flopping down next to them. Kendall gives me a disdainful sneer, but Brynn turns toward me.

"Well, that was freaky," she says.

I cock my head. "What was?"

"Uh, Mr. Perv charging into a room of naked girls?" She curls her lip with distaste.

"No one was naked," I say.

"Yeah, well, he didn't know that." She scowls. "Okay, I didn't want to tell you this because I didn't want to freak you out, but Kendall . . . saw something."

My throat gets tight. I sneak a look at Kendall. That day in Cannon Beach. Did she see more than I thought she did? Did she see me with Aiden?

Kendall purses her lips prissily. I can tell she's thrilled to have information someone wants.

"Like, okay, the other day at rehearsal I lost my phone. What else is new, right?" She glances from me to Brynn, hoping for a laugh, and then gives up. "Anyway, I came back into the theater to look for it and I found one on the edge of the stage. So I just grabbed it without thinking. But when I looked at the screen I realized it wasn't mine."

I give her a look like, *so what*?

"Well . . ." Kendall glances at Brynn. "There were, like, dozens of pictures of you on it."

I blink. "What?"

"Pictures. Of you. During rehearsal." She takes in a breath, savoring this final bit of intel. "And then Mr. Hunter came in and saw me with it and got this funny look on his face, like, really embarrassed. And he kind of laughed and said, 'Oh good, you found it.' Then he took it from me."

There's silence for a long moment. I stare at her, wondering if that's really and truly all she knows . . . or if she's hanging on to something she might have seen in Cannon Beach. I glance over at Brynn.

"Is that it?" I ask.

She raises an eyebrow. "Don't you think it's kind of sketchy?"

I shrug. "So he wants to take pictures of the production."

"Yeah, but, there weren't pictures of anyone else," Kendall says.

I roll my eyes. "Yeah, but I'm kind of the lead. Doesn't it make sense for him to have a bunch of pics of me?"

"Oh, come on," Brynn bursts out. "You don't think it's weird? He's, like, obsessed with you or something."

I've finally had enough. "You just don't like him because he didn't give you Juliet. Get over it, Brynn."

The words whip out of my mouth before I have a chance to think about them. Brynn freezes in her place. She looks like I've slapped her.

Kendall clears her throat. "Gosh, guys, I didn't mean to start any *drama*."

Neither one of us answers. We stare each other down. Once upon a time I would have apologized—I would have hurried to smooth things over. But I'm tired of Brynn throwing shade at me and then pretending I'm being too sensitive.

I'm tired of making things easier for everyone else.

It seems like forever before she grabs her purse and stalks out of the green room, letting the door slam behind her.

TWENTY-FIVE

Gabe

Let's talk. Now.

I stand in Sasha's driveway, staring up at the house. It's almost one A.M., and the windows are dark, the neighborhood silent except for the distant sound of a barking dog. I stare down at my phone, waiting for a reply. Somehow, I know she's up.

The mini-camera is in my pocket. It's maybe five ounces, but it feels like it weighs five hundred pounds.

I find her window, with its sheer white curtains. Just as I thought, her light is on. I stand for a moment, my eyes narrowed. Then I pick up a handful of the smooth white pebbles that fill the garden. One by one, I hurl them at the glass.

I see a dark silhouette look out at me. Then my phone chimes.

Coming. Meet me in the back.

I pace along the side of the pool, rigid with anger. The succulents in Mrs. Daley's garden scrape against my shins. For hours I've been roiling, furious, planning what I'd say to her, planning what I'd do. But when she steps out onto the patio, I'm at a loss for words.

The first thing I notice is what she's wearing. It'd be hard not to notice. She's in a short, sheer pink thing, trimmed in lace. I've seen Sasha in her pajamas a few times—she usually wears tank tops and shorts, nothing like this. Beneath the thin fabric I can see the outline of her navel, the swell of her breasts. She's not wearing underwear. She's straightened her hair, and it hangs like a heavy curtain around her shoulders, her skin blue in the pool's light. There's something surreal about her new look, almost uncanny, like seeing a doll made to look like a real-life person.

"Stay. The hell. Away from me," I hiss, throwing the camera at her feet. She doesn't even look at it.

"Hi, yourself," she whispers. She takes a few steps toward me, grabs my arm, and tries to drag me toward the pool house. "Come on, I don't want to wake up my parents."

"I don't care." I shake her off. "What the fuck is wrong with you? Stay out of my house. Stay out of my life, you crazy psycho bitch."

Tears fill her eyes. Her hand falls away.

"All I want is for us to be together," she says. "Why don't you want me anymore?"

It's the last thing I expect her to say. Sasha Daley doesn't beg. She demands; she commands. I gawk at her, my mind spiraling through all the things I could say. *Because you kidnapped my little sister. Because you keep sending me threatening Snaps. Because you tried to frame me for destroying your locker.* But a sick feeling creeps up inside me, and I can't quite get the words out. Because suddenly I realize why the hair is so strange.

It's Catherine's hair. Catherine's style. She's cut and dyed and styled her hair like Catherine.

Somehow this is scarier than everything else she's done—because this makes no sense at all. This isn't rage, or some play to get attention. This is something else entirely.

Mascara runs down her cheeks in slick black ribbons. She takes a shuddering breath. One strap of her nightie slithers off her shoulder, and she doesn't bother to fix it.

"You're all I've ever wanted," she says. "I need you." She steps closer to me, reaching for me. I shift away from her.

"Sasha, I am not yours anymore." My voice shakes slightly, but I try to keep it steady, firm. "I don't love you. I don't want you. I'm sorry this is . . . I'm sorry you're hurt." For a half moment I mean it. "But you have to get over it. Because we are never going to be together again."

She draws in her breath in a hiss. I tense, almost waiting for her to strike. But she doesn't. She reaches up to touch my face.

"We'll see about that," she whispers.

"Look at you. You can't change my mind—not even when you're playing someone else."

Her face twists into a sneer. "Your little sister was so easy to grab. And who did the cops believe? Fuck, Gabe, your own parents didn't believe you. I told her next time I'd take her to my lake house. Take her out in a boat. She was really excited. I told her there were mermaids at the bottom of the lake." Her voice drops to a whisper. "Maybe I'll show her."

The anger surges up in me again. I grab her wrist and pull her hand down, away from my face.

"If you come near my family again, I'll kill you. Do you understand me?"

She laughs then, her lips stretched wide. I let go of her hand, a shudder of revulsion traveling along my skin. I start edging my way back to the gate. She doesn't follow, but she watches me every step of the way.

The wind picks up, rippling the silk against her skin. The last I see of her, she's tilting her face up toward the moon, and in its pale light I can see that she's smiling.

TWENTY-SIX

Elyse

Opening night.

I pace back and forth in the wings. Oksana's gold brocade dress feels too tight across my chest. I can already feel the sweat pooling at the small of my back; meanwhile, my mouth is bone dry. I ball up the excess fabric of the Renaissance-style sleeves, squeezing them in my hands. I'm going to pass out. They'll all be waiting for me on stage, and I'll be flat on my face behind the curtains.

I glance around me. Frankie's dancing from foot to foot, trying to stay loose. Oksana's doing a quick repair on Laura's dress; Trajan has his eyes closed and is mouthing his lines. For once it occurs to me: It's not just me that's nervous. Somehow that makes me feel better.

"Places," Aiden says. He's wearing a headset in order to

talk to the kids in the lighting booth. He looks down at his clipboard. "Curtain's in two."

He pauses next to me, close enough that our shoulders nudge against each other.

"You're going to be fantastic," he whispers.

I smile up at him, but I don't have time to respond. Beyond the curtain I hear the audience go quiet as the lights go down. Aiden disappears, off to give instructions or encouragement to someone else.

I hold my breath, listening carefully to the opening lines. I hear the servants start to squabble; I hear Trajan as Tybalt, growling angrily at Benvolio. My pulse beats so loud in my ears it threatens to drown out everything else.

"Hey."

The voice is a bare whisper. I look up to see Brynn, there in her simple gray dress, her hair covered by the wimple. My fingers twist nervously around the fabric of my skirt. We haven't spoken in a week—the longest we've ever gone.

Her dark eyes are uncertain as they move across my face. "Break a leg," she says finally.

Tears spring to my eyes. This isn't how I've ever imagined this moment—barely speaking with my best friend, both of us still licking our wounds. I want to hug her, to laugh about our opening-night jitters. But that's not where we are right now.

"You too," I whisper.

We don't have time for anything else. She's up. She and Laura hurry out to center stage and start their dialogue.

I take a deep breath.

I hear my cue. It's time. I step into the light.

"How now? Who calls?" My voice rings loud and true.

We're amazing. We hit all our marks, nail our lines. Brynn's daffy nurse gets big laughs from the audience; I hear audible gasps during the big fight scene when Mercutio and Tybalt both die. My nerves disappear as I get into the rhythm of the lines. The poetry of the language is so familiar by now it's like a second heartbeat. My tongue moves deftly across the words, spinning them, twisting them, making them sad or joyous or wistful.

The audience roars its approval as the curtains draw closed. Two at a time, we all step out to take our bows; Frankie and I go out last of all. My feet barely seem to touch the scratched wooden stage. I catch Brynn's eye for a moment, and she smiles at me.

Nothing has ever felt so good, so right.

We're still in our makeup and costumes when we go out to the lobby to greet our friends and family. Brynn's parents and siblings crowd around her, feverishly snapping pictures. I recognize Kendall's family, too; her brother and sister are chasing each other around. Nessa Washington kisses her girlfriend, Tamika.

"Elyse!"

It's my mom. I know it's her only because I know her voice; I can't see her face behind the enormous bouquet she's wielding. I laugh and take it, cradling it in my arms.

"Thanks, Mom."

"You were so *good*," she says. She sounds genuinely surprised. "Where'd you learn to act like that?"

I bite the corner of my lip. A part of me—the part that's still holding on to every resentment, every frustration of the last ten years—wants to say something cutting, to point out that if she'd come out of her stupor a little sooner she might've known I could perform. But she looks so vulnerable, standing there in a skirt she's had since before I was born, her fingernails gnawed to the quick. I hug her tight.

"I'm really glad you came," I say.

Before she can answer, Aiden steps up to the two of us.

I can't help but go tense. But his dimples are in full force when he shakes her hand. "Are you Elyse's mom? It's so great to meet you. I'm the director, Mr. Hunter."

"Oh," she says meekly. I wince a little. Her small talk is rusty. But Aiden seems unfazed.

"She's a special girl," he says. "One of my most talented."

"Oh, thank you. I mean, yes, she is," Mom says. She shifts her weight. "Thank you so much. She told me you took a leap of faith in casting her. I'm so glad you did."

He shakes his head. "She's too modest. She earned this. And she proved herself."

I see some of the others slipping back to the green room to change out of their costumes, so I take the opportunity to break up the awkwardness. "Hey, Mom, I need to go get cleaned up, and then a bunch of us are going out for coffee to celebrate. See you at home?"

"Oh. Yeah, of course." She gives Aiden a little nod. "Nice to meet you, Mr. Hunter."

"Nice to meet you too." He glances at his watch. "I'd better go back there and make sure everything's put away."

We walk back into the theater together. It's quiet—I can hear shrieks of laughter coming from the green room, back behind stage left, but the stage is dark and empty. We climb up the steps.

"Tonight was . . ." I start, but before I can finish the thought he's taken me by the hand, and pulled me behind the curtains. He cups my chin with his hand.

"Amazing," he whispers. "You were amazing."

We kiss. The beaded cap that's held my hair in place comes off, and my hair spills around my shoulders. He picks up handfuls of it, runs his fingers through it.

"All night long it was all I could do not to touch you," he breathes into my ear. "You've never been so beautiful."

I close my eyes. Everything else vanishes—Brynn, the performance, my mom. Everything's gone except for our two bodies, pressed together in the dark.

Something rustles nearby. I freeze, my muscles taut and trembling. Aiden pulls away a little.

"What's wrong?" he asks.

I untangle myself from his arms and take a step toward the noise. "It sounded like . . . like someone brushed against the curtain." I pause for a moment, and then quickly dart forward and pull back the velvet.

No one's there.

I exhale loudly, my heart lurching in my ears.

He relaxes visibly, but gives an indulgent smile.

"We're both getting paranoid," he whispers.

"Yeah, well, we almost got caught at the beach," I remind him. He steps close to me again, but the spell is broken. His hand, when it brushes a lock of hair out of my eyes, is tender, but restrained.

"I know. It's been hard. But I have an idea. Can you get away Saturday night?"

"I think so. What are you thinking?"

His glasses catch the light just so, and glint keenly. "It's a surprise."

"You have to give me a hint!" I tug on his arm. "What should I wear? What should I bring?"

"Don't worry, just come as you are. You're perfect," he says. He leans in again and kisses me, a short, sweet, tender kiss this time. Then he steps away. "They'll be looking for you. You'd better go."

I linger a moment more, wishing we were back in the folds of the curtains. Wishing we had all the time and privacy in the world. But we don't. We can't.

And I don't want to miss the celebration, either. I can hear laughter from the lobby. Nessa whoops loudly. Brynn's singing something, though I can't make out what. I head back to the rest of the cast, ready to be a part of it.

TWENTY-SEVEN

Gabe

"It's so beautiful out here," Catherine says softly, tracing the surface of the lake with her fingertips. The ripples arc out behind us. "God, I can almost believe we're alone in the world."

I smile. That's pretty much exactly what I was going for.

It's a week after I found the hidden camera in my room. I haven't been able to do anything without feeling watched. Everywhere I go—the skate shop, the park, the taco truck, the convenience store—I have this sense of Sasha, lurking somewhere just out of sight. The image of her, bleached by the moonlight, leering like some kind of succubus, keeps floating up before my eyes. It's making me crazy.

So today, I picked up Catherine from a bus stop we'd agreed on, and we drove an hour outside Austin to Inks Lake, where we rented a rowboat. The instant we pushed off into the water, I felt the tension go out of my shoulders. And suddenly I was free to look around and see how perfect the day was—the deep-blue water, the brightly colored granite along the shoals. The girl across from me, fine-boned, fragile, lovely. A rare smile on her lips.

"Maybe someday we can come out here and camp," I say, before I think. But no—of course we can't come out here and camp. There's no way her dad would let her.

But she looks up at me, cheeks rosy. "Maybe," she says. "Someday."

I lean back against the hull and stare up at the clouds. This is all I want. To be alone with her. To be drifting, out under the wide blue sky.

"Have you heard from Sasha?" she asks suddenly. My heart gives a sharp lurch.

I shake my head. "No. Thank God." I haven't told her about going over to Sasha's. I didn't want to freak her out any more than I had to.

She's quiet for a moment. An awkward, self-conscious feeling comes over me. I don't know if she's waiting for me to elaborate. I pick up the oars and propel us further out, toward the lake's center. My shoulder gives the tiniest twinge of protest, but it's almost back to normal.

"I hate all this sneaking around," I say. "I just want this shit with Sasha to be behind me."

She shrugs. "Even if it were, there's still my dad to contend with," she says. "We'd still have to keep this quiet. But I'll admit, I'm kind of praying Sasha gets packed off to boarding school or juvie or something."

"I don't know why I was with her so long," I say. "She was horrible to everyone and I just . . . excused it, I guess. But I shouldn't have. I should've stood up for them. For myself too."

She gives an odd little smile.

"Said everyone who ever got out of a bad relationship, ever," she says.

"Yeah, well, I think Sasha wrecks the curve a little. Most people don't enter into long-term relationships with psychos."

Her eyes dart across my features like she's trying to piece together a puzzle. "Maybe. But that's what makes the psychos so awful. They're pretty good at getting under your skin."

I cock my head at her. "You sound like you know from experience."

She looks down at her lap. "I'm just saying, you aren't the only one who's ever been manipulated. People will always find a way to hurt each other. To use each other."

I rest the oars against my thighs. The boat bobs a little as I shift my weight. "Not all people."

She gives me an odd, measuring look. Then she smiles.

"No. Not all people." She takes a swig from a water bottle and wipes her mouth. "Sorry. I'm used to seeing the worst in everyone."

"So young, and so cynical," I say, trying to sound like I'm teasing. But I can't keep an edge of curiosity out of my voice.

Catherine gives a little shrug and doesn't reply. I let it drop.

"Well, anyway, I'm glad it's over. I feel like . . . like a different person. Especially since I met you," I say.

Our eyes meet, and my body sparks like a live wire. The sun is bright behind her, the light lost in her glossy hair. Almost without realizing what I'm doing, I leave my seat and climb across to where she's sitting. The boat rocks hazardously, and we laugh, clinging to one another, before it steadies. I rest my cheek against the crown of her head and take a deep breath.

"I do too," she says softly. I can feel the vibration of her voice against my chest. "It's probably obvious, but I was scared at first. It's been a long time since I . . . since I had anyone. I mean, friends, or . . ." She trails off. I can see that she's blushing from the pink in the part of her hair. "And the last time I trusted anyone it didn't go well."

I don't speak for a few minutes. I've known from the first time I saw her that something, someone, hurt her. You can see it in the angle of her shoulders, in the wounded curve of her mouth. You can hear it in her voice. I'm not sure if I should ask more, or let her tell me in her own time.

Finally, I swallow my curiosity. Because whatever happened, it was bad enough that it's kept her lonely and locked up ever since. She's the one who has to decide what it means. But I tilt her face upward to look at mine. "I'll never hurt you."

"Don't say that," she murmurs. "You can't promise that. Not really."

I rest my hand against her back, feeling the way her breath moves in and out, the way our bodies gently conform to one another's. "Why can't you trust me?"

"I do," she says quickly. "I just mean . . . things happen, sometimes. People get hurt."

"Give me a chance to show you," I say softly. I look down into her face again, and a desperate ache twists in my chest. "Cat, I love you."

The words are out before I can think about them, but I know as soon as I've said it that it's true. Her lips part in surprise. Then she puts her forehead to mine, closes her eyes.

"I love you too," she whispers.

TWENTY-EIGHT

Elyse

"Hey, Elyse, you coming?" Frankie asks.

It's nine on Saturday night, and we've just wrapped our last performance of the week. Everyone's gathering up their stuff and getting ready to go, but I'm still in the green room's vanity, wiping away my makeup. I'm taking my time so I have an excuse to linger behind when everyone else is gone. The rest of the cast is going downtown tonight—there's talk of trying to get into a bar, but really they'll probably just get donuts and coffee and wander around the Pearl District watching hipsters stagger from one cocktail bar to another.

Brynn's crouched next to one of the big plastic tubs we keep our props in, helping the stagehands pack the swords and things away, but I can tell she's listening. We've been tentative with each other, a little halting. I realize with a pang that we'd probably make up by midnight if I went out with them tonight. Nothing like the camaraderie of getting kicked out of a gay club, or eating too much sugar and horsing around Pioneer Square, to bring people together.

But I already have plans.

"I can't tonight," I say. "I've got work."

"The night of the performance? That sucks." Brynn frowns. "It's already ten."

"Yeah, Rita's sick. I said I could cover the last few hours of her shift," I say, smiling. "But I'll be at the cast party next week."

Trajan slides an arm around Brynn's waist. They look adorably ridiculous; she comes up only as far as his shoulder. "Text when you get off. If we're still out, I'll come get you."

"Thanks." I smile, truly grateful.

In the dressing room, I change slowly into my street clothes. When I get out, everyone's gone. I pick up my phone and text my mom.

Going out with the cast to celebrate—is it okay if I stay at Brynn's tonight?

A few minutes later, her reply comes.

Sure see u tomorrow

I grab my bag and turn out the green room's light. When I step back out into the theater, Aiden's waiting.

"Ready?" he asks.

I lean up to kiss his cheek. "Ready."

He drives toward the Columbia River Gorge. It's dark, so I can't see much, but the high canyon wall looms to our right, a slice of darkness that blocks out the sky. The moon's hidden behind the clouds. Even with the heat on in the car I can feel the crisp chill of the air whipping across the river.

We don't talk much, but it's a comfortable, intimate quiet. The radio is on low, and I lean against the window. It feels like a luxury to be driven somewhere—to lie back and trust in the person at the wheel.

After almost two hours he pulls onto a small side road that wends its way up the mountains. He turns on his brights, flooding the narrow road ahead of us with light. I can see needles of rain, lichen-covered trees. I sit up as the gloom closes in around us.

It feels like forever before we pull up in front of a small A-frame cabin. The forest crowds in on all sides, so it feels like a fairy-tale cottage in an enchanted wood.

"It's gorgeous up here during the day," he says. "Sorry your first glimpse is at night."

Inside, he snaps on a lamp to reveal a small, cozy space. There's a woodstove and a worn rag rug, and the windows are covered with hand-sewn curtains. A single queen-sized bed sits in the middle of the room. The air is cold and smells like the woods.

I suddenly realize Aiden's studying my face. He hangs back a little, frowning. "You're freaked out. I shouldn't have sprung this on you." He takes my hands in his. "Listen, I didn't bring you up here to pressure you into anything you don't want. I just wanted to be *alone* with you for a little while, so we could spend some time together without worrying about getting caught." He nods toward a ladder in the corner. "See, there's a loft. I'll sleep up there tonight, and you can have the bed. I just thought we could come out here and talk. Maybe go hiking tomorrow."

I draw closer to him and slide my arms around his waist. "I'm not freaked out. I trust you, Aiden."

It's mostly true. It's not that I think I'm in any kind of danger. But I've never been alone in a room with a bed with a boy—with a man—that I liked before.

He strokes a lock of hair away from my forehead. "You sure? Because I can take you back home."

"No!" My arms tighten at his waist. "God, no."

He kisses me softly. Then he pulls away. "Then I'd better get the stove going, or we'll freeze."

I sit on the edge of the bed and watch him start the fire. I've never had the chance to do anything very outdoorsy before—I never camped or went hiking as a kid—so I wouldn't know how to get a fire going if my life depended on it. It's kind of sexy, watching him crouched there with his sleeves rolled up, building a perfect little nest of paper and wood to catch the flame. Usually he doesn't strike me as particularly rugged, but out here, in the chill mountain air, I can see his survivalist roots.

While the cabin's warming he shows me everything he's brought. Plates of fruit and cheese; pecans and strawberries and figs; a tray of chocolates. Delicate tartlets filled with mascarpone and apricot. I rest against the pillows on the bed and he sits a few inches away, a platter of food between us.

"This is amazing." I look around the little space, marveling at how cozy and warm it feels now that the woodstove is going. "Let's run away and live up here. No one will ever bother us again. We'll live off the land."

He grins. "As easy as that, huh?"

"Yup." I pop a truffle in my mouth. "We'll forage for food and chop wood for the stove."

"Hm. There's not a lot of chocolate or brie that grows in this region," he says. "We'll have to make do with tree bark and moss."

"Delicious," I proclaim. "And we'll tame the squirrels to come be our pets."

"They'll eat all our tree bark and moss!" he says.

"And we'll go without shoes or clothes. Just . . . wander naked through the woods."

"Okay, I'm listening," he says. We both laugh. My nerves are starting to evaporate.

"Sometimes I wish we could," I say softly. "Just . . . pack up and leave. Start a new life somewhere. I mean . . . things are getting better with my mom. But I feel like I've been trapped here for so long. It'd almost be a relief to get a fresh start, without all the baggage."

He nods. "I know. I think about it, too."

I picture it. Maybe we couldn't go off the grid and hide in the woods, but we could go someplace and blend into the crowd—New York or Chicago or L.A. Get our own little apartment, with a record player and a coffeepot and a cat. Sprawl on the floor reading novels; get under-the-table jobs washing dishes or fixing leaky faucets. Go on a few auditions, maybe.

And we'd finally be alone. We'd finally be together, without anyone judging us.

"What're you thinking about?" he asks. He's watching me, his eyes almost blazingly bright.

"Oh, I don't know. Just daydreaming." I look down, suddenly unable to meet the intensity of his gaze. "I can't leave. Not really. Not while my mom needs me."

"I know." His voice is wistful.

"But . . . but this is amazing," I say quickly. "Being here, with you."

He shifts the plate out of the way, leans toward me. The kiss is soft and slow. A kiss that has all the time in the world.

"Elyse," he murmurs. "I love you."

My heart thumps against my sternum. "Aiden . . ."

"You're the only future I can picture. The only thing I can think about." He touches my chin.

I close my eyes. "I love you too."

We kiss again. Less soft, less slow. A kiss that's breathless with longing. His hands stroke my hair, my shoulders. I toy with the buttons on his shirt; I start to undo them, one at a time, until I can see the flat plane of his stomach, hard and muscular. His skin is so warm, so soft. His lips brush my earlobe and I moan, tilting my head back.

"I should go upstairs. It's getting late," he says.

I lean back against the pillows and pull him toward me. "Stay," I whisper.

He searches my face. I put my hand on his chest, feel his heartbeat warm and strong.

"Stay," I repeat.

And then we're kissing again, our bodies melting against each other, our clothes coming away piece by piece. My thoughts and fears dissolve. I'm nothing but sensation, shivering and arching.

Outside, the rain picks up again.

TWENTY-NINE

Gabe

Monday morning I break my own rule. I make my way to Catherine's locker, hoping to see her before the first bell, even though we're still trying to keep this on the down-low.

But every second she's out of my sight, I'm thinking of ways to get to her. I'm wondering where she is, and what she's doing, and where we could go to be alone.

She's there, hanging her jacket in her locker. It's almost bare—no pictures, no magazine clippings, no magnetic mirror stuck inside the door. Just a neat stack of books. I sidle up beside her, smiling. "Hey! What's . . ."

I don't get a chance to finish the sentence. She slams the locker door and turns on her heel, walking quickly away.

For a second I'm stunned. I just stare at her retreating form. Then I hurry after her.

"Cat? What's going on?"

She walks faster, trying to ignore me. I reach out and grab her elbow, spinning her around to face me.

Her eyes flash wildly. For a moment I think she looks scared. But then I realize she's furious.

"How could you do this to me?" Her whole body is trembling. "How could you . . . with *her*?"

"What?" I glance around, realizing we're dead center in the hallway. People are staring. "Can we . . . go somewhere more private?"

She gives a nasty laugh. "So you can tell me more lies? So you can talk me into trusting you? I don't think so."

"Cat—" I start, but she doesn't let me finish.

"That's not my name!" She pounds on her thighs in frustration. I take a half step back. I've never seen her so upset.

"Catherine," I try again. "I'm sorry, I want . . . I want to make this right, but I don't know what you're talking about."

"She caught you. On tape. It must have been before we found the camera." She laughs again, a strangled bark. "Maybe the same day, for all I know."

"*Who* caught me?" But dread mounts in my gut, a twisting, writhing thing. I know, before she even says it.

"Who do you think?" She pulls out her phone and types something in. Then she turns it around to show it to me.

The picture quality is grainy, but right away I can see that it's my bedroom. There's the mural Irene painted on my wall—an Aztec warrior popping an ollie on his skateboard.

There's my faded blue bedspread. My pillow, my stack of comics by the lamp.

And there, on the bed, is a girl. Or the back of a girl. The naked back of a girl. Long dark hair swings around delicate-looking shoulder blades. Her spine arches with pleasure. A guy sits on the other side of her—you can't see his face, but you can make out his dark curly hair as he kisses her neck, as he runs his hands down her sides.

Then my voice comes from the speaker. "Catherine . . ."

Everything in my body goes still. My muscles, my bones turn to stone. My lungs freeze mid-breath. I'm lost in a nightmare. I know whose shoulders those are. I've seen them dozens of times.

"It's Sasha," I say.

She snaps the phone away. "Yeah, Gabe, I know who it is. What I don't get is what kind of fucked-up game you're playing with her. With me."

"But I don't understand." I stare down at her. "I never . . . did that. In my room, with her. The only time anything close to that happened was the time she broke in, and we didn't . . . I didn't touch her." I frown. "Plus her hair was blond then. This has to be recent, because she dyed it."

Catherine gives an almost hysterical laugh. "You're thinking about her *hair*?"

"No, but the point is, I didn't do this. This isn't me." My mind can't seem to process the image. I *know* it's not me. But it's my voice, my room, my hair. For a single wheeling moment I wonder if I actually did do this and I've somehow forgotten—or if Sasha drugged me. Or even hypnotized me. But that's nuts.

Right?

"Really? Because it looks a lot like you," she says.

"I know. But she must have, I don't know, gone looking for someone who looks like me, and then broken into the house. She has a set of keys."

I see her hesitate at that. She bites the corner of her lip, and for just a moment I can tell she's not sure what to believe. But then she shakes her head.

"Whatever, Gabe. I don't know what kind of crazy shit you dragged me into. This is all over Facebook. Everyone's seen it. Everyone thinks this is me." She jabs her finger at the girl on the screen. I feel an absurd desire to cover up the screen, to shield us from view, even though I know it's not her, it's not me. "People I don't even know were asking me about it in the hall on the way to my locker."

"I'm sorry," I say, but she doesn't let me get any further than that.

"Do you have any idea what my dad will do if he sees it?" She runs her hand manically through her hair, her eyes wide. "He'll pull me out of school. He'll pack everything up and we'll be on to the next town. And I can't go through this again. I can't . . . start all over."

The idea makes me hot with anger. "He can't. That's not fair. It's not your fault."

The laugh that tears loose from her throat is frightening. It's a savage, hysterical sound. "You still don't get it. He can do whatever he wants." She shakes her head, lips trembling. "Just . . . God, Gabe, just leave me alone."

She backs away a few slow, faltering steps. Then she spins on her heel and breaks into a run.

"No running in the halls!" Mr. Perlman calls after her. But she doesn't stop.

For a moment I brace to go after her. Then I look around. People are staring, talking, laughing. A few big football player types cross their arms over their chests, and I realize it's not going to look good if I pursue her.

I turn around, ready to go back the other way, and then I do a double take. Catherine's there, by her locker again.

But no. It's not Catherine. It's Sasha. Sasha with Catherine's brown hair, Catherine's low-key tomboy look. I see with nausea that she's even bought a pair of purple Keds. She looks up at me, her face makeup free, her pale blue eyes strangely bright.

"You," I snarl. The world around her goes muted and red. I realize almost distantly that I want to hit her. I've never really wanted to hurt someone before.

"You need to be careful with that one. She's got issues," Sasha says.

A giddy hysteria swirls through me. I charge toward her, pressing her back against the lockers. "Tell her the truth. Tell her that wasn't me."

She purrs. "I always liked it when you got a little angry."

Before I can stop it, my fist slams the locker next to her head. She just laughs.

"Keep it up," she whispers. "The cameras love you."

That's when I feel them—dozens of eyes on me. Everyone's holding a cell phone. Everyone's got it angled right at me. This little snippet will be all over the Internet in seconds.

I push myself away from the lockers, hold up both hands in disgust. "Fine, Sasha. You win. Congratulations. At least now it's fucking over."

Her eyes go wide, innocent—for the benefit of the cameras, I'm sure. She steps close to me and leans up to whisper in my ear.

"Is it?"

Before I can say anything else, she slips through the crowd, dark hair swaying down her back.

THIRTY

Elyse

It's late afternoon when Aiden drops me off a few blocks from my apartment. The day is cold and gray but I hardly notice. I'm a million miles away.

Every moment of last night and this morning keeps replaying across my mind. The way he looked at me. The way his lips felt on mine; the way his hands felt on my body.

Waking up next to him. Opening my eyes and seeing his looking back at me across the crisp white pillow.

We can't kiss goodbye—it's too public—but I reach across the console and squeeze his hand. His eyes lock on mine, warm gold, warm green, almost hypnotizingly beautiful.

It takes all my self-control not to look back at him as I walk away from his car.

It's almost four. Mom should be at work, which is good—I have to get some homework done, though I can't begin to imagine how I'll focus on algebra right now. First a shower. I can still smell the woodsmoke on my clothes. I unlock the door and step inside. Then I drop my keys with a clatter, startled.

Mom's sitting on the couch, her leg bouncing nervously up and down. And sitting right next to her is Brynn.

There are a thousand things I could say in that moment, but my mind lurches clumsily, trying to catch up. Trying to make sense of the two of them, side by side. "What's going on?" I ask.

Mom stares at me, hollow-eyed. Her mouth stays tightly closed, so I glance at Brynn. Her face is makeup free, clean. It makes her look tired.

"I came by to talk to you," she says. "But you weren't here. And Sammie thought you were with me."

Fuck.

But that doesn't mean they know anything. I try to reassure myself. I can say I was out with a boy I met at the movie theater. I can keep Aiden out of this.

But before I can get a word out, Mom stands up off the couch. I'm so used to how she slouches that I always forget how tall she is—almost six feet. Now she uses every inch to tower.

"You're fucking your *teacher*?" Her voice cuts shrill through the Sunday quiet. I shrink away from her.

"What? I . . ." I stammer. But she just shakes her head.

"Brynn *saw* you," she hisses. "Messing around in the theater."

The rustling noise in the curtains. I turn to glare at Brynn. She looks down at her lap.

"That's what I came to talk to you about," she says miserably. "But when you weren't here I . . . I thought I should tell your mom."

"That's great, Brynn, thanks so much," I snap. I turn back to Mom. "It's not what you think. We're not just 'messing around.'"

"Oh no?" she sneers. "Let me guess. You're in love. He's different. He's not like other guys."

I cross my arms over my chest and stare defiantly back at her. "You don't even know him."

She snorts. "He's twice your age. That's all I need to know."

"Why does that even matter?" I ask. The dread of a moment ago has been replaced with a slowly mounting anger.

Her nostrils flare. "What does it matter? You're a *kid*, Elyse. He's taking advantage of you."

"I'm not stupid. And I haven't been a kid in a long time," I hiss. "I've been taking care of myself since I was six, Mom. *Six*. I've been feeding myself, paying my own bills, getting to and from school. Getting you to rehab, how many times now? I never had the luxury of being a kid. So forgive me if I find your sudden concern a little hypocritical."

Brynn cowers on the couch as Mom and I inch toward each other.

"Yeah, I've been a shitty mom. Why do you think this makes me so mad? You want to turn out like me? Stuck in a dead-end job, in a cheap little apartment, pregnant at seventeen? I'm trying to keep you from the same bad decisions I made," she says.

"There's no way I'll turn out like you, because I'm not a fucking junkie!" I shout. I'm beyond caring if I hurt her. I stare up at her, the world red-tinged, my hands balled into fists.

She swells up, and I think she's about to hit me. She's never hit me before. My body goes rigid in anticipation. But she just takes a deep breath. When she speaks again, her voice is softer.

"You're not to see him again, Elyse," she says.

I laugh scornfully. "Who's going to stop me?"

"I will." She puts her hands on her hips, then lets them fall to her sides self-consciously. "If you go back to him, I'll tell the school. He'll be done."

I suck in my breath. "You can't."

"I will." She's shaking with the effort of staying calm. "Even if it destroys our relationship. Even if you hate me forever. I'll do it to save you."

A scream rises in my chest. I force it down. My body's rigid with fury. I stalk to my bedroom and pause in the doorway.

"We don't have a relationship." I turn to look at Brynn. For the first time in her life, she's trying to be invisible. "And you. We're done. I never want to see you again."

I turn away from them both, and slam the door behind me.

THIRTY-ONE

Gabe

"I can't believe Sasha's gonna get away with this," Caleb says in a choked voice, after exhaling a long stream of smoke. He leans back and hands me the joint with the other.

"She always does," I say, my voice flat. I take a deep drag. I can feel the smoke moving through my chest, loosening the tight, anxious knots.

It's Friday, four days after the breakup. I've been drifting, numb. Going through the motions. Caleb, Irene, and I are sitting under one of the abandoned off-ramps that no longer connects to the highway, our skateboards at our sides. They dragged me here after school, trying to wake me out of my funk, but I mostly just watched them glide up and down the concrete. It was hard to imagine my body, heavy and slow, moving that effortlessly through space. Now it's getting dark, a chill cutting into the air.

"You hear from Catherine at all?" Irene asks, barely looking up from the sketchbook on her knee—she's planning a new midnight installment, something with a pin-up girl in a helmet straddling a rocket ship.

"Nope." I try to sound brisk, but my voice cracks. Catherine hasn't been at school since Tuesday. I feel her absence everywhere, a weird gap in the crowds, a dense and heavy feeling to the air in certain hallways. I've texted her half a dozen times, trying to find out if she's okay.

Hey, I'm not trying to harass you but I'm worried, you ok? Just answer y or n and I'll leave you alone.

Your dad hasn't hurt you, has he?

I miss you so much.

She never answers me.

Irene shakes her head. "We should *do* something. Figure out some way to get back at Sasha."

"No," I say quickly. "It's over, okay? She's already ruined everything. And I don't want to escalate shit any more. Someone's gonna get hurt."

She grimaces. "That's exactly why we should take her down."

I rest my forehead against my knees. I would love nothing better than to plan some elaborate comeuppance—to expose her, to show the world Sasha's true face. But I keep thinking about Catherine's terrified expression; about Vivi, trustingly following Sasha wherever she goes. I can't risk it.

"I'm sorry, man," Caleb says. "I really liked Catherine. She's a sweet girl."

"Yeah," Irene says. "This sucks."

I sigh, biting back a snarky reply. *Understatement of the year, guys.*

Suddenly, I can't stand it anymore. I pick up my skateboard. "I gotta get home. I promised Vivi we'd play board games tonight, and I gotta clear my head before I can manage that."

"Dude, the only way to play Candy Land is while stoned," Irene says.

"Oh man. Remember that crush I used to have on Queen Frostine?" Caleb says, his eyes vague.

Irene starts to laugh. "Uh, no. I think that must have been a personal thought you kept to yourself. But thank you for sharing."

I kick off on my board, the two of them still squabbling behind me. For a moment I feel wobbly. I haven't moved much for a few days; I've been splayed out on my bed, watching cartoons on my laptop and feeling like shit. But there's a new energy in my limbs. A new urgency pushing me forward.

I'll just skate by her house. I won't knock. I won't bother her. I'll just skate by to see if she's still there—to see if there are lights on, a car in the driveway. There's no law against that. But even as I approach her house I feel my skin crawl, as if I'm being watched. I step off my board a few blocks from her house and walk the rest of the way.

It's dark now. I slip in and out of the pools of light from the streetlamps. Acorns and dead leaves crunch under my feet as I make my way back toward the little cottage. The wind is cold. I pull up my hood. Then I put it down again, afraid it makes me look somehow suspicious.

The house's front windows are covered with thick blackout curtains. A tiny sliver of light escapes, but it's impossible to see anything through that. I glance up and down the street. A few blocks away someone's out walking a large dog. Otherwise, there's no movement in the neighborhood. Nothing stirring. Before I can talk myself out of it, I dart to the cottage's side yard, moving around to the back of the house.

I'm officially a creeper, I think, adrenaline soaring through my veins. But I can't stop now. She's in there. I have to see her. I have to make sure she's okay.

The backyard smells like fresh-cut grass, and a little like gasoline. Mr. Barstow must have been mowing. A square of light spills across the patio from a large window. Their kitchen. I can see scuffed wooden cabinets, outdated paneling along the walls.

And there, at the sink in front of the window, is Catherine.

She's doing dishes. I can just make out the rubber gloves at her elbows. She's wearing a frayed plaid shirt I've seen her in a hundred times; her eyes are cast down toward the sink. My chest feels tight at the sight of her. I stare up at the glowing square of the window. It might as well be a vision of another dimension, it's so far away.

There's movement behind her. Mr. Barstow comes into the kitchen. I sink down behind an Adirondack chair. The gasoline smell is worse over here, almost choking. I hold my breath.

Mr. Barstow lifts a handful of Catherine's hair behind her head, tugging it like a ponytail. I can see the slender line of her throat, the hard line of her clavicle. My blood sours suddenly, the adrenaline twisting inside of me. There's something wrong with this. Something about how he touches her . . .

I feel my body turn to liquid as her father leans down to kiss her neck.

Catherine stares woodenly out the window. Her expression doesn't change. She's far away, somewhere else.

Move. You have to move. You have to stop him, somehow. But I can't move. I'm weak against the chair, trembling. The image replays again and again in my head, even as it's playing out in front of my eyes. I don't know how I'm supposed to get up, to move my arms and legs, when my brain is choking on this knowledge—when it's fighting off the understanding of what's happening there, in the window, with all its might.

Then I see flames, licking along the base of the house, dark red and hungry.

THIRTY-TWO

Elyse

Monday morning, Brynn's waiting at my locker. I don't look at her as I spin the dial; I try to pretend she's not even there. But when I open the door it's with a jerk that makes the metal shudder on the hinges.

She doesn't say anything for a long time. I put my books away and hang my coat. I spend an inordinate amount of time folding a sweater and putting it neatly on the shelf. I look in the little magnetic mirror and fix my hair. I do everything I can to avoid her eyes.

"Are you okay?" she finally asks.

The question blindsides me. Of all the things to ask me. Of all the things to say. I shut the door, more gently this time, and finally look at her.

She's muted today—hair in a chunky braid, wearing a

pair of jeans and an oversized *Wicked* sweatshirt. She hangs back a little, uncertain, uncharacteristically sober.

"Oh, I'm great, thanks for asking." The sarcasm feels curved and metallic, sharp as a dagger. "What a great way to finish my weekend."

She bites the corner of her lip. "Did you get in trouble?"

I smirk. "Well, honestly, there's not a whole lot Mom can do. It's not like she can ground me. She's got a new job—she's working the night desk at the Super Eight. So she's not around to bother me too much."

It wasn't entirely true that there wasn't anything she could do, though. She'd taken my phone away the night before.

"I'm the one that bought it," I'd snarled. "With *my* money, that I earned. You were busy snorting Oxy, so you probably don't remember."

Mom winced at that, but she didn't back down. She stood in the doorway to my room after Brynn left, looking around like she didn't even recognize the place. Well, she probably didn't; everything in the room was mine and mine alone. I'd bought the bedspread, the books on the shelves, the curtains. I'd had the playbills framed; I'd bought all the clothes in the closet. I didn't owe her for any of it.

"You'll give me your phone, or I'll go to the cops," she said. Her voice was hoarse with emotion, her hands crossed over her chest. "I'll tell them all about your teacher."

I drew in my breath. "You can't."

"I will," she said. "God knows I should do that anyway. But I don't want to put you through that kind of humiliation.

So we're just going to put it behind us. But that means you can't talk to him. You can't text him, can't e-mail him . . ."

"But I'm in the play. We've got one more weekend," I protested.

"I'm sorry, but you'll have to quit," she said. Her eyes were heavy and sad, dark shadows beneath them. "I know how much you love it, but . . ."

"If you go to the cops I'll tell them you've been neglecting me." It was pathetic and desperate, but it was all I could think of. She shrugged.

"I'll take that chance if it means keeping you safe." She held out her hand.

I didn't have a choice. I gave her my phone.

Now, Brynn lingers next to my open locker door. "I'm really sorry," she says.

I laugh. "A little late for that, don't you think? Especially after you got what you wanted all along. I'm out of the play. You'll probably get to do Juliet next week, since you know all the lines by heart. Congratulations."

She looks at me like I'm crazy. "I'm not going back to that theater. I'm done. I e-mailed Hunter last night that I quit."

I do a double take in spite of myself. "What?"

"You really think I'd do something like this to, what, steal your role?" For a second she looks hurt. Then she looks pissed. "I wasn't trying to get you in trouble. I was freaking out. I didn't know what to do."

"So you went to my mom?" I snort.

"I wasn't going to. But she caught me in your lie." She

points at my chest. "I didn't know you were going to tell her you were with me. That's on you. And I can't believe you'd think I would do this to try to sabotage you. I thought you knew me better than that."

I grit my teeth. It stings that she's partly right—that it's my own fault that I got caught, using her as a cover when we'd been fighting. "All I know is that you've been jealous of me since I got this role. You can't stand it that someone thinks I'm better than you."

She gives me a pitying look and shakes her head.

"He doesn't think you're better," she says. "Just easier. You stupid, stupid girl."

I let out my breath with a sharp puff. Then I slam the locker door, twist on my heel, and walk away without looking back.

It's surreal to be at school. Especially because suddenly, everyone knows who I am. Half of them saw me on stage this weekend. People I've never talked to say hi as they pass me in the hallway. In English Ms. Cowan recites my lines back at me, dreamy-eyed. "Beautiful work, Elyse," she tells me.

It all makes me even angrier. I should be enjoying this—basking in the attention for the first time in my life. But Brynn and my mother have managed to ruin it for me. When word gets out that I'm quitting, what will that do to my reputation? Will people think I'm a prima donna, that I'm throwing some kind of hissy fit? The thought makes me so anxious I can't breathe.

I make sure not to walk past the theater department. I can't risk Brynn seeing me anywhere near Aiden. She may say she wasn't trying to get me in trouble—but I don't trust her not to go running straight to my mom. Or worse: the cops.

At lunch I use one of the school computers to log into my private e-mail. I message him at the account he set up just for me.

We need to talk tonight. Forest Park, Witch's Castle. Ten pm.

I hit Send just as the bell rings.

Cold little needles of rain prick me all over when I get off the bus near the trailhead. In the dark, the trees loom in a shapeless shadowy mass. It took over an hour to get here on the bus, across the river and up into the hills on the west side of town, but I want to make absolutely sure no one sees us.

It's a short hike to the mossy pile of stones known as the Witch's Castle, a burned-out structure that used to be a ranger station. People meet there to party in the summer. There are always broken bottles and cigarette butts all over the floor.

Now, though, at the end of November, at almost ten P.M., the park is eerily quiet.

I make my way down the trail with a flashlight. The ground is slick and muddy, and the rain rustles the leaves all around me. I pause where the trail crosses the creek. I keep thinking I hear footsteps behind me. The first time I thought it was Aiden—but when I paused to let him catch up, they went silent. It's got to be my imagination. The sound of my pulse against my bones, maybe, or an echo. The dark is so absolute here—there aren't any streetlamps to light the way. The clouds above reflect the city lights, a nauseous shade of purple, but beyond that there's nothing to see by but the wavering little light of my flashlight.

The quiet and the chill send shivers across my skin. And even though I've come down here plenty of times, there's a moment of panic when I'm suddenly sure I've turned off on the wrong trail, that I'm lost.

"Elyse?"

His voice comes from my left. I spin toward the sound and the light lands on his face. His glasses are flecked with rain, his hair covered by a warm knit cap. Without thinking I run straight at him.

My foot slips, and I fall to my knees. The flashlight goes spinning off into the bushes. My hands splay out in the mud, burning with pain. I can't see anything in the sudden dark. A strangled whimper escapes from my throat before I can stop it.

Then his arms are around me, and he's helping me to my feet. He snaps on a lantern hanging from his backpack, and its light sways and dances around us. I press my face into his chest and try to control my breathing.

"They caught us," I say, my voice muffled in his sweater. "Aiden, they caught us."

His body tenses. He puts his hands on my shoulders and pushes me away so he can look down at me. "What do you mean?"

I gulp at the cold air. I'm still shivering. My knees sting from the fall; I can feel the mud caked to my jeans.

"Brynn saw us kissing in the theater Sunday night. She told my mom."

He takes a step away from me. I stagger a little without his support.

"Shit." I can't see his face; the lantern sways just behind him and leaves his expression in shadow. "That's why she quit. I thought you guys had just had a fight or something."

I walk over to the wreckage of the little cottage. In the dark it looks even spookier than during the day, a haunted husk of a building. I sit on the steps. They're slick in the rain.

"This is bad." He's pacing, his outline tense against the violet clouds. "We shouldn't even be meeting here."

My whole body snaps backward at that. I didn't necessarily expect a welcome with arms outstretched, but his tone is strange and sharp.

"Has she called the cops yet?" He's rummaging in his pocket, pulling something out. In the flutter of the lantern I see the burner he's been using to text me. He wrenches it in half.

Fear creeps up the back of my neck. The police have only been a vague, distant threat since Aiden and I got together. I've been more concerned with keeping my friends from finding out. But now all I can see are images of swirling police lights. I get a vision of Aiden in cuffs and it makes me want to fall to my knees.

"No. She says she won't, as long as I stay away from you. But Aiden, I . . . I can't stay away from you." I want to hear him say it back: that I'm worth the risk, that he can't stand the idea of being apart from me. The naked fear in his voice is scaring me more than the threat of the cops. I think of the feel of sand whipping out from under my feet that day in Cannon Beach. The sense that the world wasn't as solid as I thought.

He stops in his pacing and turns his face toward me. I still can't see his features.

"This is a felony, Elyse. If we get caught I'll be on the sex offender registry for the rest of my life."

"I'm sorry." Tears sting my eyes. What am I apologizing for—getting caught? Coming here now? Being with him in the first place? "I don't know what to do."

The lantern finally stops bouncing around. He's taken it off his backpack and sets it down on a flat rock. Finally I can see his face—his brow furrowed, his mouth twisting unhappily. He sits next to me on the steps, but he doesn't put an arm around me.

"I don't either," he says. The hardness has left his voice. Now he just sounds exhausted. "So do you think your mom will keep her word?"

I hesitate, then nod. "She doesn't like the cops. She wouldn't talk to them unless she really felt like she had to."

"What about your friend?" he asks. "Brynn—will she tell anyone else?"

That I'm less sure of.

"I think she might be done with me," I say finally. "We talked at school today. She was pretty mad. I think she'll leave us alone."

"Think, or know?"

I hug my sweater closer around me. "I can't be sure."

He puts his face in his hands. "Fuck."

We sit like that for a few minutes. I'm still trembling, but now it's as much fear as cold. I don't know how I expected him to react—but the distance he's keeping between us makes me feel more alone than I've ever felt before.

"We should never have started this," he finally whispers. He looks up and sees my face. All at once his expression softens. "You're cold."

He takes off his fleece jacket and tucks it around my shoulders. The gesture is too much. A sob escapes my throat. I can't hold it back anymore. I break down.

"It can't end like this," I choke out.

He pulls me close. I nestle against him, his neck warm against my cheek. His fingers curl around the back of my head.

"They'll always be watching now, though," he says. "We'll never be alone. Not really."

I think about the cabin in the Gorge, tucked away among the trees, quiet and secret and ours. I know we can't live there forever, not really.

But couldn't we go somewhere else?

"Aiden," I breathe. "Let's leave."

He's silent for a minute. I feel the rise and fall of his breath beneath his shoulders.

"Elyse . . ."

"No, seriously, Aiden. Let's get out of here."

"Where would we go?" he asks.

"I don't know. Away. New York. L.A. Somewhere we can disappear in a crowd. Somewhere we can be together, alone."

He shakes his head. "Think of what you'd be giving up . . ."

"What?" I snort. "Life with my mom? Thirty hours a week mopping up spilled soda? A best friend who . . ." The words catch in my throat. I want to say "stabs me in the back," but I know that's not right. I know Brynn thinks she's helping me. Still, who is she to decide what's right for me? I've been taking care of myself as long as I can remember. I don't need her—or my mom, for that matter—thinking she knows better.

"It won't work." But he looks like he's running calculations, plotting a course. "What will we do? How will we get by?"

"We'll figure it out. You did, when you were a teenager."

"That was different. I didn't have to take care of someone else."

"You won't have to take care of me," I say. "We'll take care of each other. We'll do it together."

He exhales gently. His breath floats away in a cloud.

"I don't want you to regret it," he whispers. "But I would go anywhere to be with you."

I put my hands on either side of his face, look into his eyes. "Then let's go. Because I'm yours, Aiden."

Our lips meet, my fingers cold on his warm cheeks. He gives a little groan of frustration.

"I need a few days to get things ready," he says.

My heart leaps. "Does that mean yes?"

He gives a strangled laugh. "It means I must be out of my mind." He kisses me again. "But the thought of living without you is worse than the thought of being caught."

Every last doubt dissolves. It's all I wanted to hear. I wipe my face, tears and rain mingling together.

"Do you think you can be ready by this weekend?" he asks.

"I can be ready by midnight tonight," I say.

He shakes his head. "Friday. I'll pick you up at the bus stop by the school at midnight." He examines my face, then smooths my hair back from my forehead. "When we go, we'll have to move fast. Be ready."

I nod. I'm already making a mental list of what I'll need.

I'm already saying goodbye to everything else.

THIRTY-THREE

Gabe

The flames race along the bottom of the house, faster than I could have imagined. I'm moving before I even have a plan.

I run toward the window, waving my arms, but Catherine and her father are already moving, turned away from the window and heading into another room. My phone is in my hand, 911 already punched in. "Nine-one-one, what's your emergency?" The voice sounds far away. I pound on the window.

"Catherine!" I scream. "Fire!"

"Sir, I'm going to need you to calm down . . ."

I take off around the side of the house, looking for the nearest door. The smell of burned wood and gasoline clogs my nostrils. In my hand the emergency operator's voice buzzes low and calm. "What is your location, sir?"

"I'm at 157 Meadowlark. There's a house fire. I can smell gas. There are two people in the house. Hurry, please!" I hang up the phone as I skid around the corner to the front just in time to see the porch erupt into flame.

Fire engulfs the steps, dancing up the pillars into the eaves. I stagger back, blinded by the lurid orange light. A sudden gust of air sweeps in, and for a moment the flames dim.

Then they roar back, stronger than ever.

From far away I hear the sound of sirens. But there's no time to wait.

I grab a cinder block from the edge of the flower bed. I don't even feel its weight as I throw it with all my might at the nearest window. The sound of breaking glass is swallowed by the noise from the flames. Jumping up, I grab at the edge of the window and swing my leg over the sill.

"Catherine!" I yell. "Catherine! Where are you?"

I'm in a spartan living room. There's a plain brown couch, a small flat-screen TV on the wall, and three floor lamps. No decorations, no shelves or old granny-square afghans or anything remotely personal. I can already see a thin gray haze along the ceiling. A fire alarm shrills through the air.

Where is she?

I stumble toward the hallway, and suddenly she's there, standing in front of me, coughing into her hands. Her eyes squint through the smoke. "Gabe? What are you . . ."

Her father staggers out of one of the rooms, sliding a beat-up leather bag over his shoulder. "The window's jammed. We have to go out the front. Go. Go, go."

Then he sees me.

"What the hell . . ." His voice is a low snarl.

"The front door's on fire," I say quickly. "I broke a window in the living room. Go!"

He grabs Catherine and pushes her ahead of him, shoving past me. I stagger into a wall that's so hot I can feel the skin on my hand peel away.

A roar thunders through the house, a hot wind gusting. Something else must have caught. The house groans. I make my way after them in time to see Catherine disappear out the window. There are flames running along the ceiling now, licking up the walls. Mr. Barstow stands behind her until she's out, and then follows without sparing a glance in my direction.

I run for the window, flinging myself out shoulder first. A rush of cool air floods my lungs, and then impact, my body flattening against the ground. Mr. Barstow and Catherine are already staggering across the street.

I struggle to my hands and knees. The heat swells behind me, and I hear another roar as something else collapses. I can feel embers against my bare skin, singeing the hair off my arms. A fire truck screams up to the house just as I manage to find my feet and run across the road.

Up and down the street neighbors are out on their porches now, watching the blaze. Dog howls echo off every building, mixing with the wailing alarms. I kneel in the cool, moist grass, gulping down mouthful on mouthful of air.

I scramble to Catherine on all fours. She's coughing, her face streaked with grime. I rest a hand on her back.

"What are you doing here?" she says. Her voice is raspy.

"I had to see if you were okay. Then the fire was moving too fast, and I had to . . ."

Just then, two ambulances roar up behind the fire truck. Within seconds we're swarmed by paramedics. One, a middle-aged woman with a tight gray braid, kneels next to Catherine, wrapping a blanket around her. Another tries to lead me away from her.

"No, I have to . . . I have to stay with her."

"Come on, son, we need space for everyone to breathe." I let him steer me by the elbow a few feet away, but I crane my neck to look past him, back toward the Barstows.

Mr. Barstow's glasses are gone, his face filthy. He gives the EMT an uneasy glance, clutching the messenger bag tightly to his side. I wonder what was worth almost dying for.

The image comes back: the kiss. His hands twining around her hair, his lips against her neck. It sends a shudder through my entire frame, a shudder that turns into a cough when it hits my scorched lungs.

Before anyone can stop me I lurch to my feet and run back across the grass, dropping to my knees at her side. She has an oxygen mask pressed to her face now, but her eyes are wide and startled above it. Her pupils flare, the spinning lights reflected in their depths.

"I saw you. Through the window. I was in the yard and

I saw what he did to you," I whisper, the words spilling out of my mouth before I can second-guess myself. "Let me help you. Let me . . ."

She recoils as if I've hurt her. One of the monitors the gray-haired paramedic attached to her starts to beep more quickly. The woman stares at me fiercely.

"Look, kid, you need to back off . . ." she starts to say. But before she can get far Catherine takes the mask from her face and tosses it to one side. Her hands slam against my chest, pushing me away.

"Leave me alone." Her voice is strangled. I stare at her.

"Catherine . . ."

"No. I'm done with you, don't you fucking get it?" She's trembling. I stare into her face, trying to see some sign that this is a put-on, that she's acting for her dad's benefit. In the fire's shifting light she looks half-mad.

I put my hands on her shoulders by reflex. All I want to do is comfort her, but she screams at my touch. It's not loud—her voice is hoarse from the smoke—but it's loud enough. Suddenly two burly paramedics swoop in on either side of me.

"Jesus Christ," mutters the gray-haired woman. "Get this idiot to the hospital before he makes more paperwork for all of us."

All the strength leaves my body as the paramedics help me firmly into the ambulance. I'm like a puppet with its strings cut, limp and powerless. Behind them I catch a glimpse of Mr. Barstow, a strange, twitchy look on his face as he edges closer to Catherine.

On the far side of the street the fire still blazes against the night. And I know, just looking at it, nothing's going to stop it, no matter how hard the firefighters try. It's too hot, too out of control.

It will consume everything in its path.

THIRTY-FOUR

Elyse

It's the slowest week of my life.

I go through all the motions. I go to school, I go to work. I do my homework. When I see my mom, I speak in terse monosyllables.

There's a minor scandal at school about both me and Brynn dropping out of the play. Frankie Nguyen corners me after English one afternoon, his face livid with anger. "Kendall's going to be Juliet," he says bluntly. "You're ruining the whole show." Laura and Nessa won't even talk to me. When people ask why I did it, I just mumble something vague about family problems. It doesn't seem to help my case. I spend the whole week eating lunch alone, sitting on the floor next to my locker.

I try not to let it bother me. Soon none of this will matter anymore . . . but a part of me shrinks in humiliation and resentment. The mental image of Kendall in my gold brocade dress makes something sharp twist into my gut.

Aiden keeps up appearances too—which means he leads the rehearsals for the week, trying to get Kendall up to speed. I wonder what will happen when he doesn't show up for Saturday's closing show. By then, though, they'll barely need him. The play will move ahead on its own steam, and by the time they break down the set we'll be in another state.

Under my bed, my backpack is ready. It's packed with a pair of jeans and a few shirts, clean underwear, my toothbrush. My beat-up paperback copy of *A Wizard of Earthsea.*

At night, when I've finished my homework, I stare out the window. I whisper Juliet's lines to myself. I picture her holding her vial of fake poison, saying her goodbyes to all she's known. *Farewell! God knows when we shall meet again. I have a faint cold fear thrills through my veins . . . my dismal scene I needs must act alone.*

On Friday night, my mom has work, but her shift doesn't start until ten. When I get home she's on the sofa leafing through a magazine. The TV is on, as usual. She's watching *Jeopardy!* I keep my head down and try to walk as quickly as I can to my room.

"Hey," she says, when I'm halfway there.

I pause. Then I turn toward her. She looks exhausted—her eyes are heavy, her hair still uncombed. She probably just woke up.

"Friday," she says, with an awkward attempt at a smile. I don't smile back.

"Yeah," I say.

I chew the corner of my lip. Something tugs at me, tries to pull me to the sofa in spite of myself. I'm still so angry with her. But this is the last time I will have to stand in this shitty apartment and listen to her. This is the last time I will have to worry about the fragility of her feelings, the delicate balance of her sobriety. I don't know when I'll see her again—but it won't be here.

There's something intense, almost spiderlike about her hands when she's anxious. They creep toward her cigarettes and light up as if they've got a mind of their own.

"Remember . . . remember when you were little and we used to watch this together?" Mom asks. I shrug. She takes a drag and exhales, and her fingers stop trembling quite so bad. "Whenever you got one right, you had this dance you'd do. Like . . . an end zone celebration."

"I guess," I say.

She sighs and grabs the remote, snapping off the TV. "Come here, will you?"

"I have to get ready for work," I say, even though I have no intention of going.

"Five minutes. Come on, you can spare five minutes," she says.

I drop my backpack where I stand and trudge over to the sofa, sitting down on the far end. I'm not in the mood for a lecture, or more scolding. Not from her.

But it's the last time, says a little voice in my head. *The last time she gets to try to tell you what to do. Just play along.*

She takes one more drag, then stubs out the cigarette in her ashtray. Her hands start to fidget almost right away, but she looks at me with steady blue eyes.

"I'm sorry," she says.

I wait. I'm sure there's going to be more. A "but." *I'm sorry but you just can't. I'm sorry but you don't know what's best.* But she doesn't say anything else. The silence stretches out.

"For what?" I ask.

She leans back against the sofa cushions. "Well, you weren't wrong about what a shitty mom I've been. I've . . . I've let you down, again and again. You've had to take care of yourself for a long time. It's not fair. And I'm really, really sorry."

I don't know what to say. She's never apologized for anything before. In all the years that I've taken care of her, she's never said a word about it.

"Okay," I say warily. I don't know that I'm ready to forgive her for any of it. I don't know if I'm supposed to.

She looks down. "I know you're still pissed at me. About a lot of things. And that's okay, you can be. I just . . . it's important to me that you know I'm trying. To do better, I mean."

I can't remember the last time she said that to me.

She gets suddenly self-conscious. "Anyway. That's all."

I don't say anything, and after a while she doesn't seem to expect me to. But I sit and watch the rest of *Jeopardy!* with her. I don't yell out the answers like I used to, even when I know them. But when it's over, I lean over and rest my head against her shoulder, just for a few seconds. The sensation is so familiar that for just a moment I'm unaccountably sad.

"I've got to get ready for work," I say. I hesitate for a moment. "I love you."

She looks surprised. A little pleased.

"I love you too," she says.

I take a long shower and disappear into my bedroom. I sit on the edge of the bed for a while, looking around my little room. The things I've scavenged over the years, the things I've earned. The few things that are mine. I'm going to leave them all behind. But already the sadness is fading, and a sense of excitement replaces it. I'm getting a new start. I'm setting down those anvils I've been juggling and walking away.

I hear Mom leave for the bus. I sit still a little longer, waiting to make sure she doesn't come back for anything. Silence swells up around me.

When it's time, I grab my bag, step out the door, and walk away without looking back.

I can't see Aiden's face when he pulls up at the bus stop, but I open the passenger side door and calmly climb in. I'm surprised—I expected the backseat to be packed full, road-trip style. But it's not. He's got a single suitcase, a leather messenger bag, and two grocery bags in the backseat.

He smiles across the console at me. "Are you ready?"

I buckle up. "Let's go."

And as hard as I try to dig for some feeling of regret as we hit the highway, all I feel is free.

THIRTY-FIVE

Gabe

"Are you comfortable?" my mom asks, leaning down to fluff the pillow behind my head.

It's almost two in the morning, and we're still stuck at the E.R. They've got me lying on a wobbly hospital bed, a pulse oximeter attached to my finger, waiting to be formally admitted for the night.

I lick my lips. They're dry and cracked from the heat of the flames. My skin tingles; there are splinters of glass embedded in my face and hands from the broken window. I hadn't noticed at first; the adrenaline had been too strong. But now everything has started to throb and ache ominously. I'm lucky I didn't hurt my shoulder again, using it as a battering ram the way I did.

"Yeah, Mom, thanks." I close my eyes.

Beyond the confines of the little room I can still hear the noise: patients being admitted, being treated, deep into the night. I know Catherine's not out there; the nurse who took my vitals told me that the "other people" from the fire had been taken to a different hospital. "It's a busy night," she'd said. "The EMTs are trying to spread the love."

I can picture Catherine, on a hospital bed just like mine, the smell of smoke and gas in her nostrils. Will she be in the same room as her dad? Will he be watching her? Waiting for the two of them to be alone so he can touch her again? My skin crawls, imagining it.

I hear a soft knock. The door to my room swings open, and two cops in uniform come in. It's Huntington and Larson—the same duo who came around when Vivi went "missing." I look up, surprised.

"Hey there, Gabe," says Larson. He smiles at my mom. "Mrs. Jiménez."

Mom gives a little frown, then stands up to shake Larson's hand. "Officer. What's the problem? My son's very tired . . ."

"I'm sure he is," Larson says sympathetically. "Crazy night, huh, Gabe?"

I rub my knees through the thin fabric of my gown. "Yeah, I guess so."

Huntington sits down on the doctor's stool, wheeling it closer to my bedside. "You want to talk to us about what you were doing at Catherine Barstow's house tonight?" she says. Her voice is clipped and businesslike.

I rub at my eyes, running through all the things I could say, wondering if any of them make things worse or better for Catherine. The idea of saying it aloud—the kiss I saw through the window—makes me queasy, as if the words themselves are dirty. But maybe they could help her. Maybe they could get her away from him. It'd be worth it, even if I lost her in the process.

Then I think about how she'd reacted outside the house when I hinted at what I'd seen. Not just angry. Panicked. Almost blind with it. And suddenly I don't know what to do. I don't know if it's my call, to tell the cops about her dad. I don't want to drag her into something she's not ready for.

"I went to try to talk to her," I say finally. "But the house was on fire when I got there. So I called nine-one-one, but I knew they couldn't get there fast enough. That's when I broke a window and climbed in to help."

Huntington's lips tighten slightly, but she doesn't answer. Larson has a notebook in hand and is scrawling something down.

Mom purses her lips. "What's this about, officers?"

"We'll get to the point," Larson says. He turns to me. "We talked to the Barstows a little while ago."

"You did?" I sit up in bed. "Is Catherine okay?"

Larson doesn't answer the question. He looks down at his notepad and seems to read off it. "According to Mark Barstow, you started pounding on his window screaming for his daughter at about eight fifteen. A few minutes later the whole place was on fire. The exit routes were more or less blocked off. Now we're still waiting on the forensics, but it's pretty obvious it was arson. There were about a dozen empty gasoline canisters thrown all over the backyard."

My eyes widen. I remember the smell of gas lingering around the gate. Remember thinking about Mr. Barstow's lawn mower. Before I can process the information, Huntington starts to talk.

"Plus, we've got two different neighbors saying they saw you skulking around the side of the house about ten minutes before you called in that fire." She leans forward slightly, as if smelling blood. "Why were you sneaking around their yard? Why didn't you just knock on the door? Or better yet, call her?"

"Wait, are you saying . . . are you saying *I* started that fire?" I try to draw in my breath, but my lungs seize up. I look from Huntington to Larson and back again. "That's crazy. I would never . . ."

"Miss Barstow says you two broke up earlier this week," Larson cuts in. His voice is gentle but deliberate. "Is that true?"

"Yeah. We did." My fingers curl up in frustration. "I just wanted to talk to her."

"Like you just wanted to talk to Sasha Daley last Friday night?" Huntington says.

The silence stretches out for a long moment. On the other side of the door I can hear some other patient's racking cough, a gurney being wheeled down the hall. They're all staring at me—Larson, Huntington. My mom. I look away from her quickly, back at the cops.

"Yeah, I talked to Sasha last Friday," I say. "So what?"

"Ms. Daley's parents brought her into the station yesterday afternoon," says Huntington. "Apparently she told them that you'd been acting . . . erratically lately. They took her in to make a statement."

Her hawklike face is thin, her eyes sharp; her features all seem pointed toward me in accusation.

I can see it all with perfect clarity. Sasha almost shyly telling her mom that I have been acting "weird" lately. Mrs. Daley pressing her for details. Sasha hesitating, holding back, acting as if she doesn't want to get me in trouble. And then Mr. Daley would be involved, furious at the idea of someone besides him controlling his little girl. They'd sit on either side of her at the station, neither holding her hand, but both staring across the table at the officer—had it been Huntington?—with an expression that demanded that the police do what they're actually paid to do: protect people like them.

"She seemed really scared," Larson says. "She says you've been following her around, begging her to take you back, telling her no one else can have her."

"That's not true!" The words burst out of me, hot and fast. "*She's* been stalking *me*. She's the one who took my little sister, for Christ's sake."

And all at once, I know who started that fire.

"You should check those gas cans for Sasha's prints," I say, trying to keep my voice even.

Mom gives a little gasp, but I hold Huntington's gaze.

Huntington raises her eyebrows. "Do you have some reason to believe Sasha would attack the Barstows?"

I give a hard chuckle that hurts my lungs. "Yeah. She's been harassing me for weeks. She's been sending threatening messages."

"She's been messaging you? Do you have any of those messages saved?" Larson asks.

"They were Snaps. They disappear as soon as you look at them." I run my hands over my face, suddenly exhausted. "But she's been threatening my family, and Catherine."

"That's interesting," Huntington says coldly. "Because she showed us this."

She holds up her phone. I lean forward, trying to make out what's on there. The picture is small and grainy. But then the audio starts up, and I know exactly what we're looking at.

"I don't care. I'll go psycho on you, bitch."

It's my voice—but I never said that. Or I didn't say it *like* that. Did I?

The video is taken from the eaves of the pool house in her yard. One of her parents' security cameras.

"I don't know what you're talking about." She sounds tearful, earnest. "Please, I didn't mean to make you angry." The angle of the camera catches the tops of our heads; you can't see our mouths moving in the grainy image. It'd be all too easy to dub herself in any way she wanted.

"If you come near us again, I'll kill you. Do you understand me?"

The fury in my voice startles even me. I don't recognize myself. It's the snarl of an animal backed into a corner, ugly and inhuman. I try to remember exactly what I said, exactly what she said, but when I think about that night it's only a white-hot blur of anger.

"Ow!" The Sasha on the screen seems to recoil from something as if I hurt her. But I *didn't*. All I did was grab her hand, pull it away from my face. "You're scaring me, Gabe."

"I don't care, bitch."

Huntington smirks a little at my expression.

I shake my head. "I never *said* that. And I didn't hurt her. She's edited the video. I went over that night to confront her because she left a camera in my bedroom. She was spying on me."

"Did you keep this camera?" Huntington raises an eyebrow. My heart plummets.

"No. No, I . . . I confronted her with it." Why? Why didn't I keep it? Why did I need to throw it at her? The cops could have checked it for prints, or maybe checked its frequency to prove it was Sasha's.

"Not to mention this," Huntington goes on. She holds up her phone to show more grainy footage of me, grabbing Catherine by the wrist in the hall at school. I remember all those kids filming, enjoying the drama.

I shake my head weakly. "This is crazy. I haven't done anything wrong." But after hearing myself on the recording, my protests sound feeble, even to me. "That's not . . . we were just talking. I got upset because she wouldn't listen. But I'd never hurt Catherine. Why would I set that fire and then try to rescue her from it?"

"To get her attention, maybe. To play the hero." Huntington shrugs. "Or maybe you had second thoughts when you saw how quickly the house caught fire."

Finally, my mom speaks up.

"I think this conversation is over for now, officers." Her mouth is a trembling, pale line, but she sounds steady and firm. "I have a feeling we need a lawyer present."

"We're just trying to get Gabe's side of the story, Mrs. Jiménez," Larson protests. But my mom shakes her head.

"And he'll be happy to give it to you, after he's had a chance to rest," she says. She stands up from her chair and steps a little closer to me. "But it's late, and he's in shock, and we will not be answering any more questions until we have legal counsel."

The officers exchange glances. I feel a sudden surge of gratitude toward my mom. I've seen this expression only a few times—when she had to fight the insurance company to get Vivi's therapies covered; when she protested a developer who bulldozed a bunch of Mexican-owned businesses in Austin. It's fierce and determined and uncompromising.

"You should know we've put in a request for a search warrant for your home," Larson says. "We should have it by tomorrow."

"Then I'll put the coffee on at seven," Mom says. "Good night, officers."

After another moment, both cops are on their feet. Huntington gives me a hard look.

"See you later, Gabe," she says.

I don't answer. I watch them go, watch as my mom moves to the door and shuts it firmly behind them.

She stands motionless for a moment before turning back around to look at me.

"Mom, seriously. I didn't set that fire. I never threatened Catherine. This is all . . ."

"Gabe . . ." She sits down and rubs her temples. "What the hell is going on?"

I swallow. My lips feel cracked, my tongue swollen and sore. The idea of telling her everything is exhausting. I can feel the last of my energy spiraling down the drain.

"Sasha," I finally say. "She's been acting unhinged since we broke up. I think she started that fire."

She looks skeptical. "That's a serious accusation."

"I know." I look her in the eyes. "But remember the day she took Vivi? I swear, Mom, I didn't tell her she could. It wasn't a misunderstanding. She's . . . she's trying to hurt the people I care about."

It must be the pain, or the exhaustion, or the adrenaline wearing off, but I feel tears sting the corners of my eyes. I swipe them away quickly, but she sees. She squeezes my hand.

"I'm going to go find some coffee for me and some water for you. We'll talk about all this after you've had a chance to rest." She picks up her purse. "I'll be back in a few minutes.

And if anyone comes in here asking questions, you don't talk to them, you understand? Not until we have a lawyer."

"Okay," I whisper.

She gives me one last inscrutable look, then slips through the door.

I close my eyes, my raw hands stinging as I clench them tight. There's only one way to fix all of this. I've known it all along, but I've denied it, even to myself. But I know what I have to do.

I just hope it's not too late.

THIRTY-SIX

Elyse

We go east. We follow the Columbia, the canyon walls cradling us as we go. At first I'm too excited to sleep. I sit up in the passenger seat, fidgeting with the radio, watching the sliver of road illuminated in his headlights. I go rigid with fear at one point when I see blue and red lights behind us, then relax when the cop car swerves around us and pulls over someone ahead. Then for a while we're the only ones on the road.

I must fall asleep at some point, because when I wake up the sun is out. The river is gone; I don't recognize our surroundings at all. The dash clock reads seven A.M.

"Morning," Aiden says softly. "How you feeling?"

There's a crick in my neck. "Hungry," I say, stretching. "Where are we?"

"Just outside Coeur d'Alene," he says. "In Idaho."

The landscape has changed. Gentle, rolling mountains mark the horizon line, dark with trees. The sky is low and gray. But even with the gloomy morning weather, excitement fills my chest like a balloon. I sit up straight and look out the window.

"It's beautiful," I say. I glance back at him, suddenly realizing I haven't even asked about the plan. "Where are we going, anyway?"

He smiles. "Anywhere we want."

The idea makes me shiver. Anywhere we want? It's both exhilarating and terrifying. I've never had the luxury of doing whatever I wanted before.

I see a sign advertising restaurants, and my stomach growls. "Can we stop for breakfast?"

He hesitates for a moment. "I was hoping to get a little more distance between us and Portland. But . . . I've been driving all night. I could definitely use a break. Sure, let's do it. First let's clean up a little, though."

We pull over into a copse of woods off the road. The air is cold; it cuts right through to the bone. Aiden pulls one of the bags out of the backseat.

"I don't know if anyone's looking for us yet, but if they are they might be looking for that outfit. Better change."

I grab my backpack from the front seat. Huddled against the cold, I pull on a fresh T-shirt and sweater. I watch as he loses the button-down and puts on a jean jacket, lined with shearling. Then he rummages in the grocery bag and pulls out a brown wig with two braids.

"Here," he says. "Until we can get some dye."

I stare at it for a second, then take it. I wouldn't have thought of wigs, or dye, or any of this. But he's right. We can't look like ourselves.

I coil my hair up and pull the wig down over my head, peeking at my reflection in the car window. The style's not terribly flattering for me—it feels juvenile and makes my face look small and pale under it. I look up to see Aiden pulling a grimy baseball hat down over his eyes. He's already got a bit of stubble around his jawline, and when he takes his glasses off he's almost unrecognizable.

"Ready for a bit of acting?" he asks, winking.

I can't help it; I laugh out loud. A billowing sense of freedom, of adventure, takes hold of me. I pat the ends of my wig. "Born ready," I say.

The diner's full of old people, gray-haired couples with plates of eggs and pancakes. Waitresses in pale pink bustle around, refilling coffee and scratching frantically on their notepads. I breathe in the smell of bacon and sigh.

We sit across a sticky table from each other and order our food. The coffee tastes burned, but the French toast is sweet and delicious. Aiden orders a cinnamon roll bigger than his fist, corned beef hash, and a stack of sausage patties. I stare.

"You're going to make yourself sick," I say. He just laughs. "You never know when you're going to have another chance at a cinnamon roll. My policy is to get one while the getting's good."

I cradle the coffee with both my hands. At least it's warm. "So, what's our next stop?"

"I've got an old buddy in Missoula I want to visit. He can help us with a couple of details." He drops his voice. "Papers. New identities. That kind of thing."

New identities? I laugh a little. "You're awfully good at this. Have you gone on the lam before?" I tease.

He just smirks a little. "Survivalist dad, remember? Plus when I left home, I worked under the table. Met all kinds of, uh, interesting people that way. Some of them may end up useful now."

Missoula isn't exactly the kind of place I pictured us fleeing to. Hopefully it'll be a brief stop. We can get the things we need and move on. "Maybe after that, we can go to New York!" I say.

"Let's think about it," he says. "It's a good place to get lost in the crowd, but it's really expensive. We'll have to be careful with our cash for a while, until we find our feet."

I lean across the table and take his hand. "Come on, we can make it work. I don't really need anything but you to be happy, anyway."

He strokes my palm absentmindedly. "Which is why we don't need to go to New York. We can be together anywhere." He stands up and stretches. "I'm going to use the restroom before we hit the road again. We're a few hours out from Missoula."

As soon as he leaves, the waitress comes back to refill the coffee. "Hey, hon. Your daddy need a to-go box?"

"Oh, he's not my dad," I say. "He's my boyfriend."

I've been so eager to say that out loud—to not have to hide anymore. But I know right away it's a mistake. Her eyes narrow. She doesn't answer for a moment. Then she puts the check facedown on the table.

"My bad," she says.

She heads back to the counter with the coffeepot. I see her whisper something to another waitress, who then looks my way. My blood goes cold. I slap some cash down on the table, then get up to meet Aiden halfway from the bathroom. "We should go," I whisper.

He doesn't ask any questions. He tips his hat a little at the waitress, and then follows me to the door. Outside I tell him what happened. He frowns.

"The wig makes you look younger," he says. "It's probably fine. But we've got to be careful. Next time, just let them think what they want."

But I don't want to have to hide what we are. The point of leaving was to be together, really together. But he's already climbing back in the car.

I don't want to make this harder than it has to be. I get in after him, buckle my belt, and try to trust that we're heading in the right direction.

THIRTY-SEVEN

Gabe

By Monday I'm well enough to be back to school. My cough's subsided, but all the aches and pains linger, and the palm of my hand—where I touched the wall in the house—is one big blister.

When I walk onto campus in the morning it's like I'm in a silent bubble. Crowds part around me. I wonder how word's spread so quickly—if Sasha fomented something, or if everyone can smell the smoke that no amount of scrubbing seems to clear away. Or maybe the cops have already been making the rounds, asking about me.

They came to my house on Saturday. They ransacked my room, took my computer, my cell phone SIM card. I'm not sure if I'm supposed to get them back at some point or if they're just gone for good. Officers pawed through drawers and bins, leafed through my comics, my notebooks, my school stuff.

My parents stood by and watched. The lawyer they hired told them they didn't have much choice in the matter.

Now I make my way to my locker, feeling bitter and fierce. I almost relish the unease I can sense rippling around me in the hall. *Yeah, that's Gabe Jiménez, the freak show that set a house on fire. Don't mess with him, man, he's loco.* If everyone's so eager to believe it, why not let them get out of my way?

"Gabe. Gabe!"

I'm so mired in my own sullen thoughts I don't hear Caleb call my name for a moment. He has to grab me by the arm before I notice him. "Where the heck have you been, man? I've been texting you all weekend."

"The cops have my SIM card," I say. "The phone's bricked until I can get a new one."

He shakes his head. "Come on, we gotta talk."

He leads me down to the Lower Courtyard. I can barely keep up with him. My limbs feel heavy and dead. Irene's already there, perched on the uneven picnic table, when we arrive. A few greasy-looking smokers stand off to one side; they pretend not to notice us, but I can feel their eyes following me.

"What the hell is going on? Five-o was at my house last night. I didn't know what to tell them. I didn't want to make anything worse." She picks at one of the holes in her jeans. "So I just said you were a living cream puff who'd never hurt anybody. I don't think they liked that. They kept bringing up *my* rap sheet like it invalidated everything I said."

"Yeah, they wanted all my log-ins and text records and stuff," Caleb says. "What happened?"

I sit numbly down and tell them most of what happened—about the fire, and the cops, and Sasha's edited video footage. I leave out what I saw through the window at Catherine's house.

When I'm done they're both silent, staring at me. Caleb looks like he's about to be sick. Irene's pale with fury.

"I knew she was a bitch, but I didn't know she was evil," she says. She slaps her palm on the table. "We've got to figure out some way to show them what she's like. Like, a sting, or something. Get her on tape acting like a psycho. See how she likes a little creative editing."

"No." I shake my head.

Irene stares at me. "But . . ."

"It doesn't matter," I say. "It's over, Irene."

I don't have the energy to explain—to make them see. Sasha started that fire—I know it in my gut. And if she's willing to do that, she's willing to do anything.

There's no way to win.

I get up off the table. "I have to get to class, you guys. Thanks . . . thanks for listening. I'm sorry you got pulled into this."

Caleb rubs his palms against his knees, frowning. "Come on, man, let's just blow off school today. It's gonna be ugly up there. You know that."

"He's right. It's going to be a shitshow," Irene says. "People've been going nuts about this. I got about twenty texts from people I don't even know asking if you're a psycho or a drug addict or what."

I shrug. "Yeah, I figured. But it'll just get worse if I hide." I pull my backpack on. "I'll see you guys at lunch, okay?"

I don't give them a chance to respond. I head back inside, braced for the onslaught.

Except I'm not going to class. Instead, I head for the dance studio.

The Mustang Sallys have an early morning rehearsal before school, and usually, Sasha and her friends hang out there, gossiping and listening to music until the last bell rings. What I'm about to do is beyond stupid. My lawyer, a sharp-faced woman with a pristine crease in her pantsuit, warned me not to go anywhere near Sasha. "Don't talk to her. Don't text her. Don't go to her house. Don't go within ten *blocks* of her house. Don't even look at her, Gabriel," she'd said, her jawline tight. "You can't afford any more run-ins with this girl."

But the lawyer doesn't understand Sasha the way I do. I can't afford to avoid her.

It takes me a moment to find her in the crowded studio. It's still surreal to see her with Catherine's dark hair hanging limply around her shoulders. She's not wearing makeup, which is unusual for her. And instead of her form-fitting dance gear, she's in a sagging pair of sweats and a too-big T-shirt. She's stretching on the barre, surrounded by her friends, but she seems somehow smaller than usual, more subdued.

My feet won't move. The sight of her makes my throat seize up; my breath goes hot and panicked in my chest, and for just a heartbeat it feels like I'm back in the burning house. Every muscle in my body is tensed to bolt.

But I have no choice. Because I know now. She won't stop. She'll kill someone. Me. My sister, my parents, my friends. Catherine.

I'm the only one who can end it.

Everyone else seems to see me before she does. Silence sweeps over the room as I make my way toward her. Sasha never looks my way as I approach, but it's an act. I know she's tracking my movements in the mirror.

"I need to talk to you," I say softly, when I'm right in front of her.

My heart constricts painfully. The way she lowers her lashes and peers up through them; the way her hair falls like a curtain around her face. It's almost exactly Catherine's affect. She's been studying for this. She's been practicing.

"Okay," she says.

She leads me into the little storage area off the main studio, stacked with yoga balls, spare uniforms, and random props. My eyes dart around the room, and I realize that I'm looking for things that could be used as a weapon, just in case. I take a deep breath and force myself to stay calm.

Sasha sits down on an upturned bucket. Even the way she sits is pure Catherine—ankles crossed, shoulders hunched slightly forward. It sends a ribbon of ice down my spine. How long has she planned all this? Has she put on Catherine's personality piece by piece, without my noticing it? Or did she do it all at once?

She looks demurely up at me. "I heard what happened this weekend. It was . . . so brave of you, Gabe. To save those people like that."

"Stop it," I say. I keep my voice low; everyone in the dance studio is probably trying to overhear us. "What do you want?"

She blinks. "You're the one who wanted to talk to me."

"You know what I mean," I say. "I want to end this. Tell me what it'll take. Tell me what you want."

She looks down again. "All I've ever wanted was to make you happy," she says in a halting whisper. The impression is good—eerily good—but it's not quite Catherine. There's something cloying about Sasha's voice, something almost sickly sweet. Or maybe I'm only hearing it like that because I know that she is poison.

"I know you set that fire," I say, almost conversationally.

She frowns slightly. "I don't know what you're talking about."

"Right. So my question is—was that enough for you? Now that Catherine and I are broken up, now that everyone thinks I'm a maniac, now that you've driven her out of her house and made her dad take her out of school—are you done?"

Her eyes glisten in the dim light.

"I just want us to be together," she says.

I close my eyes.

All of this blood and fire and pain, all of this rage and madness—all of it just to keep me on my leash. A tiny voice still speaks up from the back of my mind, telling me this is crazy, telling me I can't be thinking of doing this. Asking how I think this can possibly end. But I can't fight anymore. I've already lost Catherine. At least this way I might be able to protect her.

"And if we're together, all of this insanity is done? You won't . . . you won't hurt anyone?" I ask. "You'll leave Catherine alone? And my friends, and my family?"

"Gabe, I . . ." Her eyes are round, as if she's wounded by the accusation. I shake my head.

"Just answer the question," I say.

She looks at me for a long moment, her eyes narrowing almost imperceptibly.

"I'd do anything you wanted, to be back with you," she finally says.

"I'll take that as a promise." My whole body feels like lead. I sit down next to her, still not touching her, numb and heavy.

"You mean . . ." She turns toward me, straightening up a little.

"I mean I'm yours," I say dully. "I'm all yours."

She gives a breathy little sob and nestles up against my shoulder. "Oh Gabe, I've missed you so much."

The softness of her voice is suddenly intolerable. "One more condition, though," I say. "Drop the Catherine act. Just be . . . yourself, okay?"

She smiles up at me, the gentle, timid notes gone as suddenly as if a switch has been flipped.

"I'll be anyone you want me to be," she says.

THIRTY-EIGHT

Elyse

I'm lying on the motel bedspread staring blankly at the TV screen when Aiden comes in, looking sour. He locks the dead bolt behind him and throws his jacket on a chair.

"We have to move again," he says, scowling. "The woman at the front desk is starting to ask questions."

It's been almost three weeks since we left Portland. Right now we're just outside of Pahrump, Nevada, a bleached-looking desert town with a Walmart and a legal brothel and not a lot else. This is the fifth place we've stayed; we've been here a week. I was hoping we'd be on our way somewhere more interesting by now, somewhere we could go to plays and readings, where we could see art and hear music. But instead we've just drifted through ugly little towns and barren landscapes.

I sit up and turn off the TV. "What'd she say?"

He shakes his head. "Just wanted to know why my daughter wasn't in school. I brushed her off, but she looked suspicious."

I don't say anything, but my heart leaps a little. We can't get out of this shithole fast enough for my taste.

He sits down on the bed and rubs his face with both hands. Since leaving Portland he's traded his glasses for colored contacts; they make his eyes a deep oaken brown. He's grown a mustache, too, which I hate; it makes him look geeky, and it tickles when we kiss. But he doesn't look like himself, which I suppose is the point.

He pulls a battered road atlas out of his bag. It's old and dog-eared, with notes scrawled in the margins. A few times it's led us to look for landmarks or roads that just don't exist anymore. Aiden doesn't want to use a phone or a GPS; he says the cops will be able to track us that way.

"We could try our luck in Arizona." He flips through the atlas. "It'll be warm enough through the winter that we could camp—stay off the beaten path."

"Arizona?" I make a face. "Can't we go to a city?"

"Not yet," he says calmly. "There's an AMBER Alert out for you, Elyse. Bigger cities mean more people who might recognize us from the news. We can't have anyone calling the cops."

I don't say anything for a minute. I know all about the AMBER Alert; we've been monitoring the news when we can. Aiden's kind of paranoid about searching the Internet, but a few times now we've seen something on TV or in a newspaper. They always use my freshman-year school photo, which is stupid, because that picture barely looks like me anyway; I've lost weight since then, and my face is much more angular now.

It never seems like a major search is being mounted, though, to be honest. Just a few little line items in the corner of a newspaper. I should feel relieved. It means we might stand a chance of evading them. But honestly, a part of me just feels forgotten. Why isn't my mom out there hitting the talk show circuit, passing out flyers? Why aren't my friends making sure my face stays front and center on the news?

There are a few pictures they've used for Aiden. It's surreal how different he looks in each image. Bearded, clean-shaven; glasses or none; hair blond, brown, red. Sometimes he looks like he's barely out of college. Sometimes he looks fifty. Every time I see a new one, it makes something stir in the pit of my stomach. Which Aiden have I fallen in love with? Is it the real one? And how would I even know?

Now I shake off all these thoughts. Everything would be okay if I could just talk him into trying a bigger town. Somewhere I won't be stuck in a drab motel all day; somewhere I can stretch my legs, stride out into the world. Become the person I've always been meant to be.

"No one ever called the cops in my old neighborhood," I try. "But that's because all my neighbors were cooking meth. We just need to find out where the drug dealers live."

He looks up at me. "That's an idea." He flips back to California. "Humboldt County, maybe. Redway, or Garberville. I could work odd jobs on one of the pot farms. It's not the growing season, but they might still have something."

My heart sinks. "I meant finding a neighborhood in L.A., or Chicago or something." I can't quite keep a whiny note out of my voice. "I'm tired of living out in the middle of nowhere."

"I never told you this'd be easy," he snaps.

We've been squabbling like this for a week or so. It's never over anything big—but we've been short with each other, easily piqued. I mean, there are still moments that are wonderful. A few nights ago we drove out to Death Valley and looked at the stars, and I'd never seen anything so beautiful in my life. In Idaho we played in the snow. But those moments are almost always overshadowed when some hotel clerk or waitress or person on the street looks at us a little too closely. It always puts him on edge.

Which means I should tread carefully. But I've been cooped up in this motel for days now, and I can't seem to hold back.

"We're in this together, Aiden. I should get a say in where we go next." I cross my arms over my chest, then uncross them, feeling like a petulant child.

"I thought you wanted to live off the land." There's a mean-spirited sneer on his lips; his voice goes shrill and mocking. "'I'll go anywhere, as long as I'm with you. And as long as it's a major metropolitan center.'"

"You know what?" I stand up off the bed. "Maybe you need a reminder. You're not really my father. You're not actually in charge of me."

"Then stop acting like a child," he says. "Do you even understand what I've risked for you? If I get caught I will go to *prison*." He overenunciates the word, as if I'm stupid. "Sex with a minor is third-degree rape in Oregon. Plus they'll get me on kidnapping. The FBI could get involved, because we crossed state lines. This isn't a game."

A hard laugh escapes from the back of my throat. "Oh, it isn't? I didn't realize. Because I've been having so much fun."

He slams the atlas shut. There's a hard glint in his eyes that I've never seen there before.

"Tell me, Elyse, what are you contributing to this situation, really? How are you helping us survive? Because the last I checked, I was doing everything. You talk a good game about how independent you are, but you'd be helpless without me. You'd starve to death in a fucking ditch."

Without another word I get up and go into the bathroom. I shut the door firmly and quietly and lock it.

In the mirror my face is pale and drawn, my eyes cavernous. I've lost weight—not because I'm going hungry, but because I've been too stressed to eat. I pull my hair back off my neck and splash water on my face.

A soft knock comes at the door.

"Elyse, I'm sorry. Please, can you open the door so we can talk about this?" He waits for an answer, but I don't give one. "I'm just scared. This has been hard for both of us."

"I know." I lean my head against the door. "Um . . . I just want to be alone for a little while. So I can calm down. Is that okay?"

He's silent for a moment. I wonder what he's doing, if he's still standing there.

"Okay. I'm going to head out and get us some dinner. When I come back we can talk."

"Something besides pizza," I say. "Please?"

"Okay."

When I hear his footsteps fade, I slump onto the bathroom floor, staring across the dingy linoleum. This isn't the man who took me to the ocean for the first time, who kissed the salt spray from my face. This isn't the man who put me in a spotlight and told me I belonged there. This sullen, paranoid man is a stranger to me.

And I barely recognize myself, for that matter. Not just my reflection, with its dyed-brown hair and sunken eyes, but the person I've become. Bored and bratty and irritable.

I want my mom.

The thought pops into my head out of nowhere. Which is ridiculous. I can't think of a time that I've ever gone running to her for comfort or help. I've never had that luxury. Still, right this second, all I want is to hear her voice. Her raspy "hello," followed by a pause as she lights her cigarette and takes a drag, the way I've seen her do a thousand times.

What would it hurt? It's not like she's set up to track a call. And Aiden's made clear we're leaving town as soon as possible anyway.

Slowly I crack open the door and peek out. The room is empty and silent, lit by a single lamp on his side of the bed. There's an ancient rotary phone next to it. I pick up the receiver and dial Mom's number.

It rings, and rings, and rings. I wonder if I misdialed. Mom made me memorize her cell number when I was little, and she's never changed it. I hang up and dial again. Even if she's at work or asleep or away from her phone, I should get her voice mail by now. A fresh panic washes over me.

I hang up again and sit on the edge of the bed. My stomach swims with nausea. Did she get her service turned off? Did she forget to pay her bill?

I bite the corner of my lip. Then I dial Brynn, hooking the numbers with shaking fingers.

"Hello?"

She picks up on the third ring. The sound of her voice is so familiar my eyes flood with tears. My tongue is clumsy in my mouth; I can't make it move.

"Hello? Can you hear me?"

"Brynn."

I hear the quick intake of her breath. "Elyse?"

"Yeah," I croak. I swallow hard. "Hi."

"Where the hell are you?" Her voice has shot up an octave. "Do you know how scared I've been? Oh my God, Elyse . . ."

"I, uh . . . I'm in Nevada," I say, then give a strangled little laugh. It's such a relief to hear her.

"Are you okay? Are you safe?"

"I . . . I don't know. I guess so. I just . . . I miss you so much." I twirl the spiraling cord tightly around my finger. "I tried calling my mom and she's not picking up. And I didn't know who else to call."

The line goes silent for so long that I wonder if we've been disconnected.

"Brynn?" I whisper.

"I'm still here." She's crying. I've never heard her cry for real before—only on stage. "Elyse, I'm so sorry."

"I'm sorry too. I wish I could go back and . . ."

"I'm so sorry," she says again. "But your mom. She . . . she's dead."

My lungs clench tight, the breath going motionless.

"No." I almost don't recognize it as my own voice. It seems too small, too weak.

"She relapsed. And I guess when people relapse sometimes they don't know their limits anymore, and she took too much. The doctor wouldn't tell me much because I'm not family, but her friend Norma—I guess that was her sponsor at NA?—she called to tell me." She sniffles. "It was last week. I'm so sorry."

I sink off the bed onto the floor, onto the stained and threadbare carpet. I push my face into the bedspread and scream. Somewhere near my ear I can hear Brynn talking, but I'm not listening.

My mom.

Alone in the apartment. Walking from room to room. Tense, a bundle of tics, her legs shaking, her toes tapping. Pain shooting along her spine. Pain gripping her nerves like a vise. Trying her hardest not to pick up her phone to call that doctor again—any of those doctors again. Going through the roster of useful-not-useful Narcotics Anonymous slogans. *One day at a time. This too shall pass. Keep coming back. God grant me the serenity . . .*

But she called for the refill. She poured a pill into her hand. She took one with water but it didn't seem to help. So she took another. She took a handful. She washed them down and went to bed.

My mom.

Somewhere far away I hear Brynn's voice. "Elyse? Elyse, just tell me where you are and I can be there in . . ."

Someone takes the receiver out of my hand. I look up into Aiden's face, deep-shadowed, eyes burning. He hangs up the phone with a deliberate calm more terrifying than any rage would be. His teeth are bared beneath his moustache.

"There's no going back," he says, and his voice is edged in steel.

And then he rips the phone out of the wall.

THIRTY-NINE

Gabe

"Is that all you're going to eat?" Sasha asks, hanging on my arm. She picks a piece of sausage off my paper plate and pops it in her mouth. "Aren't you hungry?"

The question makes me want to laugh. But I just shake my head. "Not especially."

Tonight's the annual Mustang Sallys fund-raiser. Savannah Johnston's dad lets the girls take over his downtown barbecue restaurant. He spends all day cooking, and they show up in their sequined uniforms to serve. For twenty bucks you get a groaning plate of meat, macaroni and cheese, and corn bread, with peach cobbler for dessert.

Usually I can be counted on to eat my weight in barbecue. But I haven't had much of an appetite in the month since I've gotten back together with Sasha.

The restaurant is packed to the gills with kids from school and their families. Most of the Sallys are working. Sasha's taking a "break" that's now spanned forty minutes. I've seen a few people shoot her exasperated looks, but no one's tried to call her out.

She's back to doing whatever she wants.

"Poor baby," she coos. "Are you feeling okay?" She toys with a piece of my hair. My skin crawls every time she touches me, but I keep my expression steady.

"I'm fine," I say. My tone must be too brusque, because her eyes narrow. I take a deep breath and force a smile.

Placated, she leans against my arm.

I'm keeping my part of the bargain. I hold her hand in the hallway. I carry her books for her. I wait obediently by her locker while she gossips and combs her hair. I do all this even though I can hear the snickering and whispering all around us. I try not to look at their expressions as we walk past; I try to keep my head straight ahead. Everything's back to a superficial kind of normal. She even called the cops to drop the charges she'd brought against me. "It was all a misunderstanding," she cooed, meeting my eyes as she cradled the phone to her ear. Of course they're still investigating me for arson—but she likes that. It makes me seem like a bad boy. It makes her parents hate me even more.

My parents are more baffled than angry. "I don't understand why you'd want to be with someone who did all the things you said she did," my dad said when he found out, shaking his head.

"Why would you risk it?" my mom put in. "She went to the *police* about you. You can't afford to get on the cops' radar, *mijo*. There are people who will assume that you're a criminal just because of the color of your skin. They'll take Sasha's side over yours every time. This girl is dangerous for you."

They don't understand that I'm doing this for them. That I'm trying to keep them safe.

Them, and Catherine.

Though Catherine might be well out of Sasha's grasp by now. She hasn't been at school in a month, and I can't seem to get any information on where she is. I logged into Sekrit on my new phone as soon as I got it, and I sent her half a dozen messages, but she hasn't responded to any. I had Caleb drive me past her house a few days after the fire—it's a wreck, a burned-out ruin with police tape across the door. So they're staying somewhere else, obviously. But where? I look back at my last few messages.

daredevil_atx: I just want to know that you're ok.

daredevil_atx: I'm so sorry about everything.

daredevil_atx: I love you.

The silence is resounding. It speaks volumes. I've given up. Just like I've given up on ever getting free of Sasha.

Sasha's hair's still dark, but at least she's not straightening it anymore. She's back to dressing like her old self, like she fell straight out of an Instagram account. She smirks up at me now.

"Too bad Irene and Caleb couldn't come," she says. "They always eat like pigs."

"Mmm," I say. She's testing me; she wants me to stand up for them, to tell her to be nice, so she can accuse me of siding with them. I'm not going to rise to the bait.

"Or is Irene finally on a diet?" she persists.

Irene is currently as far from this restaurant as she can be. She made clear that she was done with my Sasha drama. "You're nuts," she'd seethed. "You cannot get back with that psycho. I'm so over this shit, Gabe."

Caleb was a little more sympathetic, but not very reassuring. "How long can you keep this up? I mean, she's either gonna kill you or marry you sooner or later, man." The thought makes me squirm in my seat, even now. I can't think about the future, or I'll lose my nerve.

All I can do is keep her happy, here, now.

She raises a morsel of brisket to my lips, and I open my mouth mechanically and accept the treat like a dog.

"There you go," she says. "That's not so bad, is it?"

It is, Sasha. It's the worst thing. This is the worst possible thing, and it's all thanks to you.

A few of Sasha's friends make their way to our table and heave themselves onto the seats, looking exhausted. Marjorie Chin's pinned-on cowgirl hat is listing to one side; Natalie McAfee is covered with a thin sheen of sweat.

"It's crazy this year," Natalie says, fanning herself with a paper plate. "I've never seen it so busy."

"How much did we make?" Sasha asks.

"Just under five thousand so far. We'll definitely be able to get new costumes for the spring concert." Natalie smiles at me. "How's the food? I haven't been able to get any yet."

"Here." I shove my plate at her. "Have mine. I'm full."

She glances at Sasha, and I realize she's asking permission. After a moment Sasha gives an almost imperceptible nod, and Natalie picks at my food.

"How're you doing, Gabe?" Marjorie asks. "I mean, after the fire and everything?" I see curiosity in her eyes, and something else. Pity. The tiniest glimmer of it. Everyone knows I'm Sasha's bitch. Everyone knows she's won.

"Never better, Mags," I say, summoning up my jauntiest tone. "Turns out chicks love reckless heroics. Right, baby?" I kiss the side of Sasha's head. If I'm going to put on a show, I'm going to do it right.

Sasha giggles. "Oh, we're calling it heroic now? I thought you were still wanted for arson or whatever."

Marjorie's eyes widen slightly, though I know her surprise is as much an act as my good mood is. Sasha's made damn sure everyone knows the cops have been sniffing around. Just another way to keep people talking; another way to keep me humiliated.

"Not technically," I say carelessly, as if it's all a big joke. "I'm just being *investigated*. There's a difference."

My phone vibrates in my pocket. I try to ignore it. Sasha hates it when I check my phone around her, even though she spends half her life texting.

"I heard that girl Catherine set the fire herself," Natalie

says, her freckled nose wrinkling slightly. "Someone told me she moved here because she burned her school down in California."

Someone. How coy.

"You know she was a weed dealer?" Marjorie says, looking at Natalie. "She used to hang out with all the burner kids."

Me. The burner kids being me. How fun this game of telephone is.

"Guys, that's all just gossip." Sasha, being the bigger person. So magnanimous. "The truth is, we don't know anything about her." She pats me on the shoulder. "I'm just glad Gabe was passing by and could get her out of there. Someone could have been hurt."

My phone vibrates again. I can't stand it anymore. I pull it out and glance surreptitiously down at the screen.

And then I stand up.

Sasha rolls her eyes. "Can't you go five minutes without looking at that thing?"

"I have to go," I say. My voice is flat and distant. It gets her attention.

"Where?" she asks, eyes narrowing again.

I don't answer. I step away from the picnic table and hitch my backpack up my spine.

"Gabe? What the fuck?" she says behind me. Then, louder: "Where do you think you're going?"

There will be hell to pay later. But right now I don't care. Right now, all I can think is that I have to move. I have to find Caleb and borrow his jeep. I have to get out of here.

I look down at the screen of my phone one more time. The two messages, sent in short succession, are still there.

dollorous00: Hill Country Motel, room 11
dollorous00: Please hurry

FORTY

Elyse

The air is heavy, even at midnight. I roll out of the bed as gently as I can. On the other side, Aiden shifts in his sleep.

I pull on my jeans and a T-shirt and go into the front room of the spartan little bungalow. We have a thrift store sofa, a few wobbly lamps, a bookshelf where I keep the tattered paperbacks I've managed to accumulate over the past year. I thumb through a few of them, trying to distract myself, but I'm restless. So I pick up the car keys from the bowl by the door and slip out the front.

It's one of the few little rebellions I have left. He usually keeps a close eye on the keys, but I take them every chance I get. He taught me to drive as soon as we got to California; he wanted me to be able to get us out of there quickly if I had to. But he hated doing it. He hated the idea that I could get in the car and leave him if I wanted.

I like imagining it. I like the vision of myself crossing the county line, without bags or baggage, the radio blasting and my hair whipping around the open window.

But where would I go?

Outside, a tongue of lightning flickers across the horizon. I breathe deep. The air smells like rain. It feels good to get out of the cramped little house. It feels good to know he'll get in the car tomorrow morning and see the odometer—he always notices the odometer—and realize that, once again, I slipped his grasp. Even if it was just for a moment.

The car—a ten-year-old beige Toyota—starts easily. I tune the radio and find a mournful folk-rock ballad that I like. I can't remember who sang it. It was some time in my old life, back in Portland. It feels like a million years ago.

Thoughts of Portland always bring with them thoughts of my mom, thoughts of Brynn, thoughts of myself as a dumb, naïve kid. Thoughts of everything I've lost. It's like pressing hard on a bruise—a low-grade ache that suddenly swerves into blinding pain. I quickly change the station and land on an oldies channel, Ronettes crooning in harmony. I pull away from the curb and feel some of the tension leave my shoulders.

I weave slowly through the streets. I don't know where I'm going; I'm not even sure I know how to get home. The houses slowly change around me, expanding up and out from modest ranch homes to sprawling mansions nestled against the hills. There's not much traffic this time of night. I tap the steering wheel in time with the music. "Be My Baby." "Daydream Believer." "Sixteen Candles." Sugary, bright-eyed music about love and innocence.

If Aiden wakes up and finds me gone, he'll freak out. He's gotten more and more paranoid and possessive; sometimes he scares me. Sometimes, the way he looks at me—I think he'd rather kill me than lose me. I think he'd rather we both go down in flames than admit defeat.

Buddy Holly comes on the radio, voice scornful and mean. "That'll Be the Day." I reach up to change the channel again. I don't want to listen to him gloat. I don't want to listen to a man singing about a woman who's afraid to leave.

Just as my hand finds the dial, something thumps against my car.

Everything gets very bright or very dark, the contrast in my vision turned way up, glittering and lurid. I slam the brakes. I put the car in park. I sit there, my hand still outstretched, the Buddy Holly song still swaggering along. There's a shape on the ground in front of me, dark in my headlights.

Fuck. Oh fuck oh fuck oh fuck oh—

The sky opens up, and it starts to rain.

I turn off the car and grab my umbrella. My headlights fade as I step out of the car, my blood roaring as loud as the downpour, pulse screaming that this can't be happening, this can't be *happening*... but the shape stays motionless, sprawled on the pavement. Rivulets are already moving around it. This is nothing like Portland rain, that lazy drizzle. This is hard and violent and punishing. And that's what somehow gets me to move: not the fact that the figure in the street might be dead, but the fact that the rain is falling on it.

On *him*. I can see that as soon as I take a step closer. He's a kid—my age, I think, Latino, with dark curls plastered to his forehead from the rain. When I see that he's breathing I take a shuddering gulp of air myself. I kneel down to get a better look, holding up my umbrella with one hand.

He stares up at the sky with a blank, dazed expression. There's a raw-looking scrape on one cheek, and his arm is lying at a strange angle to his body. A few yards away is a splintered skateboard, one wheel still spinning.

A rattling groan escapes from his chest. It scares me for a second, until I realize he's had the wind knocked out of him. He's trying to find his breath.

"Shhhhh," I whisper, resting a hand on his cheek. "Don't move."

His eyes roll around frantically. I pull out my phone and type in 911. "I need to report an accident. Hit-and-run. There's a . . . a boy. He's hurt. It's at Merritt and Bantam. Please hurry."

I hang up before they can ask any questions.

My stomach churns. I should have been paying attention. I shouldn't have fiddled with the radio. I shouldn't have taken the car out just before a rainstorm. I should . . . but the list of what I should or shouldn't have done goes back and back for what feels like forever. I close my eyes and take a deep breath, and when I open them again, my hands are steady. I don't want to leave him here in the middle of the street, in the rain, but I have to go before the police get here. If Aiden finds out I talked to the cops he'll lose his mind.

The boy's eyes sink closed. I watch him for a moment. There's something about his face that I don't know how to describe—something gentle. Though maybe that's just because he's in repose. Maybe everyone looks kind in their sleep. For a fleeting moment, I wish I could stay. I want to hold my umbrella over him, keep him from the rain. But the faint echo of sirens cuts through the night. I have to go. I jump up and run back to the car.

Back home I let myself in the front door as quietly as I can. I'm still jittery with adrenaline, but I keep my movements careful and controlled.

"Where've you been?" The question pounces on me the moment I open the door. Aiden glowers from the kitchen doorway, holding a mug of tea.

He's traded in the mustache for a full beard, and he highlights it with silver every few weeks. It does a reasonable job of making him look even older than he is. He's taken out his contacts for the night, so I can see the gleaming hazel of his eyes, like coins under water.

I put down my umbrella and bend to untie my shoes. "I wanted ice cream," I say.

His eyes narrow.

"Where is it?"

"Oh, I just got a bar. I ate it on the way." I give him what's left of my smile. It's a ragged, paltry little thing now, but I try to make it convincing.

He disappears back into the hall and comes back with one of our thin thrift-store towels. Instead of handing it to me, he wraps it around my shoulders.

"Don't go out like that without telling me," he says. He rubs my hair a little too roughly with the towel. I flinch.

"I should've left a note. I'm sorry," I say.

He looks down into my face and finally smiles. "It's okay. I just worry," he says. "I love you."

"I love you too." The words are automatic. I don't even think about them anymore. Like many things, it's easier that way.

When he kisses me I fight the urge to pull away. I close my eyes. The image of the skater floats back up to my mind, and I imagine what it'd be like to be with someone like that. Someone my age. Someone I'm not scared of.

But it's useless to imagine something like that. I made my choice a long time ago. I'm stuck here, and there's no way out.

"Let's get you out of those wet things," Aiden says.

"Yeah," I say. "Okay."

FORTY-ONE

Gabe

It's a forty-five-minute drive to the Hill Country Motel, just outside Austin. I put Caleb's jeep through its paces, stepping on the gas all the way. The roads are narrow and rough; scrubby ranchland alternates with shaggy cedar and mesquite trees. As dusk comes, I see more and more deer bounding along the side of the road. I send up a silent prayer to whatever saint looks out for deer that they stay out of my way. I don't want to hit Bambi—but I'm not about to slow down.

Please hurry.

I don't know what "hurry" means to her—don't know what the timetable is, don't know what might be happening even now. I texted her before starting out but I haven't heard another word. Is she in trouble? Is she hurt? Every second feels like a fully encapsulated panic attack. My fingers are tight on the wheel, and I rattle over potholes and cracked pavement without slowing down.

The sun slips behind the curtain of trees and leaves a bloody smear along the horizon as I catch sight of the sign nestled against the forest's canopy. Hill Country Motel. It's a long, low building, paint peeling away in strips. The parking lot is gravel. Trees fringe the little clearing. There's nothing else around.

I pull into the parking lot and turn off the truck. Then I sit there for a moment.

I have no idea what I'm about to walk into.

But I didn't drive all this way to sit in my car. So I climb out, legs stiff, and take stock of my surroundings. There aren't many cars in the lot. It's the off season, and while it's not cold enough here to deter all travelers, it's definitely not outdoor-recreation weather. Most of the windows in the motel are dark. The trees crowd in around the property.

Almost by habit I pick Orion out from the stars above. Over to the east I see Andromeda. I remember the myth we learned about in astronomy last year—Andromeda, the princess chained to the rock. Sacrifice to a monster. The thought steels me. I start toward the motel—and then turn around. I get the tire iron out of the back.

The window for room eleven is brightly lit. I pause outside, trying to listen for sounds from within. I can hear the mutter of a TV inside. I rest a palm lightly against the door . . .

. . . and jump backward as it swings inward.

Open, all along.

"Hello?" I crane my neck to see around the door. The lights are all blazing. There's an old black-and-white movie I don't recognize on the TV. There's no luggage, save a sooty bag propped on the floor next to a dresser. I recognize it right away; it's the bag Mr. Barstow went back for in the fire.

"Hello?" I hold my breath and listen for any sign of life. "Catherine?"

Nothing. I step into the room and shut the door gently behind me. I peek in the bathroom. There's a bunch of dirty towels lumped on the counter, but no one's there.

I grab the messenger bag.

Inside is a thick bundle of paperwork. I frown, leafing through, trying to see what was so important that he'd risk his life for it. At first glance it just looks like a bunch of legal documents. It's not until I find a bundle of cards, held together with a rubber band, that I understand.

There are four different driver's licenses, all with Catherine's face—all with different names. Catherine Barstow. Sarah White. Emily Woods. Olivia Roberts.

I turn quickly through the other pages. Passports, birth certificates, social security cards. All in different names, but with the same pictures. Identities for her father, too—he's gone by Louis, James, Mark. My pulse pounds in my ears; the pages trickle from my fingers and scatter across the threadbare carpet.

Who are these people?

Then I notice something that makes my breath catch in my throat.

There's a faint red smear on the doorjamb.

I walk back to the door, almost in a trance. My fingers clench and unclench. The red is bright against the white paint. Closer up I can see the swirls and whorls of the handprint, too small to be a man's. The blood is fresh.

My hand feels far away as it pushes the door open again. I float out into the dark parking lot, my eyes darting right and left, my breath coming quick. I look for some sign. I pray, desperate, for some sign. Out beyond the motel's yellow lights it's dark; the moon is hidden behind pale clouds. There's no way for me to know where they went if I don't have a sign.

I stand frozen for a long time. Then I see it; there, on the edge of the ice machine. Twenty feet to the right. Another smear of blood.

The tire iron is a comforting weight in my hands. I follow the trail: flecks of red along the siding, on a windowpane. It takes me around the side of the motel—to the woods, black and fathomless in the moonless night.

For just a moment I hesitate. Then I turn on the LED flashlight on my phone and push my way into the thicket.

The woods are dense and dark. She could be anywhere. "Catherine!" I shout. "Catherine!" My voice echoes back to me, eerie and warped. I can hear the Pedernales murmuring on the other side of the trees. Something rustles behind me, and I spin around in time to see an armadillo waddling away into the underbrush. I take a quick, gulping breath, my fingers tightening around the tire iron.

"Fuck," I hiss.

Then, in the flashlight's bleached-out glow, I see something else. A scrap of cloth—green plaid. Caught on a branch. One of Catherine's shirts. Beyond, I can just barely make out the ghost of her path: broken branches, compressed grass.

"Catherine!" I shout.

I hear rustling again. I move the flashlight's beam left to right, trying to pinpoint where the sound is coming from.

The light doesn't land on her until she's two feet away from me.

Her face is so caked in blood I barely recognize her. Her hair is damp and tangled with dirt and sticks. I drop the tire iron and run for her. My eyes scan her body, trying to see if she's hurt.

"You came," she says. Tears streak down her face, cutting a path through the dirt and blood. "You came."

"Are you okay? Where are you hurt?" I'm afraid to touch her, not knowing where the blood has come from. But she throws her arms around my neck.

"You came," she sobs. So I pull her close. I rest my cheek against the top of her head. Even with everything that's happened, she feels like she was made for my arms.

"Of course I came," I whisper.

She suddenly pushes away from me. "We have to go. Right now, we have to get out of here. Did you bring a car?"

"Yeah, of course, I . . ." I trail off.

A man moves out of the shadows, quick and quiet. The first thing I see is the glint of the gun. Then I see a face I don't know—white, clean-shaven, tight with anger. It's not until he speaks that I recognize him.

"You're not going anywhere," says Mr. Barstow.

FORTY-TWO

Elyse

"Aiden, please," I whisper. "Please, just let us leave."

His eyes are sharp and shining. The gun is steady, but his chest heaves with his quickened breath.

"I already told you," he says softly. "No one's going anywhere."

That's when I realize that his eyes aren't glinting with rage; they're bright with tears. And somehow, that scares me even more.

The fight at the motel started small, like they always did. It'd been simmering for weeks, roiling behind every sullen glance, every passive-aggressive snarl. We'd been cooped up together all that time, both of us wondering how long we had before the police figured out who we were.

This time, it got physical. He grabbed me by the shoulders, shook me back and forth. When he let go, the momentum took me forward. I tumbled off the bed. My head hit the corner of the dresser with a sickening crack. My field of vision went white, then sickly green, the pain shuddering along my bones.

Something sticky and wet poured over my face. Blood. I couldn't believe how much of it. Next to me I could sense more than see Aiden go very still, just a few feet from me.

"Elyse . . . I didn't mean . . ."

I didn't let him finish.

The world spun around me as I shot to my feet, but I managed not to fall. I shoved him in the chest with all the strength I could muster.

Then I ran.

Now, he stands in front of us on the path, holding the gun with a taut, practiced posture. Next to me, Gabe's heart bumps heavily against my hand. His T-shirt is damp with sweat, his curls matted against his head from the run through the woods. I can tell from the way he's poised that he's ready to push himself in front of me.

I can't let him do that. I can't let this go any further.

Slowly, gently, I disentangle myself from Gabe's limbs. I hold my hands up above my shoulders. I fight to calm my breathing, to break out of the whirl of mud and blood and terror I've been tumbling through.

"I just want a normal life," I say. I fight to keep my voice calm. I have practice by now; I've been soothing and comforting him for months. "I won't turn you in. I won't tell anyone. I just . . . I don't want to run anymore."

His face looks so pale without the beard. Back at the motel, when he'd first shaved it off, I'd felt a thin little pulse of attraction for the first time in a long time. Seeing his face uncovered was, for just a split second, like seeing him as he'd been when we first met, before everything went wrong. Before my mom died; before I lost Aiden to the paranoia and the possessiveness.

"I threw everything away for you," he says. "Everything. And this is how you're going to pay me back? No. No, this isn't how this ends." He paces, two steps one way, two steps back, the gun still trained on me. "You told me we'd do this together."

I bite back the retort that springs to my mouth. *How can we do this together when you won't let me decide anything? How can we be together when you treat me like a child?* Instead I take a halting step toward him. "I know. I'm sorry."

"You said you loved me." His voice breaks. Once upon a time that would have destroyed me. Now I just feel numb.

"I do. I always will," I say. "But we can't keep going like this."

His face crumples into raw, naked sobs, a child frightened in the night. "You're right," he says. And I think, *It's working; I'm getting through to him. He's going to let us go.*

Then, before I have a chance to move, two loud *pops* tear through the night.

Smoke drifts lazily from the end of the gun. My body goes rigid. For a second I wait for the pain to come. Then I realize that's wrong—that I'd already feel it. I look down at my body. I'm a mess—clothes torn and dirty from hiding—but there's no sign of fresh blood.

From behind me, there's a soft, strangled whimper.

I turn to see Gabe, on his knees in the dirt. His mouth is a strained line. His eyes are wide and round. A small, dark stain is blooming across his shoulder, getting bigger and bigger.

"No!" I turn to go to him, but Aiden stops me short with a little hiss.

"Next one's to his head," he says.

I draw in my breath hard.

"Leave him alone," I say. "Please, Aiden, I'm begging you."

Aiden bares his teeth. "This little bastard ruined *everything*. He took everything from me."

"No, Aiden. I'm still here. I'm still yours, if you want me. Just . . . please. Don't do this." His hands are shaking now, the gun unsteady. I take a tiny step forward, and my toe hits against something hard. I glance down. It's Gabe's tire iron; he dropped it when he came into the clearing. I look up quickly, fight to keep the discovery out of my face.

He shakes his head, still staring at Gabe. "I can't trust you anymore. He ruined that."

I fall to the ground, covering the tire iron with my body and pushing my forehead into the dirt so it looks like I'm begging. "Please," I whimper. "Please, I'll do anything." Like all good acting it's a little bit true. My fingers close around the cold, hard metal, and I think it again to myself. *I'll do anything. Anything I have to.*

"Too late," he murmurs, almost to himself. "It's too late." He resets his stance, steadies his hand. His eyes are locked on Gabe.

"No!" My body is stiff from the run through the woods, from hiding, but somehow I make it move faster than it's ever moved before. I swing the tire iron upward with all my might. It connects with his arm, and the gun goes spinning out of his hand.

"Fuck!" he screams, hunching over in pain. I don't pause to think. I scramble on all fours for the gun. It glints darkly on the forest floor a few feet away.

My fingertips brush the handle. Then something slams into my torso. His boot. He kicks me again, harder this time. The dry snap of my rib cracking is almost, but not quite, too soft to hear. I fight the urge to curl into a little ball. I fight the urge to keep hiding.

Another quarter-inch reach, and I have it. The gun is heavier than I expected. I don't really know how to use it. I don't even know if there are more bullets. But I roll onto my back and point it at his chest.

His face warps into a monster grimace. He lunges down at me, fingers curled into claws.

I pull the trigger. There's heat, noise. Force pushing me into the dirt. There's a spray of something hot and wet.

And then, silence.

I don't know how long I lie there, staring up at the sky. Aiden is near my feet. He's very still.

And then the stars blink out. No—they're obscured. Gabe's form blocks them from view. He's leaning over me. His breath is ragged but steady.

"It's going to be okay," he whispers.

I close my eyes. I feel like I'm floating. In this moment, before consequences, before explanations, I feel safe.

"I know," I say.

FORTY-THREE

Gabe

We walk back toward the motel holding hands. I move gingerly, trying not to jostle my shoulder too much. The pain is getting steadily worse, roaring in like a rapidly approaching train. I focus on keeping my breath steady. There's no way Catherine—or whatever her name is—can carry me if I pass out.

My brain keeps flying back to the man in the clearing behind us. To the moment before he fell. It's frozen in my mind: Catherine on the ground, pointing the gun up. The look on his face as he lunged for her. For some reason I'm stuck there, in the instant before she shot him. That last moment before a person died right in front of me. The thought makes my legs go soft for a second; I stumble, but catch myself. The motion sends a molten wave through the gunshot wound.

"Gabe?" It's too dark to read her expression, but she clutches my arm like it's a life preserver.

"I'm . . . okay." My voice is small in the dark. For a moment the world tilts, the stars wheeling overhead. Then I take a deep breath, and everything falls still again.

"It's just a little further. Come on. That's it." She helps me over a fallen tree branch. "I'm so sorry I dragged you into this."

"None of this is your fault," I say. Then, a moment later: "Who was that guy?"

She's quiet for so long I start to assume that she's not going to answer. It startles me when she speaks.

"I used to think he was my boyfriend. I don't know what to call him now."

Boyfriend. I don't know if it's the blood loss, or the shock, but it takes me a moment to understand the word. It feels somehow abstract, detached. Boyfriend, father. Alive, dead. Whoever he was, it doesn't matter anymore.

"I'll explain everything when we get out of here," she says. "I promise. But right now we just need to focus on getting back to the car."

Through the trees I see a glint of light. The motel. We're almost there. We step out of the woods, and I feel some of the tension leave my shoulders. A wave of agony comes in on its heels. Catherine must notice; she pauses to let me catch my breath.

Something explodes; a branch shatters overhead.

Instinctually, I grab Catherine by the edge of her shirt and pull her as hard as I can behind a copse of trees.

I lean back against the bark, my shoulder screaming with pain. A gunshot. But there aren't any red or blue lights pivoting through the parking lot. It can't be cops.

And that's when I know exactly who it is.

"Sasha," I call. "Don't do this."

I hear her footsteps coming closer.

"This .40 caliber has some fucking kick!" There's a jaunty rage in her voice, a grit-toothed smile. "You know, I think I like Mom's .22 better, but she caught me playing with it the other day and hid it. All I could find was this monster." Another echoing boom, and the ground explodes a few feet from us. "Daddy's gonna be *pissed* when he sees I took it."

I close my eyes, pressing my back against the tree. After all we've been through, after what I've just seen, this can't be how our story ends. It can't.

"How'd you find us?" Maybe I can distract her, defuse her rage, if I can get her talking. "Let me guess. Some of your mom's super-spy shit."

"Yeah. I put a tracker on your phone. That's how she caught Daddy fucking his assistant last year." She laughs. "Aren't they all just dogs, Cathy? From what I've heard, you know a thing or two about that."

"Leave her alone." My voice comes out in an uneven snarl. I clutch my shoulder with my free hand, panting a little with the pain.

"It just makes me so *mad*." The laughter is gone from her voice now. "You're such a liar. You told me you were mine.

You told me we'd be together forever. And the first chance you get, you go running after her."

"The cops are on their way, Sasha," I say.

She laughs again. It's a dry, empty sound.

"I don't care anymore."

Next to me I can feel Catherine tremble. I look over at her—at her narrow features, at the slight, pensive overbite of her mouth. At her long-lashed eyes, pupils wide with fear. I lean down and kiss her cheek. Then, before she can try to stop me, I step out from behind the tree.

I don't have a plan. All I know is that Sasha is here for me. She'll hurt Catherine, but she'll do it to get to me. So I'm the one who has to stop her.

Instantly there's another shot. It disappears somewhere into the darkness past me. Sasha's about thirty feet away, gun held out from her chest in both hands. She's still in her drill uniform—a sparkly vest, a short white skirt. The sequins catch what light there is, flaring bright as flame.

She lowers the gun ever so slightly, her eyes meeting mine.

"Why do you love her, and not me?" she asks. Her voice is almost matter-of-fact.

There are a million and one things I could say. I could point out all she's put me through. I could use all the labels she hates so much: manipulative, abusive, controlling. I wouldn't be wrong.

But the truth is so much simpler, and so much more complicated.

"I don't know," I say. "I just do."

We stand like that for a long moment, staring at one another. I look at her heart-shaped face, at the thick, dark hair like a tempest around her shoulders. I look at her mouth, sagging under the weight of her bitterness.

"I'm sorry," I say. Because it's true. For whatever she's going through. For whatever I may have done to make it worse.

Her features crumple into an expression of anguish. The gun is aimed at my chest this time. No more wide shots.

Then, all at once, she turns the gun toward her own temple. The movement is so swift and so sure I realize that it's what she's meant to do all along.

"No," I say, too soft. I start to run. There's no way for me to get there in time; I know even as I reach toward her I won't make it. "No, Sasha."

I can hear sirens. I barely noticed them over the pounding of my own heart. But there are the red and blue beams, swirling across the highway. Lights go on inside the motel. Someone steps out, a silhouette in a doorway. A cop car swerves into the parking lot, another close on its heels.

Sasha's hand trembles. I stop a few feet away, holding my hands up.

"Don't," I say.

She blinks, once, twice, like she's waking up from a bad dream. She looks up at the cop cars. An ambulance pulls into the lot a moment later. The lights flash across her skin.

The gun falls to the ground. She sits down, hard, on the broken concrete. Her expression is empty, as if everything has been drained away.

FORTY-FOUR

Elyse

It's the kind of gray day I love, the kind that makes me homesick for Portland. Town Lake is dull under the heavy clouds, and while December in Texas isn't nearly as cold as I want it to be, there's a cool current in the air.

It's the day before Christmas Eve; the usual joggers and walkers and bikers are probably doing their last-minute shopping, so the park is less crowded than usual. I sit on a bench and watch a chubby guy with a beard throw a tennis ball for a sheltie in the dog area. All around is the hum of traffic, the noise of the city.

When the minivan pulls into the parking lot, my nerves shoot sparks.

It's been a week since what happened in the woods. I haven't seen Gabe since he disappeared into the back of the ambulance that night; and while we've been texting back and forth nonstop, I'm suddenly nervous to be face-to-face with him. Even though by now he knows some of the story—the news has covered the basics—there's still so much to confess, to explain.

I've never stood in front of him as myself. Not completely.

The side panel swings open, and the first thing I see is Vivi, waving frantically. She's holding a stuffed armadillo and beaming at me. "Merry Christmas! Merry Christmas!" she calls.

"Merry Christmas, yourself," I say, getting up from the bench and moving closer. She holds the armadillo out toward me. I take it and make it dance along her lap, and she squeals with delight.

The passenger side door swings open, and Gabe steps carefully out. It's surreal to be able to look at him directly in the light of day, without fear that we might be seen. There's almost a rush to it. He's wearing a loose black T-shirt that says SATAN'S CHEERLEADERS, and his curls are adorably tousled. He grins at me, that cocky sideways grin that pulled me in from the start.

Before he can even say hi, Mrs. Jiménez leans across the seat.

"You must be Elyse," she says.

I nod, not sure if I should move to shake her hand or something. I don't remember how normal teenagers talk to adults.

"It's nice to finally meet you," she says, hesitating. "How're you doing?"

I don't know how to answer, so I just say, "I'm okay."

"Mom," Gabe says. "We only have, like, an hour."

"Okay, okay." She frowns. "I'm running your sister to her playdate. I'll be back in a bit. You have your phone? Water bottle? How's your pain?"

"Mom," he says again, more firmly this time. "I'm fine. Thanks for the ride."

She purses her lips like she's about to say something. Then she sighs, and starts the car.

"Bye, bye, Leese," Vivi says sadly. She waves at me again. She makes the armadillo wave. "Bye, bye."

"Bye, Vivi." I watch them drive away, more because I'm almost afraid to look directly at Gabe than anything else. But once they're gone I can't put it off. I bite my lip and turn to face him.

"Hey," he says.

"Hey," I say too. After all we've been through it feels ridiculous to start with "hey," so I smile. And then he smiles too, and I'm almost overcome by the sweetness of it, the innocence. Our fingers slide together.

"I like your hair," he says.

I touch the back of my head. I had one of the girls in the group home I've been staying at help me with it. It's short now, just below my ears, and dyed back to the dark blonde that's my natural color.

"Thanks," I say. "I feel lighter now."

"It makes you look . . . different."

A quick surge of anxiety runs through me. "Different bad?"

"No." He hesitates. "Less, like . . . hidden. But it's good."

I lick my lips, glance around. "Should we sit down?"

"Let's walk," he says. He pats his shoulder. "It's not like I got shot in the leg."

We take the path that skirts the lake. The city skyline is reflected in the dark water below. An egret floats placidly in the rushes. I look down at my feet, more from habit than anything else. My purple sneakers were ruined in the woods—they were covered in blood—but I found a pair of slip-ons in the donation bin at the social worker's office.

"How're you feeling, anyway?" I ask.

"Okay. It still hurts like a bitch, but they've got me on some pretty good drugs." He gives a lopsided grin.

I try to smile, but my mouth feels dry. "Yeah, well, be careful with that stuff," I say. "I mean . . . not to be a nag. But it's not, like, recreational."

His expression softens. "Shit. I forgot about your mom."

"No, I'm sorry. I'm not accusing you of . . ." I bite the inside of my cheek, take a deep breath. "You know, Becky—the social worker—says the hardest thing for me is going to be learning that the worst doesn't always happen."

He doesn't answer, just squeezes my hand. I force myself to look up. I don't have to stare at the ground all the time anymore. I have to learn to look at the sky again.

"And she's right," I say. "I mean . . . you could have been killed, but you weren't. We survived."

"Yeah." He strokes the inside of my wrist with his thumb. "And with Sasha caught out there with a gun, my name's been cleared. No more po-po on my ass. She gave them a full confession, I guess . . . she told them she was the one that started the fire."

I give a little shiver, remembering her expression in the spinning blue-and-red lights the other night. It wasn't the gun that'd made her scary. It was the rush of recognition when I saw her turn it on herself. It was knowing that, while her brokenness wasn't the same as mine, there was a way in which we were sisters.

"What's going to happen to her?" I ask. "Are they charging her?"

"Yeah. But she's got the best lawyer money can buy. She'll end up with parole and some sort of court-mandated treatment program," he says, rolling his eyes. "I heard her parents are looking at therapeutic boarding schools. The further away, the better, if you ask me."

I give a little laugh. Boarding school. It doesn't seem fair, after everything she put us through. But then, who am I to claim I know what anyone deserves? I just killed a man, and yet I'm walking free.

I've dreamed about him every night. And they're the worst dreams—because they aren't about Aiden as I came to know him, paranoid, possessive, territorial. They're about the Aiden I fell for. The one who made me feel loved, and seen. And in the dream I still shoot him. I still shoot this man I love. I wake up with the metal taste of loss in my mouth, in the early morning hours before I have a chance to remember how angry I am. I lie in bed and wipe away tears, and by the time I'm completely awake I'm more mad at myself for crying than I am at him.

I'm finally free of him, but he's still got a hold on me, at least in my dreams. I wonder if I'm ever going to be able to move on. If I'll ever be able to forgive myself—not just for killing him. For everything. For all the choices I've made.

"Gabe . . ." I take a deep breath. His fingers tighten around mine reassuringly. "I'm so sorry for all of this. I wish I hadn't lied to you. I wish I . . . I'd just trusted you. Instead I dragged you into my mess."

He stops, turns to face me. Puts his palm on the back of my neck so I'm looking up into those warm, dark eyes.

"You didn't drag me anywhere." He caresses my hairline with his fingertips. It makes my breath catch a little in my throat. "And besides . . . if we got into some kind of apology contest, I don't know who would win. Sasha could have killed either one of us. Or both."

"It's different," I whisper. "You didn't choose that. She was unhinged. But I . . . I'm the one who got in that car in Portland and let Aiden drive me away. I'm the one who set my own life on fire."

A sweet little crease springs up between his eyes.

"You know you're the victim, right? That guy was twice your age. He knew better. You . . ."

I look away. "Yeah," I say quickly. "I know."

For their part, the cops and the D.A. seem to agree that I'm not at fault. It doesn't look like they're going to press any charges against me. Bit by bit the whole story's come out. It's been all over the news—KIDNAPPING VICTIM KILLS CAPTOR IN TENSE STANDOFF. Or: MISSING SIXTEEN-YEAR-OLD FOUND AFTER A YEAR ON THE RUN WITH HER TEACHER. I don't recognize myself in the story. A part of me wants to; to be able to absolve myself of all responsibility. To be able to shake off the guilt, the shame. But some other, bigger part of me can't let go of all the choices I've made in the last year. All the lies, all the mistakes.

Becky says with time, the story will change shape for me. She says I'll see it a lot of different ways—because life is messy, and weird, and hard, and no one story is the absolute truth anyway. And she says that's okay, that I can be in charge of my own story. I'm trying to believe her. I keep getting messages from journalists and true-crime writers who want to interview me, but I'm not going to talk to anyone for a while. Not until I can step back and see things more clearly. I've been manipulated enough for a lifetime.

"Anyway." I brush a lock of hair out of my face and force myself to meet his eyes. "Neither one of them can stop us anymore."

"You're right. Now it'll just be half the United States between us." He leans against the railing looking out over the water.

Tomorrow morning I'm getting on a plane to Redding, California, to live with an aunt I didn't even know I had. She's my father's sister, though she said she hadn't heard from my dad in about twenty years. Her name's Roberta—Bobbi, she told me to call her. She has two kids. My cousins. Insta-family, I guess.

Gabe glances at me sidelong. "You nervous?"

"Yeah." I play with the zipper on my hoodie. "She didn't know about me—she didn't even know Dad got married. And it's not like he ever told me anything about his family. So I don't know what to expect. But she seems nice. And Portland's only about seven hours away—my best friend might drive down to see me over her Christmas break."

I've talked to Brynn almost every day since Aiden died. I remember that first call, sitting hunched in the private room they gave me in the hospital, my heart hammering as the line rang and rang. I was so afraid she'd be mad at me.

But she answered the phone sobbing. "You dummy," she'd said. "I've been waiting."

And of course because she cried, I cried. We cried for what felt like hours. But it felt good. It felt like letting go of something.

"Why didn't you call back?" she'd asked. "Why didn't you let me know where you were?"

It was an impossible question to answer, at least in that moment. How could I make her understand how desperate I'd been, how scared? How could I tell her that I'd been embarrassed to ask for help after tossing everything so casually away? How could I explain that I'd had to stay with Aiden after my mom's overdose, because otherwise, I'd have paid too high a price for nothing?

Maybe someday we can talk about it. Or maybe we won't. Maybe we'll decide that it's more important to have fun. We can go thrifting in Redding and she'll find some Dior cocktail dress I'll have to zip her into. We'll get the sugariest drinks they make at Starbucks, and we'll drive around singing show tunes with the windows rolled down. She'll give me all the theater gossip and tell me about her conquests. I've missed that for so long now. I am ready for some lightness.

But even with Brynn back in my life, even with a new family to get to know . . . I won't feel complete. Because I have to leave this boy behind. This beautiful boy, who came for me. Who drove out into the darkness and found me.

He puts an arm around my waist now. "I wish I could come with you."

"Me too."

Would it be so crazy? Why couldn't we go together? He's seventeen, and I'll turn seventeen in May. That's not so young. Especially when I've been on my own so long, anyway.

But that answers my question for me. I've been on my own so long. And I'm tired. I don't want that life anymore, and I don't want him to have to live it, either.

"We'll text nonstop," I say. "And Skype. And I'll write letters—real ones, on paper."

He grins. "I've only ever gotten paper letters from my grandma."

"Didn't you know? I'm ninety years old." I nudge him with my hip. "And maybe . . . maybe we'll be able to meet halfway between, this summer. I can get a job, save for a bus ticket . . ."

He already has his phone in his hand. "Bluff, Utah."

"What?"

"That's the halfway point." He shows me on a map. I make a face.

"I bet we can find something more scenic nearby." I look at the map, the towns familiar after staring at Aiden's atlas so long, so longingly. "Zion, maybe. Or the San Juan Forest. Or . . ."

"Anywhere." He slides his other arm around me. I press my face against his neck, breathe in. "I'll go anywhere you want. It doesn't matter, as long as we're together."

So similar to the promise Aiden made. I close my eyes. I try to believe that the worst might not happen, for once.

I make myself imagine it. The two of us—no, why not the five of us? Gabe and Caleb and Irene and Brynn? It's *my* fantasy, so I'll invite everyone. The five of us camping together in the brilliant sandstone towers of Zion. Irene blasting music from her portable speakers, and Caleb building a fire, and Brynn in hot-pink bedazzled hiking boots, and Gabe . . . Gabe with his arms around me, laughing, telling jokes, until it's very late, the fire goes down, and we go back to our tent.

I've been hungry for family my whole life. I wasn't born with one. But somehow, maybe, I've found them along the way—in spite of everything.

Becky's going to pick me up soon; I have to go back to the group home and pack up my things. Not that I have much to pack. But I leave early tomorrow, and she wants to make sure I'm ready. I lean against Gabe, knowing we should turn back up the trail, not ready to admit it.

"Um. I haven't been able to do any shopping, what with the hospital and everything . . ." he says. He looks suddenly bashful, his cheeks pink. "But I've got kind of a . . . a thing for you. For Christmas."

Now I'm blushing too. "Oh . . . oh, I didn't . . ."

"It's okay," he says quickly. "It's nothing big. I mean, I made it. Irene helped me. I . . ." He trails off, then rummages in his pocket. There's a small lumpy package, wrapped in purple glitter paper.

I take it from his hand. It's light in my palm, the paper rough-textured. There's no box; it's a pendant, a chunk of jagged wood set in resin. The wood's painted red and white—it looks like a fragment of a design, but I can't make out the picture. Feathers, maybe? An angel wing?

"It's . . . kind of dumb," he says. "It's a piece of my skateboard. The one that got smashed in the accident? I . . . you know, since that's how we met, I wanted you to . . . to have it."

I stare down at it, my fingers curling around the sides. "It's beautiful."

He helps me put it around my neck. Light as the wood is, there's a satisfying weight to it. I can't stop touching it, the resin cool and smooth beneath my fingertips.

"Thank you," I say. "I wish I had something for you."

He shakes his head, looking pleased. "Don't. I'm just glad you like it."

Maybe it's the necklace that reminds me. It's while we're walking back to the parking lot that I remember I have one more confession to make.

"Uh. So. About the accident," I say. My stomach twists into a knot. I steal a glance at his profile.

"Yeah?"

"Um . . . the thing is . . ." I hold my breath for a moment, then say the rest in one big jumble. "I-may-have-been-the-one-who-actually-hit-you."

His mouth drops open. He stops in his tracks, and turns slowly to gawk at me. I squirm under his gaze, wondering if this is somehow the final straw, the deal breaker. After everything we've been through together—is this one foundational lie the one that makes him walk away?

But then the corners of his eyes crinkle up, and he bursts into laughter.

And then I'm laughing too, the two of us clutching each other, breathless with it.

I don't know how long we stand like that. But before I know what's happened we're kissing, a hard, desperate kiss, like we're trying to impress the memory of it into our lips. Then we cry a little, both of us. His tears mix with mine on my cheeks. I'm afraid to move, because when we move again, all bets are off. We'll have to go.

When we make it back to the parking lot, his mom's van is already there, and Becky's car is a few spots away. I wipe my face.

"Just a few months," I say. "See you in Bluff?"

He doesn't smile this time. We kiss again. It's softer. Gentler.

"Just say the word," he whispers.

I watch him climb into his mom's van. I wave at Vivi one more time. Becky pretends to text someone on her phone, trying to give me a minute, but I know she's watching.

I touch the pendant again. A splinter of wood, broken and made into something new. I don't know if the fractured picture is really an angel wing or not, but I know what Gabe has given me.

I know he's given me flight.

RESOURCES

While the characters in *A Lie for a Lie* are fictional, some of the challenges they face are unfortunately all too real. If you or someone you know is struggling with mental health or domestic violence, the organizations listed below can help.

You're not alone.

The National Domestic Violence Hotline
1-800-799-SAFE (7233)
thehotline.org
All calls are free and confidential, with advocates available 24/7 in more than 200 languages.

RAINN
1-800-656-HOPE (4673)
rainn.org
Call to be connected with a trained staff member from a sexual assault service provider in your area.

988 Suicide & Crisis Lifeline
(988)
988lifeline.org
Trained crisis workers are available to talk 24 hours a day, 7 days a week to provide crisis counseling and mental health referrals. If the situation is potentially life-threatening, call 911 or go to a hospital emergency room.

Substance Abuse and Mental Health Services Administration (SAMHSA)
1-800-662-HELP (4357)
samhsa.gov
Provides resources on general mental health and can help connect you with local treatment options.

ACKNOWLEDGMENTS

The first person on my list is Lanie "Ride-or-Die" Davis, whom I can't thank enough for her fortitude, flexibility, and insight. She met every minor catastrophe along the way with compassion, and believed in this book, and in me, throughout.

I'd also like to thank Jessica Almon, Julie Rosenberg, and Ben Schrank at Razorbill for their excitement and vision, as well as Phyllis DeBlanche, Annie Stone, and Eliza Swift, each of whom put eyes on this at various points of the process and helped it become an actual book.

Last but not least, I'd like to thank all my family and friends, particularly Matt Donaldson. Shout-out as well to the NICU nurses and therapists at St. David's Main in Austin. In your hands I felt strong enough to get to the finish line.

No thanks at all to A.D., who did absolutely nothing to help, but whom I love with all my heart anyway.